STARJUMPER LEGACY

BOOK ONE

THE CRYSTAL KEY

STARJUMPER LEGACY

BOOK ONE
THE CRYSTAL KEY

CHRISTOPHER BAILEY

Phase Publishing, LLC
Seattle

Cover art by Tugboat Design
http://www.tugboatdesign.net

Phase Publishing, LLC second paperback edition
March 2020

ISBN 978-0-9899734-1-0
Library of Congress Control Number 2013917076

For my first readers, Jeff, Doug, and Katie, for your enthusiasm and encouragement.

For my editor, Ferrell, and her amazing crew, for all their great feedback and advice.

For Brandy, for your unfailing support.

And for my Angel.
For you, the stars.

CONTENTS

ABDUCTION

Designation R.A.I.Th.-84. His name, such as it was. R.A.I.Th-84 was a little surprised that the woman had come to this particular planet. It was completely off the grid as far as the Coalition was concerned. It was way out in one of the spiral arms of the galaxy, far from the heart of Coalition power. The civilization here lacked the technology to travel much beyond their own planet.

The Resistance was clever; far more than that fool Tyren gave them credit for, anyway. He doubted that Tyren had any idea that this little world even existed.

Frankly, R.A.I.Th-84 was a little disappointed that the Resistance had been so thoroughly crushed. He rather preferred them to the Highlord's men. The Highlord. Just the title gave him a bad taste in his mouth. Or at least, what passed for taste in his complex system of sensors.

R.A.I.Th-84 sighed quietly as he watched the woman moving rapidly along the faintly lit street. The predawn air was chilly, almost crisp, the crystal-clear sky conserving little of the planet's emitted heat.

The woman was bundled up against the cold, though R.A.I.Th-84 himself wore only his mottled gray stalking suit, as he liked to call it. It wasn't insulated, but for a Theta unit, that made no difference at all. He registered the temperature to the thousandth of a degree in forty-seven different thermal measurement scales, but he didn't feel it the way organics did.

She was hurrying, though not running. He felt bad for her. For some reason, the Resistance still assumed that the Thetas were like the old Kappa units, who wouldn't pursue a target unless they were running. He'd been given a target, and he would pursue it regardless of its form of motion, or even a total lack of movement.

Then again, she probably didn't know she had a Theta on her trail. She wouldn't have seen his slight form atop the roof where he perched even if she had turned her gaze directly up to him, and she certainly wouldn't have heard him coming.

The woman, "Morgan Bennett", according to his assignment transmission, moved up the steps of a small but cozy-looking house on the far side of the street. R.A.I.Th-84 smiled. He'd chosen his vantage point perfectly and could see both her and the doorway in perfect clarity.

Another human woman opened the door. R.A.I.Th-84 mentally stored her image for later archiving. As the pair talked, he filed the audio recordings of the conversation away to add to the archive on this particular file, as well. It would all be uploaded to the mainframe when he reported back in. The Highlord liked a thorough recon job.

Morgan drew a large bundle from beneath her heavy cloak and handed it to the other woman, who looked stunned. R.A.I.Th-84 knew that she'd been carrying something, but he hadn't yet had the chance to determine what it was. His thermal and auditory scanners gave the bundle a quick inspection. He frowned to himself as he realized that it was a human infant. The woman had a child and was giving it to this woman.

He turned and spun, stepping almost casually off the edge of the roof, landing lightly and silently on the lawn below. He moved quickly closer, attempting to determine if the crystal was anywhere in the bundle. His sensors couldn't detect any sign of the crystal's unique energy signature. Peculiar that she would take such care and effort to deliver a child to this remote location but didn't bring the crystal.

Silently cursing himself, he realized that he must have missed when and where she'd hidden the little stone. Now he'd have to backtrack and try to locate it. Either that or interrogate the woman once he'd acquired her. In a few moments, he had a good ambush location picked out. He took up position and waited, still recording the last few moments of the women's conversation.

Soon enough, Morgan was on the move again. He heard her breath coming in short, sharp gasps. She was desperately trying not to cry, he realized. He felt a pang of guilt but quickly suppressed it. Morgan was moving quickly again, toward the place where he crouched behind a low fence, between two yards a few houses down.

As she passed just beyond his position, he moved, faster than a human could, faster than she could have reacted even if she'd spotted him before he struck. His hand snapped out, clamping the reddish-metal bracelet around her wrist. Her entire body instantly went rigid, and he pulled her down behind the wall again to avoid any unwanted observation.

Her green eyes stared at him in terror and confusion. She struggled to speak and, to R.A.I.Th-84's surprise, she managed to speak a few words. The Bennett woman must be incredibly strong willed, he realized. For some reason, that made him feel even more guilty.

"You're… just… a boy…" she gasped. He cocked his head to one side to regard her. He hated the fear in her eyes.

"I'm a Theta," he replied in a voice pitched to carry only a few feet. Her eyes went wider still, the fear becoming absolute panic. Apparently, she hadn't known they made Thetas in juvenile forms. They hadn't made many Thetas to begin with, and only four of them been designed with juvenile forms. They had been something of an experiment.

"Don't… please don't… my baby…" she managed to get out past her clenched jaw. R.A.I.Th-84 hesitated. His orders said nothing about an infant. Interesting that she was more concerned with the child than with herself.

"Does the child have the key?" he asked.

"No. Crystal… hidden," she said.

He considered. He didn't register its energies anywhere on this planet, so she must have hidden it someplace before he'd picked up her trail.

"The child is not relevant to my orders," he replied.

Relief flashed in her eyes, being replaced after a moment by the fear again.

"Report… he'll know…" she said. R.A.I.Th-84

considered again. She was right, of course. He couldn't conceal the existence of the child in the report. It was a complete data upload. All auditory, visual, and sensory feedback automatically transmitted with the report.

"Please…" she gasped, tears beginning to trickle from her wide, frightened eyes and running down the sides of her face.

There wasn't anything R.A.I.Th-84 could do, though he felt sorry for her. The child really wasn't relevant if the crystal wasn't here. Tyren would care, though. The offspring of any crystal bearer would be automatically declared a threat and a target.

An idea came to him; a dangerous, inspirational idea. He'd never tried this before and wasn't even sure he was capable of it. He wasn't supposed to feel anything for his victims, but he did. He wasn't even sure why he felt emotions so strongly.

Thetas were programmed for emotional response, but only as far as necessary to help them understand and predict human emotion-based reactions and decisions. It helped to imitate them when they were in infiltration mode. He'd always struggled to keep his own in check. It was going to get him into serious trouble someday.

Maybe today.

He looked into those green eyes, mentally replaying the image of her handing the infant to the other woman. Technically, his orders didn't strictly forbid him from tampering with the data before uploading, since it had probably never occurred to anyone that he was capable of it.

There also had been no orders whatsoever about a child. He had simply been ordered to track down the woman and bring her in, acquiring the crystal in the process.

She had hidden the crystal, so he would have to backtrack along her trail and attempt to discover it while he brought her in. He could probably torture the information out of the woman, and the idea of hurting her any more than he had to made him distinctly uncomfortable. Additionally, he had only been ordered to bring the woman and the crystal back. No more, no less.

R.A.I.Th-84 didn't want to bring her in at all, but he couldn't refuse or resist a direct order. It was completely against his core programming to violate an order given by any official of the Coalition, let alone his direct owner. Unfortunately for R.A.I.Th.-84, his direct owner was Highlord Tyren himself.

After several long moments, he came to a decision. He didn't want to do Tyren any favors at all, so he felt no desire to go out of his way to do anything he wasn't directly ordered to do. He could resist in this small way. It would mean he would be scrapped and recycled if his actions were ever discovered, but what was the point of being operational, if he couldn't express himself a little now and then?

He nodded once to Morgan, closed his eyes, and began to reprogram his data archives.

This should prove interesting.

CHAPTER ONE

THE AWAKENING

"Your mother wanted you to have this."

Allie's bright green eyes blinked in surprise as her adoptive mother handed her a small, rather beautiful, wooden box.

The wood of the box was dark, almost black, but with a luster that gave the wood an inner glow, the gentle grain seeming to move subtly in the light as she turned it. A spiral pattern was etched in silver on the top, with a peculiar, intricate pattern tracing the outer edge in the same shining silver.

It almost looked like writing, but like nothing she had ever seen before, with each letter seeming almost made for the ones on either side of it, flowing into a seamless row of markings. It appeared, without any of the lines quite touching, to interweave into a pattern that would make any Celtic knot envious. She turned her clear, green eyes, her only attractive feature, in her opinion, to her mother.

"It's beautiful, but when did you get it? Have you had this since…?" she trailed off, her already soft voice now barely above a whisper.

The idea that her adoptive mother had held onto this for thirteen years was hard to understand. Why hadn't she given it to her years ago?

She awkwardly ran a hand through her shoulder-length, flat brown hair. She hated her hair. It was dull, lifeless, and completely resistant to any attempts at style. It just sort of hung there, straight and boring.

"I'm sorry, Allie. I was under strict orders not to give this to you until your thirteenth birthday. I don't know why, just that your mother said that was the way it had to be." Her tone of voice was apologetic, as was the softness in her warm brown eyes. "I'll leave you to it, then. Good night, Allie," she said, and with a light kiss on Allie's forehead, stood up from the bed and headed for the door.

As she left the room, shutting the bedroom door quietly behind her, Allie found her gaze unable to break away from the surprising gift. The box was absolutely beautiful, but Allie had the strong sense that it was simply a container for the true gift within.

Her hands trembled slightly as she gripped the lid of the box. What could possibly be inside, she wondered?

Allie had been left with her adoptive mother, Katherine, shortly after her birth. Katherine had never been able to fully explain why, just that her closest friend had one day come to her door after having been missing for two long years and begged her to look after Allie. Katherine hadn't even known Allie's mother was pregnant, let alone who the father could have been.

Allie had grown up happy. Katherine took good care

of her, but she always wondered why her mother had abandoned her in such a way. Was her mother okay now? Would she ever come back for her?

She knew her mother loved her. If she didn't, she wouldn't have left Allie with someone like Katherine. Neither Allie nor Katherine had any idea if Allie's mother would ever return, though Allie had always had fantasies of it one day happening.

Now, there was this sudden revelation that her mother had left her something. Allie didn't know what to do with this new information. Should she be angry with Katherine for withholding the one thing her mother had left her?

No, she wasn't angry. Katherine was only doing as her mother had asked. She was more curious than anything else. Why had her mother left it for her? Why her thirteenth birthday? What on earth did it contain? The box couldn't hold much. It wasn't much bigger around than the palm of her admittedly small hand, and it wasn't more than two inches deep.

It was possible, she thought, that it contained a note from her mother, and she wasn't supposed to open it until she was thirteen because that's when her mother felt she would be mature enough to understand what it said. It might contain an explanation of why Allie had been given away in the first place.

Not that she minded that Katherine had raised her. She was an excellent mother, and a wonderful person. It was quite clear to Allie why her mother and Katherine had been such close friends. She'd even grown up calling her 'Mom'.

And yet, just to know what had happened, where her mother was, who her father was... that would be something amazing.

She had a picture of her mother, one that Katherine had always kept in a small, locked box in her closet. Just before her eighth birthday, Katherine had caught her breaking into the box, again, and looking at it. On her birthday, Katherine had given it to her as a present. It sat on her bedside table in a small, silver picture frame.

Her mother's name was Morgan, and she was a beautiful woman, something Allie herself secretly envied. She figured that she must look a lot more like her probably less-attractive father.

In the picture, Morgan's long, stunningly blonde hair was flowing freely over her shoulders, framing a perfect, elegant face. Her mother didn't have the kind of beauty usually attributed to supermodels. This was different. It was something more real, more substantial. Almost angelic, Allie thought for probably the thousandth time.

She turned to look back down at the small box in her hands. It felt slightly warm. Taking a long breath, she steeled herself. Slowly, she tugged on the lid. It refused to budge. She scowled in sudden frustration, then pulled, tugged, twisted, and rattled the little box until she was afraid she might break it. She let out a sigh of annoyance, her excitement and tension converting rapidly to irritation.

Allie flopped backward down on her bed, head on her pillow. The box wasn't much good if she couldn't open it, she thought. She turned it around in her hands, feeling the smooth surface of the wood.

Maybe it was like those old Chinese puzzle boxes. There was probably a trick to it, like a hidden catch or something. The box didn't appear to have any latches, buttons, switches, or even seams other than the single, nearly invisible line where the lid met the base.

Turning it over and over, she couldn't find any way to open it. There weren't any clues about how to get the lid off. It occurred to her that the pattern around the rim might well be writing in some language she didn't know. It might contain instructions on how to open the box.

As hard as Allie tried, she couldn't seem to wrap her mind around the fact that her mother had left her something that she wasn't allowed to have for thirteen years, and now she couldn't even get into it to discover what was inside to figure out why.

Even in the dim light of the bedside lamp, it seemed to shine more than the little faint natural light would account for. The silver spiral pattern on the top was a mystery, as was the odd design around the outer edge; everything about the box practically screamed "secrets". Allie hated secrets.

Looking back to the window and the glittering stars above, Allie sighed. They seemed brighter to her than usual. Slowly, her eyes drifted closed. Her final thought before the warm embrace of sleep claimed her was of her mother. Perhaps she was looking up at the same stars, wherever she was. As sleep took her, the box slipped from her fingertips to rest on the bed beside her.

A thin band of silvery light shone momentarily through the seam around the lid of the box, then faded, unseen by the young girl as she slipped into the tranquil embrace of a deep, dream-filled sleep.

Burning blue eyes flashed, going wide in surprise. The smooth, tanned skin around them grew a few shades paler. Black-gloved fists clenched in sudden shock and rage, and the deceptively handsome, clean-shaven face turned sharply to the side to cast a baleful glare on the monstrous creature beside the great silver throne on which the man sat.

The creature was vaguely humanoid, but the massively muscled arms hung nearly to the ground, hands tipped in glistening black claws. Its body, where visible beneath the oddly textured, brown leather armoring it wore about its legs and torso, was covered in distorted bulges of oddly placed muscle, poorly hidden by a layer of greasy, grayish fur.

The face that turned in response to the man's stormy gaze was grotesque, one huge tusk protruding from the lower lip, reaching almost to the thing's dead-black left eye. The other lip hung low, drooping far lower than the other side. Its sharply pointed ears curved out and back from the top of its head like horns, and they turned slowly, independently of one another.

"Did you feel that, Klythe?" The man's voice was silken, pleasantly calm, and completely at odds with the rage burning in his eyes. They shone unnaturally in the dim reddish light of the immense throne room. "Did you perhaps feel the sensation that just struck me with such a subtle, yet profound impact?"

The behemoth beside him blinked blankly, though one great ear twitched nervously. When this man spoke pleasantly, it was rarely a good thing for those he addressed.

"Your greatness?" the creature asked, its voice so deep as to be almost more felt than heard, a resonating rumble deep within the thing's chest.

The man bit back a scream of outrage at the creature's stupidity. This was what he got for working with these beastly creatures. The stupid brute was practically useless for anything requiring thoughts deeper than when his next meal was. In any situation involving violence or intimidation, however, the creature called Klythe was remarkably effective.

"A crystal has just been awakened, Klythe. Why did I go to all the trouble of attuning you to their energies, if you're too stupid to notice!" The man's tirade had started in the same calm tone, but he rapidly lost his carefully cultivated control.

"You swore to me your people had acquired them all! They were *all* to be destroyed! Go! Find it! Kill anyone and everyone near it!"

The huge beast promptly loped out of the room, frighteningly fast and agile for a beast so massive.

Highlord Tyren watched Klythe leave, seething inside. All it took was one of those stones to ruin everything for him. Decades of planning, war, and hunting those accursed crystal bearers, all for nothing if even one of those crystals remained active.

With a great deal of personal effort, he calmed himself. No matter, he thought. The entire Enclave hadn't managed to bring him down with a hundred of those stones. One nuisance with a single stone had no chance against Klythe and his people. The beast was a moron, but he was one of the best killers in the galaxy.

Placing his hand on a silvery panel on the arm of his throne caused an image to appear before him, showing a panoramic view of the stars. With quick, concentrated thoughts, he narrowed the focus and set the scanners to search for the crystal energies. This would only work for a short time after its awakening, while it was still synchronizing itself with its bearer. He had no time to waste.

Gradually, the image zoomed in on a single planet, tuning in to his conscious direction and the signature picked up by the scanners. The image filled with one small, blue, insignificant planet, in an otherwise lifeless solar system. No wonder he had missed it. This planet could have gone unnoticed forever, if the blasted stone hadn't awakened.

His computer quickly gave him a string of data about the planet and its occupants. What a worthless little space rock, he thought to himself with disgust. Another quick thought connected him with Klythe's com-system.

"On second thought, Klythe, find the bearer. Bring him to me alive."

"Yes, great one," came the growling reply. Slowly, the Highlord smiled. Perhaps some enjoyment could be gained from this after all.

CHAPTER TWO

SO MANY QUESTIONS

Allie rolled over, her thoughts heavy with interrupted sleep, and reached her hand out blindly to slap the snooze button on the alarm clock that was at that very moment enthusiastically shrieking its notice that her blissful rest was over. Her groping arm bumped the little wooden box, knocking it from the bed. It clattered to the ground noisily.

As her eyes and mind cleared, she climbed out of bed and fumbled around on the floor for the fallen object. She picked it up and sat back on the side of the bed. Putting it down next to her, she rubbed her eyes and stretched.

She sat beside it for a moment, then picked it up again, carefully examining the intricate patterns along the side, seeming drawn into them. As she stared, her focus began to pull in so tightly that everything else was momentarily forgotten. The shapes seemed to slide around as she stared, slowly making more and more sense, until finally, it clicked, and she…

"Allie? Are you coming down? You're going to be late!" Katherine called from downstairs.

Allie blinked, feeling as though she had just snapped back into reality from some weird dream.

She glanced at the clock and realized she'd been staring at that silly box for almost twenty minutes. She looked back at the symbols beside the box, but there was nothing unusual about them. They made no sense at all. It had almost seemed for a moment there… She sighed and stood up.

"Yeah, I'll be there in a sec!" she called back. In a rush, she got dressed and grabbed her cell phone from its charger. She grabbed the wooden box and tucked it into her shoulder bag before racing out the door and down the stairs.

As she slid into her seat at the breakfast table, Katherine smiled and pushed a bowl of cereal in front of her before stepping out of the room. Allie ate with one hand, opening her phone and sending a quick text to her best friend, Dav.

Get over here, I have something to show you!

She hit the send button. The reply was almost immediate. She got the impression he had been waiting to hear from her this morning. It was short and sweet, much like Dav, she thought with a grin. His response was a simple:

Coming.

She wolfed down her cereal, but before she could finish, movement caught her eye. Looking up, she burst into giggles. Dav was at the kitchen window, making faces at her. He flashed his usual, impossibly bright grin and vanished from the window, reappearing through the back door.

"Hey, Allie. How does it feel to be thirteen? Wait. Scratch that. That's a stupid question. Have you ever wondered why people always ask you that? I mean, they say you're a year older, but really, you're only one day older than the day before. Why do people always expect it to feel different?" he asked with a playful grin.

"You think too much, Dav," she laughed, which was her usual reply when he got onto one of his tangents.

He just laughed along with her, the same response he had been giving to that comment for years.

She found herself wondering, not for the first time, how one person could smile quite so much and not constantly have a sore face. Not that she minded, of course. He had a very nice smile.

"True," he said in a nearly flawless imitation of Lacy Briscoe, one of the most unbelievably mindless souls ever to walk the planet, in Allie's humble opinion. "But it's better than, you know, not thinking, like, enough. I mean, if I didn't think enough, I'd be, like, totally one of those bubbleheads."

Lacy Briscoe was an idiot, and she was mean. A terrible combination all by itself, but add to that the facts that she was gorgeous and knew it, and was the most popular girl in school... This all combined to make her instantly despised by any and all people like Allie and Dav, which basically meant anyone not interested in belonging to the popular group of mean kids at school. Allie had a strong suspicion that most of the popular kids hated Lacy, too, they just couldn't admit it without losing some of their precious status.

Allie almost burst out laughing again at his imitation, barely restraining herself for the sake of the mouthful of cereal threatening to burst forth. She chewed fast and swallowed, throwing Dav a glare, though her smile showed through anyway.

"Hey, I'm eating here! Can we not bring Lacy up at the table? It's nauseating," she protested.

Dav laughed with her and held both hands up in surrender. She rolled her eyes and went back to her cereal just as Katherine walked back through the doorway. She flashed one of her special smiles as she saw Dav. Katherine absolutely adored him and had a special smile just for him.

Katherine was convinced that Allie and Dav should be together romantically, a thought that sent both Allie and Dav into hysterics whenever she brought it up, though secretly Allie agreed.

Dav was nice, sweet, funny, and not at all bad-looking. He had sun-blonde hair that he wore just a little bit long, with a natural wave to it that made Allie insanely jealous. His clear, blue eyes that sparkled when he laughed, which he did a lot, could absolutely swallow her if she let them.

He was also brilliant, though he took care not to flaunt that fact. He was the only person she knew capable of getting straight As who didn't do it. What was more, he deliberately avoided a perfect grade average simply to avoid being thought of as a teacher's pet.

Dav was smart enough that he kept a carefully calculated B+ in each class every term. He said he wanted to be a good student, but he had no interest in being a perfect one.

Her grades were nearly identical, but she had to work hard for hers. In fact, without Dav's help, she wouldn't be able to manage even that high. Even her best subject, science, seemed to come with effortless ease to him.

His only failing was that he was a bit short, actually even a little bit shorter than Allie was, but he insisted that would change over the next few years. He swore the men in his family were always tall. Allie suspected that gene might have skipped poor Dav.

He was right about his family, though. His older brother was quite tall. His father had died shortly after Dav was born, so she couldn't judge that one herself. She didn't know what had happened to his mother. Dav wouldn't talk about that.

Dav had been raised by his much older brother, who looked a great deal like him, right down to those same strikingly blue eyes and perpetually friendly smile.

His name was Artus, which Allie thought was a weird name. She kept that to herself, though. Dav's real name was Davrelan, so he didn't like her commenting on it. They must have had weird parents.

"Hi, Mrs. Pennbrook. You look stunning today. Trying a new hairstyle? It's definitely working for you," Dav said, flashing one of his most suave smiles. Katherine laughed.

"Charmer," Katherine chided as she turned back into the kitchen, but Allie could tell she was quite pleased with the compliment. Allie shook her head and smiled.

She was certain Dav could charm a drowning person out of their life jacket, should he ever turn his mind to it. Allie was incredibly glad that he'd never turned that charm on any of the girls at school, or on her for that matter. She didn't think she could take it.

"So, you wanted to show me something?" Dav asked. Allie shook her head and finished her last bite.

"Later. I want to talk to you, too. Privately."

At her serious tone, Dav's playful smile slipped, a glimpse of his rare, serious expression underneath.

"No problem. We can talk on the way to school. You ready?" he asked.

Allie nodded and picked up her bowl, placing it in the sink. She grabbed her gray hoodie and stepped out the side door. With a quick glance up at the thick, gray mass of clouds forming an almost solid, gloomy ceiling above the rows of houses, she slipped it over her head and flipped up the hood. Dav zipped up his blue windbreaker and slung his backpack over his shoulders. Allie grabbed her shoulder bag, and the pair headed out the door.

"Bye, Mom!" Allie hollered into the house, closing the door before she heard a reply.

She glanced again at the sky and tucked her hands into her pockets. It wasn't raining yet, but it sure looked like it was coming. After only a few steps, Dav spoke.

"Okay, Allie, spill it. What's up?"

Allie sighed, feeling oddly reluctant to tell him about the box. She felt somehow protective of it, though she figured that was just because it was a gift from her mother. Dav's expression got even more serious as she hesitated.

"I got another birthday present last night," she started. Dav nodded, waiting for her to continue. "It was from my mother." Dav again nodded, but Allie shook her head. "No, my real mother."

That got to him. He blinked, his mouth opening as if to speak, but closing again before any sound came out. That was a first. Dav always knew what to say.

"Wow," he finally said.

Allie nodded. That about summed up her thoughts

on it, as well.

"Mom has been holding onto it for thirteen years. She says my mother made her promise not to give it to me until my thirteenth birthday," she said, glancing sidelong at Dav, watching his reaction.

"Wow," he said again.

Allie laughed nervously.

"You already said that," she scolded.

"I know," he replied with a small smile, "but it's the only word that seems to fit. What was it?"

"It was a beautiful little box, wooden, with a silver spiral on the top. There's an odd kind of pattern around the edge. I think it might be some kind of writing, but I can't tell for sure."

As she spoke, she pulled it out of her bag and handed it to him. She frowned when he didn't take it immediately. She looked over at him and was surprised at the expression on his face. He'd gone a little pale, and he stared at the box with an unusual intensity, and a definite look of nervousness.

"Hey, you okay?" she asked.

Dav started as if he'd forgotten she was there, and his expression was instantly normal again. He reached out and took the box casually, looking it over. She frowned suspiciously at him.

"Sure. This is really something. What do you suppose the writing means?" he asked.

Allie stared at him curiously for a moment before answering. Interesting that he didn't question her theory that it might be writing. Dav questioned everything that didn't come with a healthy dose of evidence.

"I don't really know. I don't recognize the language, if it is writing at all. I can't figure out how to get it open, though," she said. Dav nodded.

"Probably a puzzle box or something," he replied.

"That's exactly what I thought!" she said with a grin, pleased that her line of thinking had led her to the same conclusion Dav had reached.

"Could be empty, though. Maybe it was the box itself that she meant to give you," he said. She shrugged.

"I guess it could be, but what does it mean? Why couldn't I have the box until I was thirteen? It's just weird is all. It doesn't make any sense."

"Yeah. Well, to paraphrase Occam's Razor…" Dav began. Allie threw him a look, and he grinned apologetically. "Sorry. I just mean to say that if the box itself doesn't make any sense as the gift, then logically, there is something else inside." He gently shook the box, but no sound came from within. "We just have to figure out how to open it. Maybe you could come over after school, and Artus could help us."

Allie smiled warmly at him. His brilliance could be annoying when he started talking theorems and equations and junk like that, but he did it blessedly rarely. When he did, it was always related to the situation and turned out to be helpful every time.

"Okay, cool. Thanks," she said simply.

He just nodded as he examined the box. She noticed him staring at the odd pattern around the outer edge, that same oddly pale color to his face, though he was carefully keeping his expression calm.

"Weird, huh?" she continued. "I swear I almost understood it earlier. I must be going nuts."

Dav blinked and he looked up at her in something bordering on alarm. His expression went normal again as she looked directly at him.

"Hey, are you sure you're okay?" she asked. "You're not getting sick on me or anything, right? I don't need a repeat of the Halloween incident."

Dav laughed at her reference.

Two years ago, they had thrown a big Halloween party for all the other kids in the neighborhood. Dav had gotten into a dare with another boy over whether or not eating a ton of candy would make you sick. They challenged each other to see who could eat more before vomiting. Dav had lost.

The end result, of course, was that he'd thrown up all over her favorite shoes. He was horribly embarrassed, so much so that she couldn't be angry at him, though she never failed to tease him about it.

Fortunately, Dav was extraordinarily secure and didn't get upset over her frequent teasing. He had also bought her an identical replacement pair in apology, which she had worn almost every day until she'd worn right through the soles.

"Don't worry. I haven't eaten candy for a while, and those shoes aren't nearly expensive enough to be worth ruining," he said casually, returning the box to her.

She made a face at him, and he grinned playfully. As the pair approached the bus stop, she saw that the bus was already there.

"Oh, man. We'll have to run to catch it," Allie said and started forward.

Dav didn't follow.

"Hey, I forgot my math book. I have to go home and get it. I'll get Artus to bring me to school so I won't be late."

He turned and bolted back the way they had come so fast that she couldn't even get a word out before he was too far away to be heard without yelling at him.

Allie heard the bus engine rev, so she raced to get there before the driver closed the doors and took off without her. She barely made it and moved quickly to the back of the bus. Allie leaned toward the window to look out back, drawing annoyed comments from the kids she bumped with her backpack as she turned.

Just before Dav rounded the corner, he glanced back at the bus. She could swear he looked frightened just before he turned and vanished around the corner.

Dav wasn't there at lunch. They didn't have any of the same classes in the morning, but he always sat with her at lunch. Maybe he had gotten sick, she thought. Even so, it was weird.

He hadn't texted her or anything, though she'd followed the school rules and kept her phone off until lunch. Even during lunch, though, she didn't hear from him, and he didn't respond to her text asking if he was okay. He had looked awfully pale before he'd run off.

Come to think of it, he had acted weird from the moment he'd seen the box. He'd seemed fine and playful before that. And his jokes after seeing it seemed a little forced.

The more she thought about it, the more she wondered what it was about the box that had set him off. Maybe he'd recognized the pattern on the outside. He'd seemed pretty interested in that. Where would he have seen anything like it before, though?

Maybe he was just sick, but if that was it, he'd have texted, right? What if he was so sick that his brother took him to the hospital? Allie was working herself into a total wreck with worrying over him.

As she was walking out of her last class, which she'd

mentally spaced out on due to her worrying about Dav, her phone buzzed just as she turned it on. It startled her so badly she almost dropped it. She flipped it open and read the words on the display. With immense relief, she saw that it was a text from Dav. She read the message quickly.

Sorry I bailed. Didn't feel well. Artus wouldn't let me come to school, so I fell asleep. Slept right through lunch. Hope you're okay.

Allie closed her phone and sighed in relief. He was all right, just sick. She'd have to go see him, she decided. She boarded the bus, ignoring the occasional comment about her "missing boyfriend".

She and Dav had gotten good at ignoring those. People had a hard time with the two of them being friends and not being romantically involved. She couldn't help but think to herself again that she wouldn't mind if they were, though.

Dav, thanks to that smile of his, had more than a few admirers, but he was always careful to let them down delicately. Some of them had been popular girls, too. He totally could have made it into the "in" crowd if he wanted. She was extremely thrilled that he seemed to prefer her company. Yet more proof of his superior intelligence, she thought.

As she got off the bus, she headed for Dav's house, rather than hers. She sent a quick text to her mom, explaining where she was going. Katherine, of course, responded that it was perfectly all right, and to let her know how Dav was feeling. Allie walked up to Dav's front door and smiled at the meticulously maintained landscaping.

Artus was an avid gardener, though his tastes leaned

toward a more masculine design, leaving the small, delicate flowers out and bringing in some strong, wild-looking plants that looked like they'd have fit right into a tropical rainforest.

The effect was impressive, with the occasional large, exotic-looking flower bringing a splash of color to the carefully kept, yet somehow wild-looking yard.

Allie climbed the steps and knocked on the door. It was answered immediately, the door opening startlingly fast. Behind it was Artus, his stance looking somehow violent. She took a step backward in shock.

Artus, like his brother, was handsome, brilliant, and extraordinarily nice. She had never seen the kind of aggression in his eyes that she saw now. His expression instantly softened when he recognized her, though not nearly as much as she would have liked. He still looked extremely wary and was looking at her like someone looks at a nearby snake that they aren't entirely convinced isn't poisonous.

"Geez, Artus. Expecting to get jumped?" she joked, trying to lighten the mood. The look he gave at her comment told her plainly that he might well have been.

"Dav's in his room. Go ahead and see him, but you'll have to leave soon. We can't have company over tonight," Artus said, being careful not to let her too close to him as he stepped back to let her in.

She frowned in confusion. Things had gotten very weird in this family awfully quickly.

"Okay, sure. Thanks, Artus," she replied as she headed for the back bedroom Dav called his own.

Artus eyed her cautiously as she walked away from him, making the hair on the back of her neck stand up.

She made it to Dav's closed door and knocked

gently, in case he was sleeping again. He answered readily enough, calling out to invite her in, though he sounded distracted. She opened the door carefully and poked her head inside.

"Hey, Dav. You feeling all right?" she asked hesitantly.

He sounded apologetic as he answered.

"Yeah, I'm good. Better now. I mean, well, never mind. Come in, come in," he told her.

She carefully stepped inside, still not sure what was going on, but suspecting that it wasn't an illness.

As she entered, she couldn't help but look at his bedroom's walls and ceiling. They were painted a dark blue, almost black, but were covered in millions of tiny dots of paint, giving the appearance of a night sky filled with stars.

Allie had jokingly told him once that splatter painting wasn't in style anymore. His response had been a lengthy argument of the fact that they were not randomly splattered. They were each carefully placed, calculated to the exact measurements of the midnight sky as seen from some place she couldn't remember the name of, let alone pronounce, at some precise date of the year which she also couldn't quite recall.

She didn't understand a word of it. Allie had been careful not to comment on them again, but she never failed to be impressed with the effect. It really did look like a night sky.

Dav himself was sitting at his desk, a stack of his astronomy books beside him, several sprawled open atop the desk before him, almost covering the half a dozen pieces of paper he had scribbled completely unintelligible notes all over. He was great at every subject, but he had a real fascination with astronomy.

Dav looked back down to his notes briefly, then back up at her as she entered, his blue eyes seeming strikingly bright, almost luminescent in the pale, dim light of his table lamp.

His expression was intense, both anxious and excited, like a dehydrated man in the desert who had just spotted an oasis, or maybe a rescue plane.

"You weren't just trying to skip out on a test today, were you?" she asked with a half-hearted grin.

He laughed, and she couldn't help but notice that he seemed a little out of breath, as though he'd been breathing too hard for a while.

"No, no tests today, though I am scheduled for an A-on my Algebra test on Thursday," he said with his usual playful grin, though it had an edge to it she hadn't seen before.

He seemed unusually excited and a little worried about something, though she couldn't imagine what it could be. She smiled at him but knew she had to be direct. Dav appreciated directness. He had always told her that if something didn't make sense, she had to ask, or she'd never learn the answer.

"Listen, Dav," she began, pulling the extra chair over beside him.

He caught her tone and put on his serious face again, though this time it was expectant, like he knew what she wanted to discuss.

"Something is going on, with both you and your brother. He almost attacked me when I knocked on the door a minute ago. You got really weird this morning, and you're a little weird now, too. You're both on edge about something, and I want to know what it is," she finished, staring at him in her best imitation of Katherine's no-nonsense expression.

To his credit, Dav didn't laugh at her impression of a stern parent demanding an explanation. He watched her carefully, the intensity never leaving his eyes. After what felt like a long time, he spoke, his voice soft but unusually intense.

"There is something going on, Allie," he began, "and I have to ask you, as my best friend in this world or any other, to trust me completely in this. I can't tell you anything. I can't even tell you why I can't tell you anything. Please, Allie. Trust me that I'll take care of it the best that I can, and I'll do my best to make sure you don't have anything to worry about. This could be either the best thing that ever happened to us or the worst, but the end result could be something wonderful for me, my brother, and you all at the same time.

"It might get really rough for a little while as it all gets sorted out, but I promise you that no matter how things end up, I'll always be there for you, okay? As soon as I'm allowed to tell you, I will. Please don't worry." Dav took a long breath as he finished, looking at her with an expression that indicated he fully expected her to protest and pry for information.

Allie looked at him for a long moment, at the intensity in his eyes, the pleading in his expression, and the excitement still hiding underneath it all.

"Okay, Dav. If you say it's all right, I'll believe you. I won't ask you to tell me things you aren't allowed. I know that if you could tell me, you would. Whatever is going on, if you need my help, just let me know, okay?" she replied.

The look of relief on Dav's face told her that that was

exactly what he'd needed to hear.

Impulsively, she leaned over and hugged him. She'd never done that before, as she'd always tried to keep the friend boundary pretty solid, but she also felt that this was a good time for a friendly, reassuring hug. Besides, she needed one, too.

Dav tensed in surprise for a second, then wrapped his arms tightly around her like she was a life raft in the middle of the ocean. She fought valiantly to keep her mind on supporting her friend and not on how amazingly good that hug felt. He was a great hugger. Either way, she knew she wouldn't forget this moment for a long time. Too soon, Dav broke the hug and stood up.

"Come on. Let's take a look at your present," he said.

She was so lost in the feelings of the moment that she almost didn't understand what he meant. Then, it registered in her mind that he was talking about the box.

"Are you sure? We can wait if you're in the middle of something," she replied.

Dav shook his head.

"Actually, helping you figure it out will make me feel better," he said firmly.

Allie took a moment to wonder why he was so curious but decided he just wanted to help her reconnect with her mother, and maybe in some way to connect with his own through hers.

She had no idea where his mother was, either, but he had always firmly refused to talk about it, so she had stopped asking a long time ago. Allie reached into her shoulder bag to get the box out. Dav moved to the door.

"I'll go get Artus," he said by way of explanation before vanishing through the doorway.

She held the box in her hands, looking at it closely as she turned it over. Allie realized with surprise that she could hear the faintest rattle as she did so. She hadn't noticed that before.

Allie shook the box gently, holding it closer to her ear. Sure enough, the faint rattle came again. It was soft, but audible when she was paying attention. There was something inside. She felt a thrill of excitement at the thought.

A few minutes later, Dav came into view. His expression was a mixture of frustration, anger, and regret. At her questioning look, he shook his head in dismissal.

"He won't come. He says to leave it alone." Dav said in a disgusted tone.

She was a naturally curious person, so having essentially promised not to pry, her required silence was extremely frustrating. She did trust Dav, trusted him completely.

What bothered her was that she just didn't know, and she was reasonably sure that whatever was bothering him involved her, since it seems to have been her wooden box that sparked this whole thing. She couldn't imagine what the connection could possibly be, but she couldn't shake the feeling.

Dav reached out and took the box, turning the desk lamp to shine directly down on his workspace. He looked closely at the silvery spiral, nodded once, then began to analyze the pattern on the edge. He studied it for so long that she began to grow impatient.

"What do you think it is?" she asked him.

He glanced her way for a brief moment before turning back to the box.

"Well, it is writing. I can't read it, though. Artus might be able to, but he won't."

"Why not?" she asked.

"He thinks we're stirring up the hornets' nest, as he put it. 'Some things are better left in the past', he says," Dav replied in disgust.

"Why should he care about my past?" she asked, a little annoyed.

Dav glanced sidelong at her, and she scowled at him.

"To be honest, I think it has to do with your mother. I think Artus might have known her," he told her, leaning in close to the box.

Allie stared.

"Wait… what? How could that be?" she asked.

Dav sighed.

"I can't say," he replied, sounding just as frustrated by the lack of communication as she was. "Our families are connected, kind of."

"Connected how? Please tell me we're not related!"

She had a sudden flash of horror at the thought that she might have had a bit of a crush on someone who might well be her cousin. Dav laughed, though.

"Not even distantly," he reassured her with a mischievous glance out of the corner of his eye.

She blushed slightly as she realized what she'd just implied.

"No, I think my parents and yours worked together. I can't go into detail about it, but they did know each other."

"How do you know that?" she asked.

"I can't say," he replied with a shake of his head.

She rolled her eyes in irritation.

"I'm going to get sick of hearing that really soon,

aren't I," she stated, more than asked.

Dav smiled and nodded.

"Afraid so. Don't worry. If I'm right about what's in here, Artus will have to let me tell you more. We just need to get it open," he said.

She grinned.

"So, get on it, genius," she teased.

"Yeah, yeah, I'm working on it," he said with a smile.

Hours passed, and still, neither of them had figured out how to open it without breaking it. Neither of them was willing to damage the box to get it open.

They'd tried twisting, lifting, prying, tapping, sliding, all manner of pressing on the various sides and points, but nothing worked. The box, for all intents and purposes, might as well have been a solid block of wood. Finally, Dav leaned back in his chair, dropping the box on the table. He leaned way back, rubbing his eyes and stretching.

"I can't take looking at that thing another minute," he grumbled.

She could only nod her agreement.

"Okay. We'll try again later. I'm going to get home, so my mom doesn't worry," Allie said. Dav nodded. "Hey, you want to come over tomorrow morning? We can find something to do that isn't box related. Play some games or something," she said.

"Sure thing," Dav replied with a smile. "Have to find some way to kill a Saturday."

She grinned and stood to go.

Dav's expression changed slightly.

Allie paused. She could tell from his expression that he wanted to say something.

"I have something for you," he said. He opened a

desk drawer and pulled it out.

Allie couldn't see what it was, with his hand closed around it. She blinked in surprise.

"What is it? My birthday was yesterday, you know. And you already got me a present." she protested.

He nodded.

"I know. I just… I want you to wear this. For me," he said, holding out his hand.

In it was a silver bracelet. It was elegant, with a small, spiral-shaped cage carved into it, containing a tiny, but brilliant, blue gemstone. She thought it was the most beautiful thing she'd ever seen.

"Dav, thank you! It's beautiful! You didn't have to, though…" That last statement held little conviction. It really was beautiful.

"Don't thank me. Just wear it. Please?" he asked.

She regarded his serious expression and nodded. It meant something to him, so she would do it. It was as simple as that.

"I will. Every day until you tell me to stop." She smiled playfully at him.

He didn't return the smile.

"Allie, be careful. I mean, just pay attention. Anything weird starts happening, you call me right away, all right?" he said.

She frowned in confusion.

"Anything weird? Like what?" she asked. Dav shook his head.

"Weird enough that you'll know it if it happens," he replied.

"I will. You'll be the first one I call," Allie replied as she walked out the door.

CHAPTER THREE

THE BLIND JUMP

Allie couldn't help but smile as she opened the front door. Dav's hair hung wet down his forehead and plastered to his cheeks. Allie thought he looked amazing, though she wouldn't have dreamed of telling him that. He shook his hair like a dog, laughing as Allie protested loudly, trying to cover her face with her hands.

Even shaggy and wet, his hair looked great, she thought with a mixture of admiration and annoyance. She stepped aside, and Dav came in. Allie noticed he had his backpack with him, and it was so full that it bulged in strange places. Odd, for a Saturday. Or any day, really.

Katherine poked her head into the hallway, and her brow creased into a frown as she saw Dav.

"Young man, are you sure you should be out in this? Allie said you were sick yesterday." As she spoke, she came forward with a concerned look on her face, reaching a hand up to feel his forehead.

He fended her off awkwardly.

"No, no, I'm okay, Mrs. Pennbrook, really. I just had a bit of an upset stomach is all." He spoke hurriedly, trying to keep her from smothering him with her concern for his well-being.

She stepped back, but still looked at him with worry on her face.

"Really, I'm fine," he tried to reassure her. "I just came over to hang out with Allie."

She nodded but kept an eye on the pair as he tossed his jacket on the coat rack and bolted upstairs.

"Geez, you'd think nobody ever got sick around her before," Dav said in a slightly irritated tone of voice.

"Well, you never have. You know how much she adores you," Allie replied. A thought occurred to her to make her blink in surprise. "Actually, you've never been sick around me before, either," she said.

"Sure, I have," Dav replied defensively. "Remember the Halloween incident?"

She giggled but refused to let him put her off track.

"Yeah, but that was from too much candy. You've never had a cold, or the flu, or anything like that, in the whole five years I've known you. Why is that?"

"I don't know," Dav replied with a shrug. "I hadn't really thought about it. I guess this climate agrees with me."

What a lame excuse, she thought. She knew she wasn't going to get more out of him, but her mind started going over little details that she'd never really connected before.

Dav had never been sick before, except with the overdose of candy. She'd never seen him trip, or fall, or even stumble a little. He'd never had a bump, or a bruise, or a scrape in all the time she'd known him. What kind of boy never got banged up a little?

Dav always said he was never any good at sports, and he said that was why he never tried out for any teams, but based on his natural grace and obviously excellent balance, he was probably more than agile enough to be great at them.

He was intelligent and clearly knew something about the box her mother had left her almost thirteen years ago. She frowned as she considered her friend. What was going on with him?

She abruptly realized she'd been quiet for some time, and that Dav was looking at her anxiously.

"Sorry, just thinking," she said, hoping to get that terrible, worried look off his face. It didn't work, though his response was casual enough.

"No problem, it's cool," he answered. "Listen, I had an idea last night. About the box."

"I thought we weren't going to talk about the box," she said with a frown.

"I know, but this will probably work. I think I know how to get it open," Dav replied.

She perked up.

"Really? Cool, what do we need to do?" She moved to grab the box from her bedside table.

"We need the vacuum cleaner," he replied.

She froze and looked at him in disbelief.

"We need... the vacuum cleaner," she repeated in astonishment.

He nodded, grinning slightly.

That certainly got her curiosity going. She handed him the box and then went into the hall closet for the vacuum. As she came back in with it and began plugging it in, Dav spoke.

"You're good at science, right? What happens to an airtight container when it's sealed in a low-pressure environment?" he asked.

"I don't know," she answered. "I guess it stays low pressure inside even if the outside pressure changes, since the air can't get in or out. Right?" She looked at him questioningly.

He nodded approvingly with a smile.

"Exactly," he continued, "and what happens when that low-pressure container is moved into a higher pressure area?"

"Same thing. The inside pressure should still stay low unless it breaks," she replied.

Dav's grin broadened. The wind outside picked up, sending the rain pattering a staccato rhythm on the window of her room.

"Right."

He took the hose from the vacuum and pulled a large, clear plastic box out of his backpack.

It looked like it had once been a tiny fish tank, but it was obvious that he had modified it. He had attached a clear plastic lid, sealed tightly around the edges, and with a hole in the middle just a bit bigger than the hose. He also drew out a roll of duct tape. Her eyes went wide as she realized where he was going with this.

"Wait, if it was sealed inside a low-pressure environment, the lower pressure inside would suck the lid on if you tried to open it in a higher pressure environment. The low pressure inside would keep the lid held tight!" she exclaimed.

Dav winked at her.

"See? Told you that you were good at science."

"You're going to create a low-pressure environment

to open it in!" she said excitedly.

Dav nodded as he put the wooden box inside the larger plastic one. He positioned it near one corner. She noticed that he'd installed a long, wire hook through a tiny hole on the top, which had been sealed around the wire with some milky-white resin. That would keep the pressure and still let him move the hook, she assumed. He put a bit of tape near the base of the box to hold it down while leaving the lid free.

Dav put the hose into the hole on the top and began sealing it with a liberal application of carefully placed duct tape.

"This wouldn't work for anything long term, but for as long as the vacuum is running, we should be able to drop the pressure in there by a good margin. I'm glad you have a good vacuum cleaner," he said with a laugh.

Thunder rumbled outside, some distance off.

After a few moments, he appeared satisfied with the taping job, latched the lid down tight, and nodded to her. He took hold of the top end of the metal hook as she flipped the switch.

The vacuum roared to life, sounding oddly high-pitched with the intake being closed in an airtight space like it was. Dav began fiddling with the wire hook, trying to tug at the lid by the tiny seams.

Several minutes later, Dav nodded to her to switch off the vacuum cleaner. She did so and looked at him curiously.

"I really thought I had that one," he said, sounding extremely disappointed.

Allie gave him a comforting smile.

He opened the container and reached in, pulling out the wooden box. He turned it over in his hands, clearly frustrated with his inability to solve the puzzle. After a moment, he handed it back to her.

She took it, looking it over herself.

"I thought you did, too. I can't even imagine a puzzle you couldn't figure out," she told him.

"Thanks," he replied with a small smile, "but I'm not as smart as you think I am. I really wish Artus would help us out."

"Me, too," she replied. "I'm surprised that he won't, actually."

"I tried to talk to him about it," he said, "but I couldn't get him to see things my way. He always has his ideas of what is supposed to happen, and he won't budge. He won't even tell me what he does think should happen, except that we shouldn't be helping you open the box."

Allie looked over at him for a moment, then shook her head. She didn't understand what was going on with Artus any more than Dav seemed to. Allie desperately wished she knew more about what was going on than she did, but she'd promised Dav not to ask.

She turned her eyes back to the edge of the box, where the stylized writing edged the lid. They seemed so precise, so elegant. She couldn't understand why she couldn't read them.

It looked just familiar enough to seem like it should make sense, but only practice could help you actually read that way. Like a mirror, she thought.

As though the words themselves were the key, her perspective of the writing instantly flipped backward. Everything else around her seemed to fade, the lettering on the box brightening and growing in her vision until nothing else existed.

A part of her mind registered that Dav was still talking, but her mind no longer processed his words. Like a switch flipped in her mind, she suddenly understood the writing. She began to read it, backward from her English language perspective, following the letters from right to left.

Oddly, this simple shift in perspective made the entire language make sense. Her mouth began forming the words as she read. *Entrindi lo'urvaithe maur Vimbrandh.* Somehow, she knew what they meant, "Breath of the Bearer".

As quickly as they had fallen into place before, the letters seemed to reverse themselves again, and she found herself no longer able to read them.

Dav was shaking her.

"Allie!" he was saying, as if he'd called it several times before. "Allie, are you okay?"

She blinked, clearing her mind as awareness returned to her.

"Yeah, Dav. I'm fine. Why?" she asked, trying to pretend that nothing had happened.

"You totally zoned out for several minutes there. I couldn't get you to respond. You just kept mumbling something," he said.

"Mumbling? What was I saying?"

He looked at her for a long moment.

"I didn't understand it. It sounded familiar, but it wasn't English," was his anxious reply. "Are you sure you're okay?"

"Yeah, it's just… I knew what the words on the box meant," she told him.

He stared at her in surprise and shock.

"No, really," she continued. "It was like, all of a

sudden, the language changed into something I could understand."

"Well?" he asked with a hint of exasperation. "What does it say?"

"It says the same thing, over and over. 'Breath of the Bearer', repeated all the way around the box," she told him, looking at the pattern again. It didn't make sense anymore. Once again, it had become a meaningless, though pretty, design.

"What does that mean?" he asked.

"I have no idea," she replied with a shrug. "Could be anything."

"Not anything," he said. "It has to mean something specific, related to the box."

"Yeah, but it could be anything about the box," she argued. "It could be the title or name of the person who owns the box. It might be the signature of the artist who made it. You know, like a painter signs their work. For all we know, that could be the name of a hotel, and this box was something bought from their gift shop."

Dav looked at her wryly.

"A box like that, from a hotel gift shop?" he repeated disbelievingly.

"Okay, so that's a stupid example," she admitted with a scowl. "I'm just saying that unless we know more about the box, we can't just assume that the words actually matter."

"Fair enough," he replied. Dav paused a moment, considering. "How did you understand the writing?"

"I'm not really sure," she admitted. "I just sort of stared at it, and it started to make sense. Like the letters decided to rearrange themselves."

Dav watched her for a moment, then glanced down

at the box.

"Do they still make sense?" he asked.

She shook her head.

"No, it was only for a minute, while I was staring at them like that," she replied. "I had to kind of… I don't know, think about them differently. Backward, almost."

"Can you do it again?" Dav asked.

She shrugged, feeling uncertain.

"I don't know. I could try it, I guess," she answered.

He nodded encouragement for her to continue, and she turned to look at the writing again.

Allie stared at the lines of script, trying to shift perspective again. She stared for a full minute and was about to give up when the writing fell into place in her mind again. It seemed as though her mind had to look at it from just the right angle for it to click. The room seemed to fade out around her again as the words brightened.

"*Entrindi lo'urvaithe maur Vimbrandh,*" she read aloud softly, whispering. Over and over again, she read the words, her whisper gradually growing louder as she spoke the foreign sounds.

They seemed so natural to her, so comfortable to speak. She felt as though she'd been speaking this language her entire life. She didn't notice when Dav reached out and slowly lifted her hands, holding the box higher. He kept lifting until the box was just below her face.

"*Entrindi lo'urvaithe maur Vimbrandh,*" she said again.

A glow began to pour over the edge of the lid, seeping fluidly through the almost invisible gap between box and lid. It poured down like liquid light, seeming to evaporate just as it fell beyond Allie's hands. With a faint hum, the light faded.

Unlike last time, as the room came back into focus, the words stayed clear to her, and she found she could still read them without any trouble. She blinked as she reoriented herself.

Dav was looking at her expectantly and with a look of concern.

She shrugged and pulled on the lid. It came free effortlessly.

Allie suppressed a gasp of excitement as she removed the lid. It wasn't hinged, so she removed it completely and set it aside.

The inside edge of the box looked singed, as though it had been welded shut, or perhaps had just been burned open. Just beyond the blackened seam, the inside of the box was lined with a dark, velvety fabric that looked impossibly soft to the touch.

At any other time, she would immediately have been drawn to the elegant material, touching and feeling its texture. Just now, however, her eye was drawn to something much more interesting.

It was absolutely beautiful. It was a small, oblong crystal, perfectly shaped, perfectly clear, and perfectly smooth, though little markings seemed etched into it just below the surface of each facet. The markings looked identical to the ones on the box, elegant lines seeming to flow together without actually touching. The angles of the facets alternated and slanted in such a way that it practically begged to be spun.

It hung on a silver clasp, as though intended to be hung as a pendant, though there was no chain. As she stared into it, the light entering it seemed almost to hesitate before leaving it, though she wouldn't have been able to describe exactly what that meant, or how she knew it. It sure was a strange effect, though.

She reached out and picked it up by the clasp between her forefinger and thumb, then spun it in her palm.

Immediately, Dav's hand clamped down around it, a look of absolute terror on his face.

"Please… don't… do that," he said, clearly and carefully.

She scowled at him, a little annoyed at his sudden interference.

The look on his face stole the fire from her response, though. Thunder rumbled again, closer this time. The sound struck her as ominous.

"Why not? It's my crystal," she replied, knowing it sounded petulant.

Dav's serious look told her quite plainly that he wasn't playing around.

"I can't tell you," he replied, clearly emphasizing each word.

She frowned before making the connection.

"Does it have something to do with…" She trailed off, not knowing how to end her question.

Dav didn't answer, but the intensity in his eyes plainly told her it was true.

Somehow, her crystal, the gift from her mother, was involved in whatever was going on with Dav. That meant…

But it couldn't be, she thought. He looked so much like he wanted to tell her. That alone made her feel better about the fact that he didn't. She knew he would if he could.

A tremendous boom tore through the air outside.

Allie flinched.

"Wow, that lightning's getting serious out there," she said, glancing at the window. Dav nodded his agreement.

"Yeah, I'd better get home. Artus will worry. See you tomorrow, and don't spin that crystal!"

And with that, he was gone out the door.

Allie shook her head. He was awfully flighty lately. The whole situation was just weird. She sat down at her desk, intending to try and pull her thoughts together long enough to finish some homework.

She sighed as she set the crystal on the desk and dug out her books, but her gaze kept sliding back to the unusual pendant.

What was it made of, she wondered? Was it quartz? It couldn't be a diamond. A diamond of that size and cut would be worth an awful lot of money. She got the feeling it was something else entirely, though she had no idea how to test that theory.

Forcefully, she pulled her attention back to her math book. She opened it up to the proper page, picking up a pencil from the little box on the corner of her desk. Her gaze slid back to the crystal. Outside, another rumbling peal of thunder sounded, feeling like a promise of destruction.

The landing precisely coincided with a resounding crash of thunder, and the craft landed in a small clearing, surrounded by thick trees over twenty miles from the town where Allie now lived. The resounding shudder that ran through the ground as the solid craft touched down simply blended into the rumbling growl of the raging storm.

The ship was a rusty, reddish-brown color, though the dull-looking metal was in prime condition and a far stronger alloy than anything the humans of this world had developed.

It was huge, shaped something like a hammerhead shark, a slender, aerodynamic body with a broader section at both the front and tail ends, narrowing briefly into a cylindrical form before broadening again in the middle.

The effect was predatory, heightened by the numerous jutting attachments all over the ship that couldn't be anything other than weapons.

The massive hatch on the top of the ship cracked open and lifted. The beasts that crawled from within the craft would have been perfectly at home in the nightmares of the residents of this world.

They were huge, twice the size of a man, broad, and covered in weirdly bulging muscles. All three of the creatures had identical, greasy, gray fur, the same tall, pointed ears, and similarly random, mismatched leather armoring. Each had the same malicious expression on its face, and the same dark glint in its midnight-black eyes.

The only real difference between each of the behemoths, to anyone foolish enough to take a closer look, was the size, angle, and placement of their tusks, which seemed to have been almost randomly placed in the front of each beast's mouth.

The largest, and arguably the ugliest of the three, grunted and growled something in their guttural language. It would have sounded like mindless snarling to anyone listening, but the snarls and grunts translated loosely into something like, "The scent is strong. Our prey is not far. We will have it by the time this tiny planet's sun descends."

At this, all three broke into a deceptively ungainly, loping run, covering frightening amounts of distance at a startling pace. The leader of the three let out a howling roar, warning any who might be between the pack and their prey to stay clear. The beasts vanished into the distance, intent on their impending kill.

It was a long time before the animals nearby dared move again.

The sound was terrifying. Allie had first thought it was just more of the rumbling thunder that had made her fidgety all day. It lasted too long, though, drawn out for several seconds, not fluctuating or changing pitch. It sounded more like a roar than a peal of thunder. She shook her head to clear it of that unpleasant thought, chills running up her spine.

She hadn't heard from Dav since he left this morning, but she hadn't really expected to. He was probably nose deep in those books again, though what he was looking for was beyond her.

Allie stood up and stretched, a little pang in her stomach reminding her that it had been some time since lunch. She picked up the crystal and slipped it into the side pocket of her jeans.

Descending the stairs with a dragging slowness brought on by a combination of boredom and anxiety, she made her way into the kitchen.

She had barely made it through the kitchen doorway when the side door burst open, and Dav practically leapt through. He wore his usual, jeans, a t-shirt, and his now soaking-wet windbreaker. His hair was slicked against his forehead, droplets of water streaming down his face. His expression was one she'd never seen before. It was like panic, but stronger somehow. He looked brave, noble, and urgent.

"Allie! Let's go!" he shouted over the screaming storm outside.

She hadn't realized the wind had gotten so bad, until the door was opened, and she could see the trees across the way thrashing in the gale, the rain coming down almost horizontally.

"Dav! What is going…" she began to protest.

"No time!" he insisted, moving forward to grab her arm. He paused a moment, looking down at the bracelet on her wrist, as though checking it were still there. "They're here already, far too quickly. They must have already been in this sector. We have to go, right now! Artus can help!" he said, pulling her forward with shocking ease.

She struggled to pull free, but his grip was like iron.

"Where are we going? What about Mom?" she asked desperately.

"She'll be safer if we're not here!" he replied firmly, moving her quickly to the door.

"Wh… what do you mean safer?" she stammered, suddenly frightened.

Dav opened his mouth to reply, but a terrifying roar from somewhere beyond the window silenced him.

That was definitely not thunder. It sounded some distance off, but even so, it sent a terrible chill through Allie's entire body. It sounded angry, hungry, and large.

"What on Earth was that?" she asked Dav, not sure

she wanted to hear the answer.

"Nothing on Earth. That's the problem. Come on. We have to get you and that crystal to Artus, fast. You have it, right?" he asked.

She nodded. It was in her hip pocket.

"Dav, what's going on? I know I promised not to…" she began.

Another roar cut her off. It sounded much closer this time.

"Go!" Dav shouted. He grabbed her arm and shoved her through the doorway.

She happily obliged him, her fear of that sound overwhelming her curiosity. Dav was right behind her, but Katherine came into the room just at that moment.

"Did you children hear that? We need to get into the basement right now," she said, her tone clearly stating she would tolerate no argument.

Allie opened her mouth to reply, but Dav stepped quickly toward her. He raised a hand in front of her face, a small, round object held between two fingers.

Katherine paused in confusion, then slowly dropped, eyes rolling back and closing as Dav reached out and caught her, lowering her smoothly and effortlessly to the ground despite his being a full head and shoulders shorter than she was. Allie stared in shock and horror for a long second before reacting.

"What did you do to her?" she screamed at him.

"I put her to sleep! It's not after her, it's after you! If she's anywhere nearby when it catches up, it will kill her, too!" Dav shouted back, grabbing her arm and moving towards the door.

As she suspected, he was frighteningly strong, and she couldn't have resisted no matter how much she might have wanted to. Another roar sounding almost right outside convinced her that she needed to be somewhere else right then, so she rushed behind her suddenly mysterious friend.

Dav bolted into the storm. The wind was incredible, driving the rain straight into their faces, pelting them with every step and stinging her eyes. She couldn't remember the last time a storm like this had hit the area. The howling scream of the wind was almost deafening, but it didn't seem to diminish the clarity of the earth-shaking roar that tore through the air from right behind her house. Dav didn't slow as they ran, but he did let go of her arm once she showed no sign of turning back.

"Move faster, Allie! We'll never outrun it at that speed!" he shouted over the wind.

She could barely hear him, though he was right beside her.

"I can't!" she shouted back, already running out of breath.

Dav cast a look over their shoulders and flinched.

She started to look back to see what had caused his reaction, but Dav quickly swept her off her feet.

Incredibly, even carrying her, he ran faster than he had been before. Even with the extra weight, he could have easily outrun her at her best speed.

Allie felt a shiver that had nothing to do with the wind and rain. Who was this person she'd known for years? She didn't even know her own best friend.

Dav ran at an astonishing speed for two long minutes, nearing his own house much faster than they'd ever made the journey before. She wasn't sure they could have driven there that fast. Not without violating a few speed limits at any rate.

Without warning, he swung her down and set her on her feet, still several hundred yards from his house. She stumbled but didn't fall.

"Run as fast as you can to Artus! He'll protect you!" he shouted and gave her a little shove.

"But what about you?" she called back.

"I have to buy time! Go!" he shouted, giving her a slightly harder shove toward his house.

Then, she saw it. The beast was enormous and terrifying. It was horrifically ugly, her eyes taking in the deformed beast, but her mind almost refusing to process what she was seeing.

As it ran with blood-chilling speed, it used its long arms to run on all fours, though it didn't have to lean far forward from an upright position to do so. It looked almost like some kind of mutated gorilla, she thought with an odd sort of clarity.

She couldn't even force herself to scream; her throat and lungs had constricted tightly in her fear. In complete terror, she turned and raced away from it, heading directly for Dav's house, clinging desperately to the thought that Artus could protect them both.

It took her several seconds to realize Dav wasn't following and that he'd already told her he wasn't going to follow. She stopped dead and spun around.

Dav stood facing the thing as it charged, crouched down in an odd stance, as if he was about to fight. She screamed his name, but he didn't so much as turn his head her way. The beast drew closer to him, each lope covering several yards of distance. It looked eager as it charged the small boy, who looked even smaller in the path of such a beast.

She screamed, unable to turn away.

A vicious warning snarl cut the air, tearing through even the howling wind. To Allie's shock, she realized it was coming from Dav!

The beast seemed to backpedal in shock, pulling to a halt ten feet from her best friend. The thing looked confused.

Dav's growl came again, sharpened to a ferocity that scared even her. Apparently, the beast thought the same. To her complete amazement, the towering, hulking brute looked momentarily reluctant to attack her short friend.

More confused than ever, she watched as Dav leapt at the creature. It flinched as Dav moved, but then it snarled and grabbed for the boy, its fighting reflexes taking over.

Dav was too quick, though. He'd moved in closer than the beast had expected in the sudden leap. Dav's right fist came slashing through the air, connecting solidly with the thing's grotesque face.

Allie blinked as silvery-blue energy arced around the point of impact. The beast staggered backward, roaring in pain. Where Dav's fist had hit it, a scorched, black patch now lay, emitting tiny wisps of smoke.

Dav took the opportunity while the thing was momentarily disoriented to shout over his shoulder.

"Go, Allie! I can take one, but two more are coming!" he yelled. As if to punctuate his words, another roar rumbled in the distance. Too close.

Unable to comprehend anything going on around her, she simply did as he'd told her. Dav knew what was going on. She trusted him. She had to trust him. Allie turned and ran as fast as her legs could carry her toward Artus, and her only hope of safety.

Moisture blinded her vision as she ran, though she

couldn't tell if it was from the rain or her own tears. The wind howled in anger, though she barely heard it. She stumbled more than once, barely keeping from hitting the ground hard.

Get to Artus, she told herself over and over. Get to Artus. She desperately tried not to think about Dav's safety, for she knew if she did, she'd turn and run back to him.

A thundering roar coincided perfectly with another peal of thunder, making the whole world seem as if it were about to shake itself apart.

Allie froze and rubbed water out of her eyes. Less than fifty feet ahead of her was Dav's house. Less than twenty feet away was another of those horrible monsters. She screamed as it roared again, obviously excited for the kill.

Dav's front door burst open, and Artus leapt out. His leap cleared the entire flight of steps, and he ran with blinding speed to her aid.

She had another oddly calm thought in the chaos of her mind that Artus and Dav were definitely brothers, both able to move that way.

Only a few feet from the unknowing behemoth, another of the creatures seemed to come out of nowhere, catching Artus in a full flying tackle from the side.

The beast before her began to charge.

She had no hope, she knew. Dav was battling behind her, Artus ahead of her, and no one was left to save her from this one. She closed her eyes, hoping it would be quick.

"Spin the crystal!" shouted a voice from what sounded impossibly far off.

Her eyes snapped open. It felt like an eternity before

her mind registered that it was Dav, but it couldn't have been more than a fraction of a second, since the beast charging her hadn't yet reached her.

"Spin it!" repeated Dav urgently, sounding closer.

He must be running toward me, she thought, her mind feeling oddly detached. She realized that she had the crystal clenched in her fist. She wasn't sure how she'd gotten it out of her pocket, or why.

The creature lunged for her.

As quickly as she could, trusting Dav, she opened her hand. The crystal dangled from the clasp between her fingers, and she flicked the crystal into a spin. Once given momentum, it accelerated by itself, spinning faster with each passing moment. It seemed to pull light into it, spinning faster and faster.

The creature seemed to slow in mid-air, as though it were a video, and someone was playing with the remote. It crept toward her, slower by the second as the crystal spun faster, seeming to hum inside her head.

A blinding flash of light abruptly tore through the air all around her. She felt as though her skin would be ripped from her body, as though something was pulling her in every direction at once. Allie tried to scream, but there was no air in her lungs. She gasped frantically, but there was no air outside, either.

In a panic, she tried to turn around, but her feet found no purchase, as though the ground beneath her had disappeared. She couldn't see anything, blinded by the swirling, mind-numbing light threatening to burn right through her eyelids.

The noise of the wind and thunder was gone, replaced by an odd sort of keening, a high-pitched whistling, like the highest note of the finest piccolo played frighteningly close to her ears. It went on and on until she was afraid her skull would shatter. Then, everything simply went away.

CHAPTER FOUR

BIOLOGY CLASS IS USEFUL

Slowly, sound returned to her. Birds chirped all around, and something that sounded vaguely like monkeys chattered in the distance. It was all odd, though. Different somehow, and not quite normal.

Her eyes opened slowly, aching from the abuse they had just suffered. Allie blinked in shock as the sights around her registered in her mind. The monster was gone. So was Dav. So was the town.

She was in a rainforest. A thick, heavy rainforest, though she seemed to be lying in a small clearing. Her first thought was that she had died, but this wasn't nearly cheerful enough to be Heaven or anything, and it was far too beautiful to be the other place. Taking her aches into account, she was likely not dead.

As she stood painfully and turned slowly in place, she couldn't help but think that something was wrong.

Besides the fact that she was nowhere near where she should be, of course.

Something about this rainforest wasn't normal. The birds sounded wrong, the plants looked wrong, it even smelled wrong, though she had no idea how a rainforest was supposed to smell.

She also felt weirdly heavy, as though she suddenly had weights strapped all over her body. It took more effort to move her arms around, to stand, to walk than it should.

The plants looked somewhat more blue than green, she noticed. A faintly luminescent sparkle flecked randomly around the plant life. The little glowing specks seemed to be moving slightly. She leaned closer to one, and gasped as she realized the little glow came from a tiny bug.

No, she thought as she leaned even closer, not a bug, a lizard. No larger than a ladybug, and glowing faintly green, but a lizard nonetheless. She glanced around at the foliage. There had to be millions of the little things! The whole rainforest seemed flecked with the small, green, glowing lizards.

Her heart was still pounding from fear and anxiety, but it was no longer from the panic of nearly being crushed by whatever those monster were. Definitely not in Kansas anymore, she thought to herself.

She straightened and looked up to the hot, humid sky. The sky, from what she could see through the canopy of trees surrounding the edges of the clearing, was a delicate lavender color.

She looked down at the normal-looking crystal sitting in her hand. What on earth is this thing, she wondered? What were those huge monsters that had attacked them, and why were they after her? What did Dav have to do with all of this? What exactly was Dav anyway? Obviously not human, she thought ruefully. She found herself desperately wishing Dav were here anyway, human or not.

This thought sent her mind into a whirling tailspin of fear for Dav. What had happened to him? He wasn't here, so he must still be back there, in the storm, with those creatures. He seemed capable enough, frighteningly so, and Artus seemed just as potent, physically. But could the two of them handle those three beasts?

Allie slid back down to the ground, her breath coming in short, sharp gasps. Her heart pounded so loudly she could barely hear the many strange sounds coming from the jungle all around her.

She was lost someplace she knew nothing about. For all she knew, this wasn't even Earth anymore. Some of Dav's comments started to make a bit more sense. After all, Earth certainly wasn't supposed to have a sky that color.

The plants were wrong, the animals were wrong, the sky was wrong… Maybe my little Oz joke wasn't that far off, she thought. Maybe I've been knocked unconscious and am having the strangest dream of my life.

She felt the hot sensation of tears rising to her eyes and swallowed hard, clenching her jaw to bite them back. Now wasn't the time for a breakdown, she knew.

It took her some time and several long, deep breaths to clear her thoughts, struggling to get the air past the knot in her throat.

Dav always told her not to worry over things she couldn't fix, and instead to focus on what she could do something about. He'd told her that about a math test she'd failed, trying to cheer her up and encourage her to study harder for the next one, but the concept applied here, too. Right now, all she could do was try to figure out where she was and how to get home.

If it was a dream, she couldn't do anything about it but wait until she woke up. If it wasn't a dream, she sure didn't want to sit around and wait for some mutant creature from the jungle to show up and eat her.

Allie almost broke down again at the realization that there probably were predators here, but she managed to keep herself under control. She wiped at her eyes with the back of one hand and looked at the crystal still clutched in the other. It felt cold to the touch, though not uncomfortably so.

This is what brought me here, she thought. Dav must have known that it could do this, or he wouldn't have told her to spin it at that exact moment. Well, that sure explained why he hadn't wanted her to spin it before.

Allie considered spinning it again. Maybe it would take her home. Unfortunately, she didn't know for sure and was afraid to try it. She would just have to trust that Dav would know best and would either come for her or help her come home.

She could stay here, hoping Dav would come for her soon, but what would she do if he didn't? She would need food, clean water, and shelter of some kind. Allie silently thanked summer camp for at least covering the basics of wilderness survival in her time there.

Allie looked around again. It looked pretty much the same in every direction. One way was as good as another, she supposed. She began to walk toward the trees. If she could climb a tree and get a good look around from a higher vantage point, she might be able to figure out where she was, or at least how to get somewhere a little more secure.

Allie knew she was vulnerable out here. She had some idea what kinds of animals lived in rainforests, and she was pretty sure she didn't want to meet most of them. Although, she thought, this is clearly not like any rainforest I've heard about, so who knows what kinds of creatures could be lurking nearby.

She quickly reached a tall enough tree and grabbed on to begin climbing. Immediately, she jerked her hands away in disgust. The bark of the tree was sticky and spongy. She barely kept from gagging and tried to rub the sticky substance off onto her jeans. She felt for a moment like she was just making things worse, but gradually, the sap seemed to lose its stickiness. Though in its place were dirty-looking patches on both her hands and jeans.

Allie frowned in irritation. She would have to be more careful. She obviously didn't know much about rainforest plant life. For all she knew, that tree's sap could have been poisonous. She looked around, but all the trees seemed similarly sticky, now that she knew what to look for.

A high-pitched shriek sounded in the distance, like nothing she'd ever heard before, causing Allie to flinch. She grabbed a decent-sized rock from the ground in her momentary panic, not caring that it was a fairly pathetic excuse for a weapon.

She spun toward the sound, though it had sounded some distance off. Despite that fact, her heart had begun pounding again, all her work trying to calm herself vanishing in a single breath.

Allie stood that way, rock upraised, for several minutes, waiting for a repeat of the sound, or for whatever made the noise to attack her.

Nothing happened, just the hum of what she assumed were insects, and calls that were not too different from birds and monkeys that lived in the kinds of rainforests she was more familiar with. None of the current sounds she heard seemed aggressive or hungry. Slowly, she put down the rock and took another deep breath.

Moving was important, she decided. Allie continued on a little way, spotting a dry-looking stick on the ground. She tentatively reached out and touched it with one small finger.

It felt normal enough, so she picked it up and began using it to tap trees along the way. It wasn't large, but it might make a useful weapon in a pinch and worked nicely for tree-testing in the meantime. She kept hoping to find a tree that felt more solid, but the further she went into the depths of this peculiar rainforest, the less hope she had of finding a climbable tree.

The sounds of the rainforest were frighteningly loud, unfamiliar, and occasionally eerie. The constant cawing of the bird-like calls was punctuated by frequent hoots and shrieks of something Allie couldn't help but picture as a large ape, though she was no longer at all certain.

Every so often, a blood-curdling shriek, snarl, growl, or roar would cause the other animals to grow silent for a few moments. The odd, clicking hum of countless creatures she thought might be insects around her seemed enough to drive her insane.

Frequently, animals moved in the brush around her, though she never saw a single one, and none of them seemed inclined to move toward her. That didn't stop her from holding her breath and jumping every time she heard movement. Which happened a lot.

Allie had been walking for almost an hour when, without warning, her occasional squishy tapping at a tree trunk struck something solid. She stopped and looked more closely.

As her gaze ran up the grayish trunk, and into the empty, barren branches, she recognized immediately that the tree was dead. She looked down at the stick and then back to the tree. What an odd place, she thought. Perhaps these trees only lost that sticky, spongy texture when they were dead.

She was about to try the tree but was held back by the knowledge that dead trees weren't usually safe to climb. The dry branches and trunks were often brittle and could snap without warning. The live trees around here, however, were totally out of the question.

The tree was thick, the trunk nearly twice as wide as she was tall, and that gave her hope. Maybe she'd be safe if she stayed near the trunk and didn't trust herself to any of the extending branches. It was also a bit taller than the other trees around it, so it might give her a good vantage point to check out the area.

Resigning herself to her task, she knew she'd never find anything just wandering around in the rainforest. Something would catch and eat her sooner or later. Besides, she was getting hungry and thirsty. She needed to get the lay of the land and work on some kind of plan.

Dropping her stick, Allie jumped up to the lowest and thickest of the branches. It held, so she slowly pulled herself up, using the trunk to brace her feet.

It took an extreme amount of effort, far more than

she thought it should have. She felt so heavy here. This planet must be massive, she thought, for the gravity to be so much stronger than she was used to. Bigger than Earth, at least. The more she thought about it, the more she became convinced that she was no longer on Earth.

Allie was amazed at how fast this heat and humidity and her extra weight sapped her strength. Her muscles ached, her breath came in short, irregular gasps, and her hair hung plastered to her cheeks and neck, dripping wet from the humidity and probably some of her own sweat, she thought with disgust. She managed to keep climbing, but it was extremely difficult.

As she neared the top, the tree began to creak and moan ominously. She held tightly to the trunk, eyes closed and unmoving for several seconds, for a brief instant convinced that the tree was going to snap, and she'd drop all the way to the ground. The tree once more grew silent, and she climbed a few more feet. As the tree once again voiced its protest, she stopped, deciding it was probably a bad idea to move up any further.

She set her position, hooking her legs over the sharp V shapes made by some of the thicker branches, and looping her arms around the trunk. She leaned back slightly and looked slowly around. Her breath caught in her throat. The sight was beautiful, and the height was dizzying.

An immense rainforest stretched as far as she could see, rolling slowly over gentle hills, the treetops a dark blue, with a definite green tinge. A pale lavender sky arced from horizon to horizon, soft, blue-gray clouds drifting across its face. They looked light and airy, not like the dense, gray, storm clouds she'd recently left, though the blue color seemed a little odd.

The sun that blazed in the sky seemed enormous to her, as though it were far too close. It, like the sky, had a soft but warm purple color. She smiled to herself. This would make a nice painting, she thought, though everyone would complain about the colors all being wrong. She thought it was pretty, at least.

Allie wondered if anyone else had ever seen this place, or if she was the first person ever to be here. A pair of birds flew by in the distance. No, she realized, they weren't birds, they were insects.

They looked kind of like moths, though the wings were elongated to either side and trailed long lengths of hair at the tips. They were a brilliant blue color, almost a neon shade. The creatures moved away from her at an angle, and she watched them until they vanished from sight, gliding on gentle strokes of their wings just over the treetops.

Looking back down toward the landscape, she found that she was glad that she'd climbed this tree. She could easily have wandered this expanse forever and never covered more than a few miles worth of ground.

As far as the eye could see was the rolling expanse of rainforest. She'd been traveling slightly downhill, she realized, her perch on this tree letting her see for miles, but her view the other way was much shorter, due to the trees looming higher than her position on the incline.

She shifted her gaze to the other side of the trunk and felt her heart leap with excitement as she spotted something unusual coming from the endless expanse.

In the distance, she could see a tiny tendril of smoke rising into the sky. If she hadn't been looking carefully, she would never have spotted it. Smoke meant fire, and the fact that it was a tiny bit of smoke meant it was a small fire. Probably controlled, which meant people.

Allie smiled smugly to herself, thinking that Dav would be pleased with her use of logic, and tried to memorize the landscape between her current position and the small line of smoke.

It wasn't even that far, she thought with excitement. Even as slowly as she guessed she'd been moving, she could make it there in another half an hour or so. At least, that's what she figured. After several minutes, she felt reasonably certain that she had a good mental map and carefully climbed down. All she had to do was keep going downhill.

Allie took a good look at the tree, positioned herself the same direction she'd been facing when at the top of the tree, and pointed in the direction she wanted to go. She would have to keep setting goal points ahead of herself to keep from getting turned around.

Taking a deep, steadying breath, she set off again into the thick, bluish rainforest. It would be hard, since her visibility in the dense underbrush wasn't more than a dozen feet or so, but otherwise, she was sure she'd get lost again in ten paces or less.

She needed to hurry, Allie knew. She was getting thirsty fast and could feel her stomach beginning to voice its usual hunger protests. Allie had missed dinner in that faraway kitchen back home. She wondered just how far away home was now.

Despite her best efforts to stay positive, she couldn't help but worry about whether she would ever see it again. It took all her willpower not to burst into tears right then and there. Dav would save her, she reassured herself. Dav was something else, something special, and he was her best friend. He would save her.

CHAPTER FIVE

PEOPLE OF THE TREE

Three hours later, though Allie would have sworn it had been much, much longer, she still hadn't found the source of the small fire. She was tired and hungry, but worse than anything else, she was thirsty. Odd, how all that moisture in the air didn't seem to help her thirst one bit.

From above and behind her, an odd chittering sound echoed through the rainforest. It sounded close. She jumped and spun around, her stick held up like a sword. The creature didn't sound dangerous, though. More like a curious monkey than anything else, though not quite like a monkey. She hoped that's all it was, anyway.

The noise came again from a slightly different direction, and she turned her head to look up into the trees, trying to locate the source of the sound, though she hadn't spotted anything she'd heard since coming to this world. Not one creature in hours of traveling, except the moths she'd seen from the tree, and the tiny, glowing lizards which were still crawling all over everything.

Allie took a few more steps but kept her eyes on the trees. With her head turned the way it was, she didn't see the fallen branch across her path, and she fell hard. Her knees hit a patch of rocky earth, and her hands splashed into a small puddle between the trunk of a tree and a small stone.

Forgetting everything else in the sudden contact with the water her body was screaming for, she greedily cupped her hands into the murky liquid and began to bring it to her mouth.

She paused as a random thought crossed her unfocused mind. Last year, in biology, hadn't her teacher Mr. Bradley told her something about parasites found in puddles like this?

What was the word he had used? Oh, right, 'stagnant'. Parasites tended to breed in stagnant water, that's what he had said. The last thing she needed was to get sick out here, too.

Allie dropped the handful of water with a supreme force of will, but she knew it was safer this way. She'd have to find some other way to get water. If she were lucky, it would rain soon. This was a rainforest, after all, right?

She tried not to remind herself that this wasn't anywhere near home, and for all she knew, the plants here pulled their moisture right out of the air. It was certainly humid enough for it, she thought. Pity she couldn't do that herself.

With the urgency of the moment gone, her knees began to hurt. She stood up carefully, brushing the moist dirt from the front of her pants, wincing as her hands touched her knees.

They didn't hurt badly enough for her to be worried about bleeding, but it was enough that she knew it was going to be uncomfortable walking. Well, she thought, time to find another tree to climb.

Allie looked around for a likely subject, but once again, her choices were few and far between. The trees, if anything, seemed bigger, healthier, and stickier than they were when last she tried to find a good climbing tree. With a frustrated sigh, she continued in the direction she thought she'd been heading.

After a minute or two, she realized that she'd forgotten about the odd chittering noise. It had stopped when she'd tripped and hadn't returned. Good, she thought. No reason to try her luck further by being followed by an unknown creature. After all, she had no idea wha…

Never mind, there it is again, she thought to herself. It still seemed just above and behind her, almost close enough to reach out and touch, but she saw nothing when she looked back. She stopped when she did so, though. She didn't need to fall twice to learn that lesson.

Allie turned forward again and resumed her slow pace. A faint, strange scent reached her nose, becoming slightly stronger as she walked. She'd been trudging through the same heavy smell of thick vegetation for hours, but this was different. Sweet and appetizing, almost like warm ginger cookies.

Her stomach gave an audible growl, loudly stating its opinion that she should follow the scent. Having nothing better to do at this point than look for food and water sources, she tried to sniff out the source of that mouth-watering aroma.

It was surprisingly easy, making her feel like quite

the accomplished tracker. It had a definite direction, and she simply headed straight toward the smell. Almost without warning, she came across the source.

The scent was coming from a small, round, blue tree, almost more of a bush, with nearly a dozen large, brightly colored fruits growing on it. Each fruit was about the size of a grapefruit, though they more closely resembled yellow pears with vertical red stripes than anything else. They looked firm and juicy.

Little orange blossoms sprouted from the tip of each branch, the fruits growing far closer to the center of the plant, though readily visible and within easy reach, if she took a few more steps forward. She had no doubt that the fruits were the source of that incredible scent.

Three more quick steps brought her almost within arm's reach of the bush, when a harsh screeching sound came from above. She looked up and stepped back but saw nothing but the heavy growth of the trees above her. The sound turned almost instantly into the inquisitive chittering noise she remembered from before.

Frowning, she stepped forward once more. The chittering changed into that awful screeching noise again. She wondered for a moment if the creature felt that the bush belonged to it. She was annoyed, tired, thirsty, and hungry. She had no intention of passing up such a fine meal.

In a rush, she bolted for the plant, stick held high. From entirely the opposite direction she expected, the creature appeared, leaping down from the side.

Allie slid on the damp dirt as she backpedaled, trying to avoid the thing. In the moment, it seemed huge. Although, as she staggered backward, she saw that the thing was actually quite small.

It landed in front of her and screeched its warning, but it did not pursue her as she scrambled back. She continued backing up until she was far enough to feel somewhat safe.

The odd little animal did indeed look something like a monkey, though the face and fur texture were just a little wrong. Of course, the purple color of the animal's fur didn't help. It had two little teddy-bear ears, and big eyes, though they seemed to be all blue, with no white around the outside, and only a darker spot of blue in the middle showing where the iris was.

Its long tail was probably half-again its body length and forked two-thirds of the way down into two smaller, fringed appendages. From the way the two parts of its tail were moving, she figured they were probably strong and agile, even more so than the tails of the monkeys she was familiar with. The fur almost seemed feathered, though not like real feathers, more like tiny purple fern leaves. It looked incredibly soft.

Its three-fingered hands seemed like they weren't sure what they should be doing, alternately flexing, showing tiny, black, sharp-looking claws, and curling the fingers underneath. The claws were retractable, she noticed, as the little hands opened and closed.

From the moment she began to back up, all signs of aggression were gone, save those twitching claws. It chattered at her curiously, cocking its head slightly to one side, then the other.

Allie couldn't help but think the thing was really quite cute, when it wasn't flying at her face. She began to take a step toward it, but the animal leaned forward aggressively and hissed, baring twin rows of sharp, vicious teeth.

They looked serrated, like a shark's teeth, but she couldn't tell for sure at this distance. Not that she wanted to get any closer to them to check.

She stepped back, and the animal calmed right down. It chattered softly, contentedly, and she frowned. Maybe it really was just trying to protect its fruit.

"That fruit is quite lethal," said a voice from behind her.

Allie was so startled by the sudden noise, and shocked by the sound of another voice, that she spun around and fell backward, right towards the monkey creature. She held her breath as she fell, waiting for those nasty-looking teeth to sink into her flesh. Allie landed more softly than she'd expected, probably due to the sponginess of the wet soil.

After a moment, she opened her eyes. The little creature sat squarely on her belly, staring at her with its head cocked to the side. It was so light that she could barely feel its weight. The voice that spoke earlier chuckled slightly.

"See? If it wanted to hurt you, you'd be dead already." Allie looked over the monkey-thing's shoulder to see who was speaking.

A strikingly tall, impossibly slender man with dark skin stood before her, dressed in such an array of bluish-green, leafy clothing and brown face paint that if he took even a single step backward, he'd likely vanish into the underbrush.

His long, brown hair, accented by the leaves woven into it, helped to break the silhouette of his face, making it even more likely that he would be invisible in the thick plant growth.

"You speak English," she stated in complete

surprise, the only coherent thought that she could bring forth. The man's expression turned to one of puzzlement.

"No, child. You speak Ayarani. Quite well, in fact."

"No, that can't be. I only speak Engl… Oh, never mind," she said in frustration, looking back at the little creature on her stomach.

It wasn't the weirdest thing that had happened to her today, by far, so she decided not to argue this particular point at the moment.

The little animal was scarcely taller than her arm from elbow to fingertips, and up close, it was decidedly adorable. It chattered happily as she gave it a tentative smile. Something the man had said a moment before struck her.

"Wait, did you say if it wanted to hurt me, I'd be dead already? It has sharp teeth, and those claws look pretty intense, but is it that dangerous?" she asked.

The man's slight half-smile spoke volumes. She looked nervously back at the little thing, but it simply chattered softly and began grooming itself. She slowly eased herself upright, and the creature hopped off her stomach, only to return rapidly to her shoulder once she stood. The man blinked in surprise.

"It really does like you. They are often protective of people, as it was with you just now, protecting you from the fruit, but they usually avoid direct contact. No one is quite sure why."

"Don't you mean us? Aren't you a person, too?" she asked, intending to be sarcastic, but her remark drew only a sharp bark of laughter from the man.

"Not in the strictest sense of the word," he replied as he turned and walked into the leafy foliage. "Coming?" he asked, just before he vanished.

She hurried to follow and spotted him a few moments after she entered the brush herself. She got the distinct impression that she could only see him because he wanted her to. It was a little unnerving.

The little creature rode on her shoulder, seeming completely comfortable perched there. It held on easily with its four-toed feet, and its long tail twined companionably around her upper right arm.

It had three fingers and one opposable thumb close to the wrist. The hands and feet looked nearly identical, appearing as well made for tree-walking as they were for picking up and manipulating objects.

As she made slightly nervous eye contact with the thing, it chirped happily at her, seeming pleased she'd looked at it, and she couldn't help but smile.

They traveled for a little over twenty minutes when, as if by magic, she found herself standing at the edge of a small village. It was built between the trees, and the undergrowth seemed to have been cultivated into the forms of small huts.

Many others like her strange guide were walking calmly about their business. Each one wore similar leafy clothing and had leaves tied into their long brown hair.

Allie could see no difference between men and women, and even the children seemed to have precisely the same body proportions, only in varying sizes. Her guide turned and smiled at her, spreading his arms wide in invitation.

"Welcome to my home. Here, your needs will be provided for, and you can remain as long as you like, as long as you follow our only rule. Do not harm any of the plants here. Under no circumstance will you damage so much as a single leaf, or you will no longer be welcome among my people. Am I understood?" She nodded her agreement.

Allie didn't know why that was the only rule, but she certainly wouldn't object to such a simple rule in exchange for food, water, and shelter until she could figure out what to do next.

"Come then," he said, and walked into a nearby hut.

She followed, fascinated. Heads turned toward her calmly, then away as the people around her continued about their business, displaying a surprising lack of curiosity.

The inside of the hut was even more amazing than the outside had been. The plants seemed to have grown into shapes resembling chairs, a bed, a small table, even shelves along the wall had grown evenly into place.

Her guide gestured her to a chair and retrieved a gourd from one of the shelves. As he took it down, she heard a sloshing sound and was once again painfully reminded of her thirst. The little creature on her shoulder held on calmly, chirping quietly to itself as she leaned forward eagerly.

As he handed the gourd to her, she drank from the opening in the top greedily, the water within tasting better than anything she'd ever had before. It was cool, wet, and sweet.

Allie gulped until the gourd was empty, drawing another of those soft chuckles from her host. She gasped for air as she lowered the gourd, not having paused long enough to breathe as she drank. She handed the gourd back with some reluctance, despite its emptiness.

"Thank you. You probably just saved my life," she said.

The man simply nodded, accepting her thanks and

statement with the same quiet ease he seemed to do everything with.

"I am called Ghier. And you are welcome."

"I'm Allie Bennett," she replied with a smile.

"Tell me how you come here, Alliebennett," Ghier said, stringing her first and last names together. "Other than my own kind, few come this far across the Jivai on foot. You are not well suited to this land." Ghier moved smoothly to the chair across from her, sitting and leaning back comfortably.

Allie hesitated but felt surprisingly at ease with this strange man. Somehow, she knew he would simply accept her remarkable situation and help her, no matter what she told him.

"Just Allie," she corrected him, "and it's kind of a long story," she said.

Ghier nodded.

"I have time, and I cannot help until I know what your trouble is," he replied calmly.

She considered a long moment, then nodded. He might be the first person she'd met since leaving Dav, but he'd been helpful so far and seemed to want to do more. She needed all the help she could get.

"This morning, I was at home, and everything was normal," she began. "My mother, I don't really know her, she left me with someone when I was really young, left me a present for my thirteenth birthday." She pulled the crystal out of her jeans pocket and held it out for him to see.

Ghier leaned forward enough to see it but made no move to touch it. She noticed, however, that his dark green eyes had grown intense. It struck her with surprise that he recognized the crystal. Dav had, too. She paused, then slowly continued.

"Anyway, my friend Dav…"

"Dav?" he interrupted.

She frowned and nodded.

"Yeah. It's short for Davrelan. Why?" she asked curiously.

He'd seemed suddenly more attentive when she'd spoken the name, but Ghier simply shook his head.

"The name is familiar," he answered dismissively. "It is not too uncommon a name, though. Please, continue."

Allie sighed and decided to tell him the full story. She spent the next hour telling him everything that had happened, right up until he'd found her. She couldn't begin to describe how much better it felt to have someone to share the story with, even if the listener was as odd as the story and belonged right in it. When at last she had finished, he was quiet for some time before speaking again.

"There are things in your story that are familiar to me, and things that are not," he began. "Knowledge of other worlds comes to us but rarely, though knowledge of our own world travels faster than the wind.

"The beasts you spoke of are called maruck. Their people serve Highlord Tyren, who styles himself as the ruler of this galaxy. His war has destroyed countless lives." He took a breath and sighed, a sound like a breeze in the leaves. "I am sorry, Allie. You cannot stay here. Your story has told me of the danger you, and all those near you, face.

"I do not mind such danger myself, and I will help you as I can, but I cannot allow you to remain with my people. Highlord Tyren and the maruck will hunt you and kill all those around you. We will rest here tonight, and then begin travel with the dawn. I will take you to the city, Teleth, where you should be able to get to where you need to go."

Allie blinked at the sudden change of plans but nodded. He had certainly told her more in a few sentences than Dav had since he'd first seen the box. She was bothered by several points, however.

"Why would this Highlord guy be hunting me? What do those creatures want with me? I'm not anything special. I didn't even know about this war until you just mentioned it to me," she protested.

Ghier nodded.

"Yes, but you have the crystal key and can make it work. I do not know much of such things, only that Highlord Tyren seeks the death of any who can operate the crystal keys, and the destruction of the keys themselves," he responded.

Allie shook her head in confusion. "And what's a crystal key?" she asked.

Ghier gestured to the pocket where she had placed the crystal.

"That which you carry around in your pocket. I do not know much of such things. It is not an Ayarani tool. We cannot use them. I only know that they allow the people who can use them to travel almost instantly from world to world. I do not know its limits, nor do I know why Highlord Tyren wishes them destroyed. I only know that he does," he replied.

"But I really don't know what's going on. He can have it, for all I care. All I want is to get home, and to be left alone!" she said.

Ghier shrugged placidly.

"Such is the way of men like Highlord Tyren. He seeks a goal, rational or otherwise, and will pursue it to its end regardless of the cost or the innocent lives lost. Do not worry, young one. When we reach Teleth, everything will be taken care of," he reassured her.

She nodded, and her stomach growled. Allie blushed in embarrassment, but Ghier only smiled slightly and nodded, rising from his seat.

He went to the shelves again and brought down a woven vine box filled with long, purplish fruits. They were cylindrical, tapering into rounded ends, perhaps as long as, and thicker around than, her forearm.

Ghier handed one to her, taking one for himself. He sat again and demonstrated how to eat them. He cracked it open in the middle, like a chimp with a banana, and began rolling the tough but thin skin back. The inside of the fruit was purple and also fairly tough.

As she imitated Ghier and took a bite, she was pleasantly surprised. The fruit was tough in texture, but no more so than a good steak, and the flavor was delightful; spicy in a cinnamon kind of way, and just a little sweet. Though it was surprisingly filling, she ate the entire thing.

Her thoughts ran rampant while she ate, trying to understand why she could use this crystal key, why her mother had left it for her, why her mother had had it to begin with, and a thousand other things she could barely identify as they sped through her mind.

"There," Ghier said, interrupting her thoughts. "Now that you have had food and water and relieved the burden of your story, I suspect you will wish to sleep?" He toned it as a question.

She nodded, the weight of her weariness coming

upon her quite profoundly. Allie yawned, and Ghier stood, gesturing toward the bed before walking out of the hut. She stood, stretched, and moved to the bed. On impulse, she reached into her pocket and closed her fingers around the crystal. It was warm again, and she was reassured by its touch, though she wasn't sure why.

She lay down, her last thoughts of Dav. She hoped he was okay, that he'd survived his fight against the creatures, the maruck, and that he was already somehow coming to save her again.

And then, sleep took her.

CHAPTER SIX

WORMHOLES

"We have to, Artus!" Dav shouted at his brother. "She has no idea what's going on, and it's all thanks to that stupid vow of silence you made me take!"

"We can't, Dav. We don't have the firepower to take on a single Coalition Guard ship, let alone the fleet of them that I am sure Tyren has sent after her by now, and let's not even discuss what will happen if he sends more maruck ships after us," Artus replied. "We have to travel to Kerilus and see if we can find any survivors of the Resistance."

"Allie might not live that long! If you hadn't made me promise, I could have told her from the beginning, and we could have had her prepared for this!" Dav protested angrily. Artus shook his head.

"This is bigger than just her, Dav. There's a surviving crystal key. If we can get it to the Enclave…" Artus began.

"The Enclave is all either dead or in hiding! The only ones surviving would be the ones smart enough to allow their crystal keys to be destroyed and never use another!

"None of them still alive would never touch one, even if it fell into their laps, for fear of Tyren tracking them down. What if she's the only person left alive in the entire galaxy still willing and able to use the key?" Dav argued. Artus shook his head.

"You would put her in the line of fire for our sake?" Artus asked quietly.

Dav scowled.

"It isn't as simple as that Artus, and you know it," Dav snapped. "It's not for our sake. Getting home has nothing to do with it. We could have gone back at any time. It's for everyone's sake. Countless lives could be saved if we can stop Tyren.

"I am willing to risk my life for that, and if Allie knew what was at stake, she would be, too. I know she would. And we'll never know unless we ask her. What if she had known? What if she would be willing to stand with us against Tyren, and we just let her die alone out there?"

"It wouldn't have mattered," Artus replied with resignation. "She Jumped blindly, Dav. We don't even know where she landed. The Resistance has trackers we could use to locate the source…"

"I know where she landed, Artus!" Dav said, his tone a bit smug. "You can't Jump blind on an unprogrammed key. It had its first destination pre-set, or she wouldn't have been able to Jump at all; not without knowing what the key does.

"Her mother gave her the crystal on her thirteenth birthday, the age where she should have been able to begin using the key. Her mother knew that, sooner or later, she'd activate it and end up somewhere. Her mother would have set an intentional first destination. If her mother knew she was going to be taken by Tyren, where do you think she would have programmed it for?" Dav raised a brow in a demanding, expectant expression. He knew he'd won when Artus frowned, then lit up in surprise as he made the connection.

"Any member of the Enclave wanting to hide," Dav spoke Artus's thoughts aloud, emphasizing his point, "while intending to come out of hiding and fight later, would have to go where they wouldn't be suspected. Somewhere they could expect to live long enough to fight when the time was right. A smart member of the Enclave would have gone someplace to do all of that while simultaneously keeping tabs on the political situation. Which means…"

"Pahrvic…" Artus said softly.

"Exactly. And since you can't Jump directly to Pahrvic because of the rogellium deposits, she would want her rescuer to Jump to…" Dav urged.

"Ayaran!" Artus shook his head slowly in wonder.

"Sometimes, little brother, your brilliance amazes even me," Artus laughed.

"Don't put me too high on that pedestal. I gave Allie a tracking bracelet. I already knew she was on Ayaran," Dav laughed, holding up a small, palm-sized tracer unit.

"Devious, little brother. Very devious." Artus said in disbelief.

"If we can get there quickly enough to get to her before Tyren's goons do, we can beeline for Kerilus and then look for the remaining Resistance with both the key and the bearer, Allie," Dav continued.

"We'll never make it. Ayaran is at least twelve arcs away, maybe more, depending on the wormholes. It will take us a week, at best."

"I have you beat there, too. I've been tracking the wormholes," Dav responded. "Remember that 'silly project' you've been teasing me about for the last two years? I told you I knew she was the one, so I've been trying to stay prepared. We can use Wormhole 446-8 to cut the distance in half."

Dav pointed to a red, curving line on one of the dozen star charts he had spread across the bed in his room. "It's stretched all the way past Ghildan right now, but only for the next twelve hours. From there, we can use 386-7, which for another week will let us out right next to 901-0, which should bring us out right next to the Sylus Loop. Just like the freeways.

"I can have us there in under four days, as long as we leave right now," he finished, straightening and crossing his arms over his chest, daring Artus to argue.

Artus spent a moment studying the star charts, and then studying his little brother, before nodding his resignation.

"You're right, kid. We can make it. Under four days still makes it a tight call, though. It won't be more than a day or two before the maruck we dealt with here will be missed, and the trackers will be activated. Once those are online, we won't have more than two days before they'll have found her," he said.

Dav nodded.

"Then we'd better make it less than four days. I can be ready to leave in ten minutes. How about you?" Dav challenged.

Artus shook his head with a laugh.

"Sometimes, Dav, I think you should have been Firstborn. All right, we'll do it your way. It will take me half an hour to prep the Runner. If it only takes you ten minutes to get your things ready, that should leave you twenty to pack mine. Better get to it," Artus said with a sigh.

Dav grinned, more than happy to do his brother's packing in exchange for leaving that much sooner. He practically dove across the bed to get to his dresser.

Artus sighed and walked out to prepare the Runner.

Dav opened the bottom drawer of the dresser and pulled out a black, polished metal case, about the size of a briefcase. He set it reverently on his bed and pressed a small button on the side. A control panel opened out of one seemingly smooth side, and Dav began pressing buttons and scrolling through a list on the small screen.

He needed tactical suits for both of them, as well as the appropriate equipment for whatever problems might arise in the near future. He selected quickly from the scrolling menu, entered their respective clothing sizes, and activated the machine. He grinned.

Nanotechnology was beautiful. These humans almost had it figured out, too. Not much longer and humans here on Earth would have machines to do this, or something very much like it.

If given a proper supply of raw materials, the machine could produce, molecule by molecule, any number of interesting objects. Within the next ten minutes, it would make two tactical suits, complete with helmets. Within an hour after that, it would have made all the equipment they would need in case of trouble.

Dav could program it to produce a reasonable supply of clothing, as well, over the course of their four-day trip. Though, sooner or later, the machine would run out of raw materials. He suspected this machine had enough left for their immediate needs, though. It was called some complicated, hard-to-pronounce name after the scientist from Ghildan who invented it, but he called it a crafter.

All that left for him to pack was sentimental belongings. Into his backpack went some of his most treasured possessions. Not the star charts, though. All of that information was on the Runner's computer, except his own data on the wormhole patterns. He quickly folded that particular chart and stuffed it into the bag.

He also took the pocketknife from his bedside table and tucked it into his jeans pocket. He had better tools at his disposal, but that knife was lucky. The last thing he grabbed was a small photograph from the fair last spring, taped to the mirror on his closet door. He paused a moment as he looked at the picture.

Allie stood, grinning, arm draped over his lower shoulder, her free arm giving the peace sign. He stood beside her, trying to look cool, arms folded across his chest and a grin on his face.

Dav sighed sadly. He hoped she was okay. Ayaran had some dangers she wouldn't be aware of. A lot of them, in fact. It was possible, however, that the Ayarani themselves had taken her into their protection. They were generally good people, even if the term tree-hugger was something of an understatement where they were concerned.

As long as she hadn't landed too deep in the jungle, they would have found her before she got into too much trouble. For all he knew, she may have ended up directly in one of the port cities. He actually hoped for the jungle, instead. Much safer than the cities on Ayaran.

He would make it in time to save her from the

maruck, he was sure. Nobody could fly a Runner class starship like he could. In a good Runner, which theirs was, he could out-fly anything. At least, he believed so, based on his and Artus's training expeditions. Artus freely agreed, with a certain degree of awe when he spoke of it.

Dav took a deep breath and pocketed the photograph. He glanced at the machine. It had already sprung up its holographic representation of the first tactical suit, hovering horizontally above the black surface of the case, and was constructing it from the boots up. It had made it past the ankles already. They always had to de-construct the suits every time they came back, since storing them was a bit risky.

Technically, storing the case was risky, too, but the case had been programmed to his and Artus's physiology. It would have cloaked itself if anyone other than he or Artus had opened the drawer. A pretty neat trick, he thought with a small smile.

He'd tested the cloaking system once. It was impressive watching the thing simply vanish. A small shimmer across its surface, and it was just gone.

Too bad the power required to accomplish that cloaking was so extreme. It would have been seriously cool to have had a ship capable of it. The crafting system would have burned nearly all its stored material to power the cloak on a full starship for even a few minutes. Even his extremely brief test of the system had cost a full cartridge of carbon, and half a container of nitrogen.

He ran across the hall into Artus's room, grabbing his brother's duffel bag. Not entirely sure what he would want, he began stuffing in various small knick-knacks and photographs until it was full. He then grabbed

Artus's pillow and ran back to his own room.

He had to wait another minute or two until the machine finished his suit, but the moment it had, he quickly stripped down and pulled it on, taking out the pocketknife and photograph and setting them to one side as he changed. The suit itself was actually a remarkably impressive piece of technology, though by now outdated in the core sectors, he was sure.

You wore nothing beneath it, since it read and monitored all your systems, automatically adjusting its own temperature to keep the wearer body temperature at its ideal.

It also contained a small tube emerging on the inside of one sleeve. When sucked on, it produced a fluid perfectly molecularly designed for his own nutritional needs, which were also monitored by the suit. If he was drinking the liquid regularly, his body excreted no waste, and he needed no additional food or water. The suit had enough material in the belt pack it fed from to keep him sustained in virtually any environment in perfect health for as long as two weeks.

The suit could protect him from extreme heat, including fire, and extreme cold, including temperatures as cold as liquid nitrogen, without any discomfort. It would even sustain him deep underwater, or in space itself, as long as he had the helmet locked on. He was completely protected from lack of oxygen for as long as three days, as well as the extreme pressure, or lack thereof, of nearly any environment.

Additionally, they had body armor plating that would absorb an amazing amount of force before becoming damaged. They also absorbed and redistributed kinetic energy, converting a lot of it into stored energy in another part of the suit.

The plates were only about a quarter of an inch thick, and they weighed almost nothing, but Dav was pretty sure he'd survive being hit by a fully loaded semi-truck at freeway speeds if he were wearing the suit at the time. He'd probably even be able to just get up and walk away from it. Not that he had any intention of ever testing that theory.

The suits allowed full range of motion, without being at all bulky. They actually looked pretty sleek, in Dav's opinion. With the dusky gray, non-conductive coating on the plates and the helmet, the overall effect was like something out of a video game.

Remarkable, really, he thought. Pity the humans here didn't have access to them. They would sure save a lot of trouble, although the humans would probably just use them for warfare.

He tucked his pocketknife and the photograph into one of several airtight belt packs.

Dav grabbed his own pillow, the backpack, and Artus's pillow and duffel bag and raced down the stairs as the machine finished Artus's suit. He ran into the garage and down the secret trapdoor, which was currently open, revealing the stairs into the hidden hangar beneath the house.

He hurried down the stairs, though as always, he couldn't help but pause halfway down to admire the Runner from his elevated perspective. She wasn't huge, only about the length of an RV camper, though with her wingspan, she was quite a bit wider. What impressed him was how fast she looked.

She was low and sleek, barely tall enough for Artus to stand up inside, but wide enough for a small galley, two small bunks, a storage bay, and the cockpit. She wasn't intended to be inhabited for long periods of time, but like an RV, she'd hold a couple of people for a week or two if need be without much trouble.

The hull was mirrored silver and highly polished. The wings swept forward like a stylized bird in flight, the cockpit windows also mirrored, though in a darker hue, arcing across the nose of the ship.

Dav grinned and hurried down. He'd never had the chance to ride a wormhole before. They were supposedly extremely difficult to pilot through at anything close to high speed. Most people dropped into a much slower cruise speed to navigate the intricacies and dangers of the wormhole.

Dav wanted to hit them at full tilt. Not because he was crazy and really wanted to see if they could do it, or at least, not only because of that, but because he had to get to Allie as quickly as physically possible. He hoped Artus would be willing to fly at that speed through the wormholes.

He ran to the tail, where the access port was. The door was down, forming a ramp into the ship. Dav jogged up the ramp and tossed the bags and pillows on the bunks, his own on the top. Artus preferred the bottom, which Dav thought was weird, but it worked out well because Dav preferred the top.

"Ten more minutes, and we can fly, little brother," Artus called from the cockpit.

Dav ran back out and up the stairs. He would be ready before the ship was, but that was okay. As long as they were getting out as quickly as possible, he would be happy.

He took the stairs two at a time, making it back to the

room before it finished Artus's suit. His excitement and running were wearing him down, he thought. He was a bit thirsty. He took a quick sip from the wrist valve and felt a little better.

A quick trip to the kitchen and he'd packed enough supplies to easily last them the four days they'd take to get to Allie, and the three of them for another four days after that, if they were careful. No reason to deplete the suit's nutritional supplies unless they had to. He loaded the food in the Runner's galley, grateful for the stasis storage unit to keep much of the food unspoiled.

Dav ran back to his bedroom, snatching Artus's suit and the helmets to both suits off the bed, then closed the case and grabbed it, too. Immediately, he was heading back to the ship. He ran up the ramp again, setting the helmets on the rack against one wall, made for just such equipment. Dav tossed the suit at Artus, who grabbed it from the air without looking.

"Take the modulator controls, Dav. I'm going to change," he said, standing up from the pilot's seat.

Dav nodded and slid into his place. He placed his palm on the controls, focusing his thoughts on the fine adjustments necessary to stabilize the potentially erratic energy fluctuations as the Jump drive powered up.

It wasn't anything like the crystal keys and wouldn't make it much more than a billion miles at a Jump, but it was a good way to get out of a planet's atmosphere, and a great way to do so unseen, especially during the daylight hours.

The Jump drive was finicky, though, and took constant adjustments to the power balances while it powered up, or it could explode. Dav wasn't worried. He'd practiced this a hundred times.

A moment later, Artus slipped into the navigator's seat, wearing his newly crafted tactical suit. Dav moved to get up, but Artus shook his head.

"No, stay. You're the better pilot, Dav," he said. Dav started to protest, but Artus cut him off. "It's true. I didn't want to say anything before, I thought it might give you a big head about it, but the fact of the matter is that I can't fly a wormhole as fast as I think you can, and we need to move as quickly as possible."

Dav took a long breath and nodded, excited that Artus was going to let him, but a little nervous. He'd done some intensive practice through the Kuiper belt that ran around the edge of this solar system, but a wormhole was something else entirely.

"I can do it," Dav said.

"I know it, kid," Artus said, clapping him on the shoulder. "That's why you're flying. Whenever you're ready," he said with a grin, snapping on his five-point harness.

Dav used one hand to do the same while still monitoring the Jump drive. When it was ready, he looked at Artus, who nodded once.

"Initiating Jump drive," Dav announced, triggering the displays which projected onto the window in front of him. "Setting destination point. Engaging in three… two… one…" Dav flipped the mental switch, his thoughts sent instantly to the ship's control center.

Light seemed to explode from all around them, and that peculiar tearing sensation inherent in any Jump pulled them in all directions at once.

Dav found himself wondering what that felt like without the protection of the ship around them. He felt a pang of guilt at telling Allie to spin the crystal. There had been no other way, though.

Someone watching from outside would have felt, rather than heard, a low vibration for a split second before the Jump, followed by a bright flash of light pulsing upward, leaving a faint, misty energy haze in the hangar for a moment after.

Dav and Artus reappeared just this side of Saturn, well outside its atmosphere, floating serenely in space beside the giant planet as though they'd been there all along. Only that misty-looking energy haze around them gave any indication of their recent appearance.

"Okay, I have the course set in. The opening to 446-8 isn't too far from here. Are we ready?" Dav asked.

Artus simply nodded. Dav placed his hand once more on the sensor bar at the end of the arm of his chair, connecting himself again to the system mentally and kicked up the throttle.

The window display showed their coordinate position along an axis system, similar in concept to the one used by the humans of Earth. It was the simplest way to identify a specific location in any three-dimensional space. It also displayed their rapidly increasing velocity. Dav loved this part.

He banked sharply, turning toward the target location, and maxed the throttle. They were now moving at a speed that would have had every scientist at NASA salivating over the possibilities. Many, many times faster than light.

The trouble with matter was that it didn't handle traveling at speeds as fast as light very well, but several technologically advanced species had learned that the trick was to make the ship phase slightly, just out of sync with normal matter. It was a combination of matter phasing and space-bending that allowed a speed like this, but even with a phase drive, the wormholes were faster.

In about four hours, they had reached their destination, the position of the wormhole mouth. Or at least where it would be for another few hours. Wormholes were inherently unstable. They tended to move over time. There were certain wormholes whose position could be tracked and calculated, based on fairly reliable patterns, though many of them were completely unstable and impossible to predict.

Dav always thought of it like geysers on Earth. Based on previous eruption times and durations, it was possible to calculate the next eruption time and duration with reasonable accuracy, though only with certain geysers. Others were so erratic that no mathematical formula could predict it. Dav had charts and books on every traceable wormhole and had been following the wormhole patterns for years. He knew this one would be here.

He stopped the ship and mentally activated the frequency scanner. This would allow the ship to identify the correct molecular harmonics frequency necessary to fall into the wormhole, and then create a field around the ship at the appropriate frequency to keep them from being torn apart at the atomic level.

Almost immediately, the hum of the field kicked on. They must have been right on top of the mouth of the wormhole, exactly where Dav knew it would be. The ship tilted sideways, as though falling sidelong over a cliff. Wormholes seemed to have a gravitational pull of their own, though it wasn't consistent. Probably had to do with the energy of the hole itself, which was inherently unstable. That didn't help with trying to fly through one at all.

As they fell through, inky blackness surrounded them. Not blackness like you find in the depths of a dark and stormy night, or in the basement closet while playing hide and seek. This was a total absence of light.

Wormholes didn't form *in* regular space. They formed *between* regular space. Light didn't enter them any more than matter normally did. It took special circumstances, or artificially created energy fields, to enter one at all.

There was an odd sensation of movement, though that was measured more by the change in the gravitational pull of the hole than by a feeling of actual movement. Since anything inside a wormhole didn't exist in normal space, it didn't move normally, either.

Ripples of something pulsed in the darkness, like bolts of lightning that you couldn't quite see, appearing as nothing more than a slight change in the quality of the total blackness. They flashed chaotically all around. The way Dav understood it, as the wormhole brushed close to normal space, it arced energy across its inner walls, like static electricity jumping from your finger to the doorknob. It was intense, erratic, and almost impossible to see.

Fortunately, the scanners on the ship had been designed to read them. As the system adjusted to the wormhole, the computer displayed the not-quite-cylindrical shape of it in a red simulation on the cockpit windows.

The bolts of energy would begin to form, building up an energy field surrounding the point where it would burst forth. The computer could read those fields, and give notice displayed digitally on the window a second or two before their occurrence. This gave the pilot a bit of notice to avoid them.

The problem with flying too quickly through them was that the computer's scanners could only read those fields at a fairly close range. Flying as fast as Dav intended to, he'd have less than a second's notice to react to each burst of energy.

Since the mouth was directly touching normal space here, there wasn't that arcing of energy, so he felt safe waiting here until the computers adjusted to the correct frequencies in the scanners.

Once the computers had adjusted, Dav watched the energy pulses, oddly disquieted by the fact that there was no sound here. Not that there was in space either, but this was different. It felt oppressive and heavy. And those bolts looked like they should be loud.

It took him a moment to work up his nerve. Those bolts came in fast and hard. If they so much as got clipped by one, they would be completely destroyed.

Once the computer had tuned to this wormhole's frequencies, Dav was ready. He grinned to himself. This was it, time to show off. He mentally slammed the throttle all the way forward, and the ship seemed to launch like a bullet.

There was no gradual increase in speed. One moment, they were stationary, and the next, they were tearing through non-space at over a million miles per second.

Each hand on one of the control bars, Dav steering by thought alone, they tore through the wormhole at the ship's maximum speed.

Runner class ships were built for speed, used for

rapid deliveries of important and valuable cargo. No ship in the galaxy was as fast. At least, there weren't any ten years ago when Dav and Artus had come to Earth on the Runner. If there was a faster ship now, and there probably was, Dav wanted one. Until then, the Runner was still a beautiful piece of machinery.

Dav danced the lightning. He banked, rolled, and dove in rapid succession. Artus said not a word, though his hands clutched the sides of his chair with white knuckles.

A bolt came down directly next to them, and Dav banked away. At the last moment, he corkscrewed, another bolt coming down precisely where their wing had been a fraction of a second earlier. The ship slid up and then down again, rolling over a bolt that blasted across horizontally.

Dav's eyes slid across the displays, mentally spotting and taking note of every bolt coming down within the scanner's range ahead of them, reacting with split-second maneuvers. Seconds, and then minutes passed, Dav never slowing an inch, never hesitating a second.

Almost without warning, they burst out of the wormhole. The full-speed transition from null space to real space hit the ship with a tangible jolt. The ship shook, like turbulence on a plane.

Dav gritted his teeth and held steady until it subsided. Just like that, in less than ten minutes, they were more than three-fifths of the way across the galaxy.

Once they were gliding through empty space effortlessly again, the ship having adapted once more to real space, he looked over at Artus. That was unquestionably the most exhilarating experience of his entire life. He tried to keep his tone calm.

"One down, two to go," he said with a smile.

Artus exhaled long and hard.

Dav wondered if his brother had been holding that breath the whole ten minutes through the wormhole.

"Little brother, I have never in my entire life seen anything even close to what you just pulled off in there," Artus said, his voice shaky. "If you aren't the best pilot in the entire galaxy, I'll eat my flight suit. If you can pull that off two more times, I'm buying you your own ship," he said.

Dav grinned, the tension slowly easing out of him.

"A Striker class?" he asked with excitement.

Artus gave him a playful scowl.

"Why, so you can use those piloting skills to blow things up? Don't push it, kid," Artus replied.

"Oh, well. It was worth asking," he said, shrugging melodramatically.

A Striker class ship, while not quite as fast as a Runner, had enough additional maneuverability to more than make up for the minor loss of speed, and the incredible firepower those little ships carried more than made up the difference. He'd have had a great time in the Kuiper belt blasting asteroids at top speed in one of those.

Dav adjusted course toward Wormhole 386-7. One down, two to go, he thought again.

Hang on, Allie. I'm coming.

CHAPTER SEVEN

FURRY AND FIERCE

Allie woke up the next morning feeling quite refreshed. The bed was remarkably comfortable, and the food and water seemed to have rejuvenated her beyond what she would have expected. She felt ready for another adventure.

The little simian creature was curled up against her side, its soft snores sounding halfway between a cat's purr and a bird's chirp. She smiled at the thing. For some reason, it looked like it wanted to stick with her. If it came with them when they started their trip this morning, she would give it a name, she decided.

She sat up carefully, but she still woke the sleeping creature. It yawned, and she was struck by how frighteningly effective those teeth looked. It gazed up at her and chirped happily. She grinned and held out an arm. It scrambled up her sleeve and perched atop her shoulder again. She was glad those claws were retractable.

Allie stepped out into the little village and froze. It looked like the entire population was standing in the center of the village, arms outstretched, bare feet planted firmly on the ground.

No, she noticed, their feet were planted firmly *in* the ground, not on it. She froze in shock at the revelation. From the sides, and, she assumed, the bottoms, of each of their feet, small tendrils of a wood-like substance emerged. Like roots.

A beam of sunlight was coming in from between two large trees, illuminating the people and the leaves in their hair. Again, she was forced to correct herself as she began to understand. The leaves were, in fact, part of their hair, soaking up the sunlight.

As she watched the people, arms turned out to absorb the light, faces aglow with the warmth of the sun, she came to a realization. Ghier was right. They certainly weren't people, exactly. They were plants.

They planted their roots to draw moisture and nutrients up from the soft ground. How often, she didn't know, but that appeared to be what they were doing. They absorbed sunlight for food, but she had seen last night that Ghier also ate solid food. Perhaps they weren't really plants or humans, but something in between.

Allie watched in fascination for several long minutes, before they began to slowly lower their arms and open their eyes, looking peaceful and contented.

Ghier spotted her and smiled, walking over, his foot-roots nowhere to be seen.

"I thought you were kidding when you said you weren't a man," she remarked quietly. He chuckled and nodded.

"On your world, they do not have people like me?

Only humans?" he asked. She shook her head. "That does not surprise me. Of all the known humanoid races, mine are the least inclined to travel. It is difficult to get the proper soil and sunlight in space," he said with a smile.

She grinned in return.

"I can imagine. We don't have any other humanoid races on Earth, you call them. Only us humans," she said, but immediately realized that wasn't true.

Dav and Artus were on Earth, and they weren't human. How many others were on her planet, not of her world, and the humans just didn't realize it? We really are an ignorant species, she thought.

"Some planets are like that. Mostly those in the outer arms, far from the core systems," he said with a nod.

That made sense, she figured. Though something else he said made her brain click into gear, and she made a connection she hadn't thought to question before.

"We're not on my world, right? But you know about humans. Have you met humans before?" she asked.

He glanced down at her as he led the way into the hut.

"I have. Humans, in their basest sense, are undoubtedly not native to your world. No one is certain on which planet humans originated, though most of the more primitive human populations are convinced that it happened on their own planet," he said.

She blushed, having been just about to point out that it was, in fact, her own planet humans had come from. He caught the expression.

"Ah, you too, then? I meant no disrespect, of course. Some planets are simply more advanced than others. Yet perhaps you still think they originated on your planet." He cast a sly smile her way.

She shrugged noncommittally.

"Let me ask you this, then," he responded. "Your people have studied evolution, correct?" At her nod, he continued. "Did it never strike you as odd that your people, while theoretically evolved from some species on your planet, seemed to have evolved from that primitive species almost overnight? There are few, if any, bridge species, so to speak?"

Allie frowned, not really sure. She remembered hearing something in biology about the evolutionary leap between the primitive ape-like men and the sudden appearance of homo sapiens, but biology wasn't her best subject. She wished she'd paid better attention. On this world, her biology lessons seemed surprisingly relevant.

Dav would know more about this.

At the thought of him, her heart gave a little twinge of sorrow. She missed him. She feared for him. And yet, some part of her still fully expected him to come riding in to her rescue on a great white horse or something. The image made her grin.

"You're right, actually. I hadn't thought about it before, but you're right. There was a huge evolutionary leap on my planet to the human race," she answered.

Ghier snapped his fingers.

"See there? Before any of our people existed, the original race of man seems to have made quite the expedition clear to the outer rims of the galaxy, 'seeding' planets, if you will. Inserting DNA overwrite viruses into the local animal population.

"The animals targeted for the procedure were most often similar in basic structure to the original humans to begin with, though, as is evident in my case, not always. Within relatively few generations on each world, humans were born.

"There are some subtle differences between humans of different worlds, of course, and some of the species took massive deviations from the genetic standard, but a substantial number of the races share nearly identical genetic patterns now. Close enough to interbreed without either race noticing the difference in the offspring.

"Many of the humanoid species became so different that they can no longer be called human, however. My people, for example, are descended from the genetic crossover between the original human DNA and that of a local plant here on our planet. We are so far biologically removed from your species that we cannot properly call ourselves human.

"Even the maruck are descended from a human mutation. It's remarkable what genetic experiments, when left neglected for hundreds of thousands of years, can do," he chuckled lightly.

"So, all the species out there that look kind of like humans," Allie began, trying to process this revelation, "and those of us that, I suppose, stayed close to the intended form, are nothing more than a genetic experiment? All from some race of humanoids tens of thousands of years ago who ran around the galaxy messing with others' genes?" she asked, astonished.

He nodded.

"In essence, though, it was less an experiment and more an attempt to broaden the scope of their society," he explained. "Not every planet was used for this, either. Some planets already had intelligent life well enough developed for the humans to leave them in peace.

"Many species exist and travel in space who are not

even close to humanoid in appearance or culture. Nobody knows where the original humans went, though. Their technology had developed phasic space travel hundreds of thousands of years ago. They should be so far advanced by now that they should rule the entire galaxy, if not multiple galaxies, but they do not.

"It is possible that the very same genetic abnormalities that struck random other worlds to create some of the more deviant races also destroyed others, including their own. Their arrogance in playing with evolution may have been their downfall," he said.

Ghier handed her a vine-woven bag and began filling it with the odd purple fruits. "All things in moderation, as they say. A bit more caution probably should have been used in that project," he said.

She looked at him curiously. Her planned next comment worried her, since she thought he might be offended, but he did seem remarkably calm-natured. She went ahead and said it.

"You seem to be awfully well educated for a talking tree in the middle of the jungle."

Ghier laughed outright at this, easing her fear that he would be offended.

"I do, indeed. But you see, all the knowledge of our people is within the earth of this rainforest. Each of my people learns a large piece of our people's collected knowledge with each rebirth," he replied.

"Rebirth?" she asked. Her curiosity only seemed to be creating questions faster than she had the chance to ask them.

"Yes. Each cycle around our sun, as we enter our winter, we each go dormant. Like dying for a season. During this time, our roots dig firmly in, our leaves die, and our minds delve into the earth.

"As the season passes, our minds connect with the minds of many others of our kind. This connection allows for information transfer far faster than speech could accomplish. To a lesser, more local degree, it is done each morning as we rise with the sun, though distant messages can be transmitted that way if it's urgent enough.

"Mostly, though, we learn what we need from our brothers around the world each passing winter." He gestured for her to exit the hut.

Allie stepped out, slinging the bag of fruit over her shoulder. It was heavy.

Ghier knelt beside the doorway and picked up several more water gourds, each sealed at the top with some kind of wax and threaded with slender vine straps. He slung the half a dozen of them over his shoulder, and she no longer felt so bad about her own burden. The gourds were not small, and she knew water was heavy.

"Is that why you speak English?" she asked him. "You learned it through the others?"

Ghier gave her an odd, sidelong glance.

"I told you before, I do not speak English. I speak Ayarani, as do you," he replied, his tone indicating he was beginning to worry she wasn't right in the head.

She shut her mouth and didn't argue.

"Shall we begin, then?" he asked.

She nodded and followed as he set out.

The little purple creature hadn't left her shoulder once the entire morning. She ate one of the purple fruits as they walked.

"Tell me more about the crystal key. I don't understand how it works, or why my mother would have one," she asked between bites.

Allie wasn't having as much trouble following him as she had the day before, but that could be because her little friend kept its eyes on the man at all times, so she just had to follow the little creature's gaze if Ghier started to fade into the thick undergrowth.

"I'm afraid I don't know much. Highlord Tyren will kill any who oppose his will to destroy every last key, and any who can use them. He killed many people to acquire and destroy them. He primarily targeted the Enclave, a group of people who gathered together to use the keys to further peace and prosperity across the galaxy.

"I suspect your mother belonged to the Enclave, or she would not likely have possessed a crystal key, and it would explain why you are able to use it. Only a select few seem able to do so, and I suspect it is an inherited trait. Possibly, your father was able, as well. It is difficult to say. You will be able to learn more about them in the human city. My people do not interact with yours often, and much of your war-like history is beyond us."

"Your people don't have war?" she asked in surprise.

"No. We do not fight. We have no weapons. Our people live in peace with our world and with one another. War is an almost exclusively human trait, although in fairness, Highlord Tyren himself is not human, nor are the maruck.

"Perhaps I should say instead that war belongs to those races of men who were created from hybridization with more predatory species. The combination of predatory ancestry and a degree of intelligence seem to be the keys that bring about such a level of conflict."

"Tyren isn't human?" she asked, surprised. She had pictured him as human, though for no particular reason.

Ghier shook his head.

"He looks human enough to pass for one of you, but his physiology, and that of his people, is so far removed that they cannot be called human any more than I can. I also look mostly like a human, despite my roots and leaves, yet if I were to be cut open, I would have no organs or blood, only sap and plant tissue. Highlord Tyren's people are like this. Not like plants, I mean, but almost as different," he replied.

Allie marveled for a moment at how small her world now seemed. She looked up as they moved beneath a small opening in the canopy. The lavender sky beamed happily down at her.

She supposed it was all a matter of perspective. When you lived your whole life in one city, the city seemed fairly large, until you were able to leave it. Once you had seen other cities, and learned how many more of them there were, your city didn't seem so big anymore.

Her reality was no longer just her world. It was one of apparently tens of thousands similar to it enough to be kin, but different enough to still be alien.

"What about my friend Dav? Do you know what he is?" she asked.

Ghier thought for a long moment before answering.

"I suspect, from what you tell me, that he and Highlord Tyren are of the same people, the Sy'hli," Ghier said thoughtfully. "They are the… nobility, if you will, of the human race. Perhaps the most closely related to the original species. They claim as much, anyway.

"They are stronger than most, faster than most, and smarter than most varieties of man. Only a few extreme mutations surpass them in any one of these traits. None surpass them in all. It is for this reason that the Sy'hli have ruled this galaxy for tens of thousands of years.

"From what I have learned from brother tribes, Highlord Tyren killed his entire family so that he could claim the throne. The Sy'hli might be the rulers, but they cannot control the crystal keys.

"Because of this, Highlord Tyren demanded the Enclave swear fealty to him, using their crystals only at his command. They refused, and he declared war. Until you, I had thought that every bearer had been killed, and all of the keys destroyed. You must be careful who you tell. The reward for your capture and return to Highlord Tyren would be great," he finished.

Allie considered this. She hadn't realized the crystal itself was what was putting her at risk. It made sense, she supposed. Even with incredibly advanced technology, the power to go anywhere you wanted in an instant would be a valuable resource. She was glad that the first person she'd encountered was so trustworthy.

They continued for hours, pausing only long enough to take drinks of water, and catch her breath. Ghier didn't seem to need to pause for breath like she did, though he was sympathetic to her own biological needs. She supposed he had no lungs, either.

Her mind wandered as they walked. In this city, Teleth was what Ghier had called it, were more humans like herself. Ones close enough to her to be called human, anyway. Most humans from Earth would sell her out for the right price, too.

Allie decided it would definitely be best to be cautious. What worried her most was that Ghier said that she would find the way to get where she needed to go in

Teleth. Home was where she needed to go, but what if she took a ship or something back home, and Dav was on his way here to find her? Would he even know where to look for her?

Maybe it was like what they told little kids about what to do if they were ever lost in the forest. Stay put, they said. If you wandered, it was harder to find you.

And yet, in the whole galaxy, how would Dav ever track her down? He was brilliant, but the galaxy was immense, and for all she knew, the crystal key could have sent her here randomly. With all the worlds out there, it would be a thousand times worse than looking for a needle in a haystack. A thousand thousand times worse. More like looking for a specific grain of sand on a beach, she thought ruefully.

She just had to trust that whatever she did, Dav would expect it. He usually knew what she was thinking before she did. Except when her thoughts were about him, anyway.

Allie smiled at that thought. She was careful not to let too much slip, but she could have snuggled up beside him, held his hand, and played with his hair all day long, and he probably wouldn't have noticed that she liked him. That actually sounds like a nice way to spend the day, she thought to herself.

He was such a boy in that regard, dense and completely oblivious to the interest of anyone else toward him unless they told him in clear and unsubtle ways.

Girls usually had to do that where Dav was concerned. He always turned them down once he realized how they felt about him, though, which was why she had never said anything herself. She didn't want to jeopardize their friendship like that. It was far too valuable to her to risk over a crush, even when that crush had been going on since the day she laid eyes on him.

"Caution," Ghier whispered, pulling her from her thoughts.

She realized that the little purple creature had gripped her shoulder warningly, as well.

"There is a nest of insects nearby that we do not wish to disturb. Move as quickly and quietly as possible," he whispered, leaning close to her to minimize the volume of his speech.

She nodded, becoming worried.

The whole time she'd been in this jungle, there'd been no signs of anything truly dangerous, excepting only the fruit tree that she'd been narrowly rescued from. Insects didn't sound bad, but Ghier's warning made it clear that this was not a trivial issue.

She remembered the size of the moth-creatures she'd seen flying earlier.

They crept further along the invisible trail Ghier seemed to be following, moving as fast as they could while still trying to maintain a bit of stealth. She walked as quietly as she could, but she wasn't trained for stealth. She stepped on a dry twig, causing a loud snap.

Ghier froze, and she did the same. A peculiar clicking screech came from her left, followed by another from slightly behind and to the right. She hadn't realized that when Ghier said 'nearby', he had meant 'all around us'.

She leaned over to peek between the leaves of a large, curly, fern-like bush on her left. When she saw it, she nearly screamed.

It was huge, maybe seven feet tall, and held some

resemblance to an ant, although it was a bluish-gray color, and had eight legs like a spider. The legs had too many joints, however, each bending and folding in at least half a dozen places.

It had a double set of huge, serrated mandibles that clicked open and shut independently of one another. The thing's sickly green, pupil-less eyes scanned the foliage. It also had six long antennae sprouting out of its head, which moved around in what appeared to her to be random, erratic twitches. They looked strong and whip-like, with little ridges running down their sides. They had the distinct look of a weapon about them. These insects definitely looked deadly.

The creature had its head turned her way, probably in response to the snapping twig. After a moment, it began to move toward them.

She started to pull away, but Ghier's hand on her arm kept her steady. The little monkey-creature abruptly leaped off her shoulder and flung itself straight at the insect-thing, shrieking aggressively. The insect pulled back a step, a process that involved a complex series of joint movements on the unusual legs.

The little critter ran around like mad, shrieking and making false charges at the insect. The insect seemed unsure of what to do.

The moment the animal had the insect facing away from them and thoroughly distracted, Ghier tugged on her arm. She followed him, moving quickly.

Allie marveled at the creature. It really did want to protect her, it seemed. Without any idea why, she could only be grateful and accept it, she supposed.

She wasn't worried about her little friend. He was fast, obviously smart, and apparently could handle himself. He would be fine and would catch up quickly enough. She just wanted to get away from those things as fast as possible.

Allie and Ghier rushed through the underbrush, moving quickly around trees and over fallen logs, and straight into another bug.

It froze, having been moving their way, as it nearly ran into Ghier. She wouldn't have thought a face like that monster had could be expressive, but it seemed genuinely surprised to see them. Almost as surprised as they were to see it, in fact. It hesitated only a moment, however, before lashing out at Ghier with a hook-bladed foreleg.

Ghier jumped back, nearly bowling Allie backward. She stumbled to get out of Ghier's way as he backed up to get out of reach of the insect.

It jumped forward to attack Ghier, but instead caught a ball of flying, feathery purple fur straight in the side of the head. The insect shrieked in momentary panic and evident shock. She got the clear impression that these creatures were decidedly unaccustomed to such aggressive behavior from other animals, especially one that small.

The tiny ball of purple fury moved with blinding speed, shrieking its rage with every move. It raced around the head of the insect, biting and clawing with surprising effectiveness against the exoskeleton-armored brute. Black, razor-sharp claws that she had forgotten that the monkey-creature had were tearing through the rigid carapace like a sharp knife through paper with a sound like tearing metal.

Ghier grabbed her arm and dragged her around the struggle and into the jungle once more. They ran full speed now, not bothering with silence. The rest of the nearby insect-like creatures would be drawn to the sounds of the struggle and were almost certainly on their way to investigate.

For a good five minutes, she could still hear the angry screams of the insect and the shrieking of the little furball, fading into the trees behind them. When she could no longer hear it over the sounds of the jungle, she took a deep breath.

"That furry beast is insane!" she said to Ghier, though they continued to move at a rapid pace.

Ghier laughed lightly.

"Few creatures are foolish enough to draw the anger of the jicund. They are small, they are fluffy, and they are fierce!" He laughed again.

"Jicund? Is that what he is?" she asked.

"Yes. Although, in this case, the word 'she' would be more appropriate," he replied.

She grinned. The little creature was a girl? Maybe that was why it wanted to help her so badly. Us girls have to stick together, she thought with an unavoidable trace of smugness.

It wasn't until another half an hour later that the jicund showed up again. The creature looked completely unscathed by her encounter. She landed lightly on Allie's shoulder from somewhere in the canopy after a light chirp of warning.

Allie reached up and scratched the jicund's teddy-bear ears, causing it to produce a satisfied little trilling sound. She glanced down at the hands again, but she saw no traces of the claws, only small slits along the backs of the fingers. Retractable, like a cat's, she thought with amazement. She'd forgotten that fact.

"Thanks, little friend. You're crazy, though. You know that, right? A total lunatic. Hey, maybe that's what I'll call you!" she exclaimed.

Ghier glanced back.

"Luna?" he inquired.

"No, Tic!" she replied with a laugh, getting the desired effect.

He blinked in momentary confusion, shook his head, and turned forward again.

"Do you like that? Can I call you Tic?" she asked the little creature.

It simply trilled its pleasure at being scratched.

Allie decided to take this to mean yes and mentally dubbed the creature 'Tic'.

She couldn't help but feel better, knowing that she had two such good friends helping her as Ghier and Tic, and knowing that Dav was undoubtedly on his way to bring her home.

Frankly, she was a little surprised that he hadn't arrived yet, although she had no idea how far she'd traveled, and it might take him some time to catch up. She didn't have the slightest idea how fast space travel was.

He was coming, though. Of that, she was sure.

CHAPTER EIGHT

REPTILIAN EYES

"We can't stop! We don't know how long we have left to reach her!" Dav protested angrily.

"Dav, we can't go flying directly into enemy territory without finding out the situation. Stopping at Irifal Station won't take more than a few hours, and it could save us all kinds of trouble when we get to Ayaran," Artus replied.

"Ayaran isn't even a prime planet, Artus. There won't be more than a token military outpost there. Worst case scenario is we fly in, grab Allie, and fly back out. They won't have anything that can catch us," Dav argued.

Artus shook his head.

"It may not be a prime planet, but it is firmly in Tyren's control. Besides, I've been out of the news loop for ten years, and our information is vastly out of date. So is our ship, I'm sorry to say. The Runner was the fastest in the galaxy ten years ago. Today? Who knows?

It's entirely possible that it might be like riding a bicycle and trying to outrun a Ferrari."

Dav sighed, knowing his brother was right. The delay still irritated him, though. The more time passed, the more he worried about Allie's safety. She was bright, and Ayaran didn't have much in the way of danger to speak of, save for some of the jungle wildlife and the token military outpost. And the cutthroats at the shipping ports, he reminded himself.

Chances were slim that she would have landed near enough to the outpost to alert anyone to her presence, and the jungles of Ayaran, while fierce, did not cover more than a fifth of the planet's land surface. Everywhere else was fairly docile, as far as the flora and fauna were concerned.

As long as she didn't land in any of the outposts or towns, and steered clear of the jungle, she'd be safe enough.

"Fine, but we do this fast. Get in, learn what we need, and get back out again. We can't waste time, Artus. Allie doesn't have much left," he stated with finality, hoping the severity of the situation was adequately impressed on his brother.

"You've got it, little brother. I want to help her as much as you do," Artus replied before casting a calculating look his brother's way. "Almost as much, anyway."

"What's that supposed to mean?" Dav snapped. He knew his nerves were on edge, worrying for Allie, but he couldn't help himself.

"Oh, nothing," Artus replied, all too innocently.

Dav glared at him. He knew full well what his brother was implying, and he didn't appreciate Artus nosing in like that.

"She's my best friend, Artus," he said simply.

Artus nodded, all playfulness and teasing gone. He knew his little brother well enough to know that now was not the time to tease him about his potential love life.

They flew for another hour before approaching the station. It's immense, Dav thought in awe. It had to be at least three or four hundred miles in diameter. Knowing the specs and actually seeing the massive station were two very different things.

It was vaguely spherical, though it had numerous sharp outcroppings and several extended docking arms reaching out in odd locations and random angles. Almost as though a giant magnet had been activated, pulling in trillions of tons of scrap metal toward its center to create an immense jumble of metallic garbage.

"Wow, that thing is huge!" Dav exclaimed. Artus chuckled.

"It's grown since I was here last," Artus commented. "This is Irifal Station, able to support almost five billion humanoid life forms at once, though not more than a few million are permanent residents.

"It's one of the biggest trading ports in the quadrant. Merchants from all over the galaxy come through here, selling anything from rare minerals or metals to information and experiences. We're here for information. Switch on the com channel, would you?"

"Roger that," Dav said with a grin, mentally triggering the main com switch.

Despite his irritation at the delay, he had to admit he was excited. He was barely a toddler when they came to Earth, and he didn't remember much from before. In essence, this was his first real deep space outing.

Artus touched his control bars, mentally reaching out and linking his mind to the ship and opening the specific channel needed to reach the station.

"Irifal Station, this is the Runner 477-6 requesting permission to dock," he said.

A moment's pause, and a reply sounded in the cabin of the ship.

"477-6, we have nothing about your arrival on our docking schedule. What's your transfer code?" came the gratingly nasal reply, thick with an accent Dav couldn't identify.

"Transfer code A-113-U75. Our visit was a last-minute change of plans. Some supply purchases need to be made," Artus replied.

Dav listened curiously. Artus had clearly done this before.

"A-113-U75?" came the voice, thick with cautious surprise.

"That's correct, Irifal," Artus said, almost smugly. There was a long hesitation before the voice came on again.

"Transfer code is authorized. Runner 477-6 is cleared for docking on Port T-67-B. Coordinates are being transmitted now. Have a pleasant stay."

"Thank you, Irifal, you've been most helpful," Artus replied with a grin, closing the com channel. "Perfect! I know Port T-67-B. It's much closer to where we need to go than I had anticipated," he said to Dav.

Dav was mystified.

"What exactly just happened?" he asked his brother.

Artus gave him a wicked smile, his bright, white teeth flashing menacingly.

"They politely asked who we were. I told them we

were Tyren's personal spies. They decided it was in their best interest to cooperate," he replied.

Dav blinked.

"Tyren's… isn't that going to get us in some serious trouble?" he asked.

"It certainly would if they ever figured out that we weren't really spies for Tyren," Artus replied with a nod, "which is why while we're on the station, you are to keep your mouth shut. I don't mean to be rude, Dav, but we're in way over your head. One wrong word from you, and we could both be killed before we even find our information dealer. Am I clear?" Artus's serious tone was firmly in place.

Dav didn't need the tone to understand how ugly this could get.

"I hear you, brother. Not one word," Dav replied.

The coordinates flashed across the display, and Dav adjusted their course to reach the assigned port.

It took ten minutes to circle around to the correct docking arm, and another ten to properly navigate the jumble of ships clustered around and moving between the mess of smaller docking ports. As he slid the Runner into position, the bay doors behind them drifted closed almost lazily.

A few moments after it had completed its slow, languid journey to a downward position, the sound of rushing air informed them both that the bay had been pressurized and oxygenated for their convenience. As Dav began putting the ship in standby mode, Artus grabbed their helmets.

"What do we need those for? They oxygenated the bay," Dav inquired.

Artus glanced at him.

"They certainly did, but if things turn ugly, they may de-oxygenate it before we get back to prevent our leaving. Personally, I'd rather be prepared."

This made perfect sense to Dav, and he mentally berated himself for not thinking of it himself. He unbelted and moved back into the hold. Reaching down onto the lower cot, he grabbed several pieces of equipment that he'd had the crafter making for him while they traveled. He tossed a belt to Artus, who caught it with surprise, drawing and studying the pistol from the holster on the belt. He looked up at Dav with approval and a touch of excitement.

"You had a gun made?"

"Two, actually. I know what you're going to say, Artus. I'm too young to have a gun, and it was irresponsi…" Dav began.

Artus interrupted him.

"You did well, Dav. Strap yours on so we can get going. This is plenty dangerous enough for us both to go armed. I was going to have to buy a couple of these for us on the way in. I didn't know the unit had the materials for them."

"Well, technically, I had to do without certain other necessities to make them, but I figured that weapons would be a priority. If the chance arises, we should probably find a merchant who sells the material packs for the crafter. Otherwise, our nutritional resources are going to be a little shorter than we'd first planned," Dav replied.

Artus thought about this, then nodded.

"You're right. We need the weapons more right now. We'll see what we can find. Are you ready?"

Dav had just finished belting on the gun and

strapping it to the side of his leg. It would keep the weapon from jostling about if he had to run. He looked at his brother.

"Let's go," he said simply.

The pair moved to the exit hatch, and Artus hit the release button. The hatch opened slowly, and Dav took an experimental breath. The air was oxygen-rich but smelled faintly of reptiles. This made Dav nervous. Why would a space station smell like lizards?

He followed Artus's lead, each of them holding their helmets in their off hand, their dominant hands near the guns. They made it almost to the door leading into the station before it opened, three men walking in. The one in the center wore some kind of silvery robe and held his hands pressed together in front of his chest, like a priest.

He wasn't a large man, and he was balding severely on the top of his head. What remained of his hair on the sides was a greasy black, slicked back against his scalp. His eyes were small, beady, and mean-looking, while his broad smile practically oozed malevolence.

Despite the man's expression, Dav almost smiled. Apparently, all of Earth's stereotypes about futuristic, space-aged garb was correct. He'd always thought it was funny that spacemen in movies always wore silver. It seemed there was some merit to that. The man's long, silver robe, with sharply angled cuffs and collar, looked just like it came from an old space movie.

The other two men did not wear silver, however. Instead, they wore deep crimson and black uniforms that seemed far more utilitarian than showy. They looked something like military fatigues, though with fewer pockets and more armor plating.

They also carried large, vicious-looking guns. Rather

than barrels, the weapons had two long, narrow, slightly curved metal blades arcing toward where the barrel on a standard rifle would end. The two blades didn't quite touch at their points, an inch or so between them.

Dav wasn't sure how they worked, but they were clearly guns of some kind, based on how they held them, and he had no intention of watching them in action.

The men were also both tall and heavily muscled. Either one could have made it in professional wrestling back on Earth, Dav thought. As he sized them up, they did the same to the two brothers. Evidently, they were not impressed, based on their twin expressions of condescension and distaste.

The little man in the center spoke, and his voice immediately irritated Dav. It was not the same man who had spoken to them over the com channel, but they could easily have been brothers. If anything, this man's voice was even more nasally.

"Greetings, travelers. And welcome to Irifal Station. We are the berythel of this Station, and we are called Xynde. We are so pleased to have... men... of such stature visit our humble port." He turned a contemptuous eye on Dav.

"It has been some time since we have had a visit from your people," he continued, "and we would like to know if there is anything we can do to assist you in your... shopping," he finished. Dav couldn't figure out why the man kept referring to himself as 'we'.

"Thank you, Xynde," Artus replied, and Dav blinked at him.

Artus was using a tone Dav had never heard. It reeked of arrogance, self-assuredness, condescension, and a dismissive tone that practically screamed that this man before him was not worth the time it took to speak the words.

"We have no need of your assistance at this time, though you are most gracious to offer. The best help we could ask is that you and your men do not interfere with our acquisitions."

The berythel blinked in surprise, then bowed deeply.

"Of course, good sirs. If you should change your minds and have need of our assistance, you have only to ask," the man said, sliding backward toward the door. The two guards moved with him, not one of the three turning their backs on Artus.

When the door closed behind them, Artus looked down at Dav and breathed a sigh of relief.

"That went well. Nice and easy. If the rest of this trip goes as smoothly, we'll be out of here in under an hour." He winked at Dav and led the way into the corridor.

Berythel Xynde and his thugs were nowhere to be seen.

"Artus?" Dav asked hesitantly.

"Yes, Dav?" came the response.

"What exactly is a berythel?" Dav inquired.

He was hesitant to ask what was probably a stupid question, but he always figured that if you came across something you didn't know and you didn't ask, you couldn't expect ever to learn anything.

"Sort of like a manager. Not the big boss, but probably the supervisor of this port ring."

"Why did he keep calling himself 'we'?"

"He's grundewa. They have sort of a hive mind, though with a little bit more individuality than your average bee has. It's part of why they make such great berythels. If there's a problem in one sector, all the other sectors know about it immediately. No chance for error or misinterpretation.

"What it means for us," Artus continued, "is that by now, every official on this station knows we're here. As long as they think we are who we hinted at being, we're fine. Let's not give them the time to start to suspect otherwise, hmm?" he finished.

Dav nodded his agreement.

They walked fast and quickly emerged into what looked like an entire carnival thoroughfare, only incalculably larger, louder, and more colorful.

There were booths, shops, stands, kiosks, and carts everywhere, literally as far as the eye could see. Dav couldn't see any walls to the massive chamber, except for the one they had just emerged from through the large doorway. That wall extended beyond sight in either direction. It was eerie.

Not far away, there were stairs, and an area around them open both above and below. They passed near enough for Dav to look both up and down. It looked similar to the big open spaces around escalators he'd seen in some of the larger malls, to make the place feel bigger.

This place didn't need the help, though. More floors extended beyond his vision in both directions, and from the sound and what little he could see, they were all as packed and busy as the one they were on.

People were everywhere, crowded in so tightly that nobody moved faster than a slow walk as they tried to navigate through the throng. Merchants and shopkeepers shouted their wares so loudly that Dav couldn't make out a word of any of them. The people were more diverse than anything he had ever seen on Earth.

There were men, women, and many others he couldn't identify. Adults and children, though with many of the individuals Dav could see, it was hard to tell the difference. Some of the shortest people were clearly adults, if here to judge by facial hair and wrinkles, and some of the tallest looked like overgrown toddlers with sweet, chubby faces.

For that matter, he thought, he couldn't assume that facial hair or wrinkles meant anything, since the individuals in question may or may not be even remotely human, and those standards probably didn't begin to apply.

Hair, skin, and eye color came in red, blue, green, purple, yellow, orange, and every shade in between, plus a few hues the human eye wasn't even capable of seeing.

Dav's eyes could see a broader spectrum than the human eye could, including several shades of ultraviolet and infrared. He promptly decided that humans had no right to judge another person based on skin coloring until they had seen someone walk by with infrared skin and ultraviolet hair so bright that it was physically painful to look at directly.

Everyone visible looked vaguely similar to humans, though few seemed exactly right. Some deviated more from the human standard than others, including some that had too many limbs, or not enough, and others that had features that Dav could, if he tried hard enough, loosely identify with various animals he had seen or read about.

He tried desperately to stay close to Artus, resisting the urge to reach out and grab onto his brother. He moved through the crowd trying not to touch anyone, unsure what the socially acceptable conduct was here.

Artus seemed to know where he was going, though, so Dav stuck close by him.

They walked for nearly fifteen minutes, and Dav had so many random items shoved in his face by salespeople that he hadn't even had time to identify ninety percent of them. Most of what he had identified, he almost wished that he hadn't. From animal parts to odd technical gadgets to pungent and eye-watering perfumes, the wares being pitched were remarkably varied.

Artus turned and entered a long, cylindrical tube running from floor to ceiling through a small hatch. It looked big enough to fit ten or fifteen people without too much trouble, but nobody else was in it right now. It took Dav's overloaded mind a moment to process what he was seeing before it made sense. They were in an elevator.

Artus spoke a few words in a language Dav didn't know, and the elevator dropped. As quickly as it moved, Dav had half expected it to feel like free-falling. They must have inertial adjusters in this thing, he thought. It barely felt like they were moving, though the floor numbers on the projected display were flashing down so fast that they were almost impossible to read.

Several hundred floors later, the elevator shifted direction at a right angle and began moving sideways. An odd experience, Dav thought, watching a different set of numbers beside the floor number flash by.

He glanced up at Artus for reassurance and was gratified to see that his brother looked completely self-assured. Dav breathed a little easier at that thought. If Artus felt confident, everything was okay.

Without warning, the elevator stopped, and the door opened onto a scene that looked very similar to what they had just left, only much less colorful.

As they stepped out into the crowd, Dav noticed a distinctly hushed feeling here, though the sound was just as loud as the other floor had been. The goods pushed by the vendors here were also advertised much more discreetly. He also noticed that Artus's hand was almost touching his gun. He felt suddenly less reassured. Dav made a note to keep his own hand near his gun.

They walked quickly again, Dav becoming more and more uncertain, until Artus ducked into the front of a small, tent-like shop. It looked just like a hundred others Dav had seen, but Artus chose this one without hesitation.

The tent was a dirty gray, and there were no windows. It was only big enough for a half a dozen people to fit comfortably in, and there was almost nothing inside, except for five chairs, two of which were on one side of a small table. Both were occupied. A small, glowing stone sat in the center of the table, casting a pale greenish light around the tent. Artus moved straight into one of the chairs, and Dav followed suit.

The two chairs behind the desk held a man and a woman, both of whom looked vaguely reptilian. Dav realized that he had seen several others like these two on their brief, but interesting, trip through the station.

This was probably why it smelled faintly like lizards, he thought. Maybe the dockworkers in the bay they had landed in were of this race. That scent filled the air here more strongly than it had outside.

The male had a gray-green, scaly skin, slitted pupils in his yellow eyes, and a predatory smile. His nose didn't turn down nearly as much as a human's would, revealing slitted nostrils. He had no hair on his face or his head, and his chin curved in too fast, leaving the bottom of the head looking somewhat rounded.

The woman was almost elegant in comparison, her skin a brilliant emerald shade, almost iridescent, and her eyes shone a vibrant gold. Her features looked more human than the male's, though still not quite there.

The woman's smile was also less predatory, especially as her golden eyes turned toward Dav. Her smile was almost soft. Dav instantly liked her, though somewhere in his mind, he felt that he probably shouldn't.

"Caranis," Artus said simply. The male's smile widened, though the slits in the eyes narrowed.

"Can it be?" the man asked.

His voice, to Dav's surprise, sounded completely normal. He didn't even have an alien accent. If Dav hadn't seen the man, had only heard the voice, he might have guessed the man was born and bred American. Possibly even a southern gentleman.

"After so many years?" the strange man continued. "Artus, my friend, everyone believes you to be dead. You know that, right?"

Artus smiled back, but Dav noticed the smile was superficial and closely guarded.

"I do know that. I wanted it that way, and I prefer it to stay that way, if you understand my meaning," he replied, his tone cold and menacing.

Caranis held up both hands in a gesture of surrender.

"I would not share any of your information, Artus. You know that. Not without consulting you first."

"Not without proper payment, anyway," Artus responded drily.

Caranis grinned.

"And not without being directly asked. If everyone thinks you are dead, there is no reason to ask, am I right? Your secret is safe with me," Caranis replied.

Artus thought for a moment, then nodded.

"Obviously, I need information," Artus said.

"Of course, of course. Anything for an old friend," came the reply. The cold, reptilian eyes darted lightning quick to Dav.

Artus caught the movement, and his eyes darkened.

"The boy is no concern of yours. If you mention to anyone that you saw a boy today, for any price, I will come back and personally tear out your kidneys. All four of them," Artus warned, his tone going from cold to freezing.

The woman spoke for the first time.

"You have my word, Artus. The boy was never here."

Her voice was warm, soft, and carried a faint accent that Dav would have called Irish, if he hadn't known better. Her golden eyes looked at Dav, her expression reassuring.

Dav believed her.

So did Artus, it seemed.

"Thank you, Sinara," he said sincerely.

She smiled that same soft smile at Artus.

"All right, fine," Caranis grumbled, casting a disappointed look at the woman Artus called Sinara. Dav noticed his expression softened considerably when her eyes met his in response. "What information did you need, Artus?" Caranis asked, his tone almost sullen.

"I need to know the situation on Ayaran," Artus answered simply.

"Ayaran? Really? What do you need to know about that little hunk of foliage for?"

"It's personal, Caranis. How much?"

"For you? I'll tell you everything you need to know for five thousand keros."

Caranis' grin told even the inexperienced Dav that he wasn't offering anything near a fair deal, though Dav had no idea what a kero was. It was so obviously a bad deal that Dav was stunned when Artus didn't barter.

"Done. Start talking."

It took a long moment before Caranis realized he'd just had a lucky break. His smile became huge; wider, in fact, than any human could have managed.

It was an eerie effect, as the edge of his mouth slid up and back along his cheeks, nearly to where his ears should have been, but weren't. He showed not two rows of white teeth, but two jagged ridges of what looked like bone jutting from his grayish gums.

"We have a deal, then. Very well, Ayaran is currently one of the least interesting planets in the sector. There is a single Imperial outpost there, manned by six maruck and a Commander. They patrol the Three Cities occasionally. Not on any consistent schedule, just whenever they need to restock on food, as far as my sources can tell.

"The only interesting thing on the entire planet," Caranis continued in a bored tone, "is the fixed wormhole just beyond its moon that takes you to Pahrvic, but you knew that already. Rumor has it, however, that five maruck cruisers have just been sent in that general direction.

"I hadn't made any connection to Ayaran before. Why would I? But this happening directly before you coming in here and asking me about Ayaran, the two can't possibly be a coincidence. I suspect your interest and theirs is... similar?"

Caranis stated this last as a question, hoping to get some information out of Artus, Dav thought. Artus gave none, and after an awkward pause, Caranis continued.

"The Pahrvic wormhole is heavily guarded, though from moon-side, not from space. Sixteen prism turrets, any one of which could quite handily blast whatever hunk of junk you're cruising around in into tiny little pieces of space dust. If you're planning on making the trip to Pahrvic, I might suggest speaking to old Zebo for a cargo ship and a freight pass. Or taking the long way around."

"And the Ayaran scanning system?" Artus asked.

Caranis grinned again, and Dav got the impression that Artus had just asked a relevant question about information that Caranis wouldn't have volunteered, had he not been asked.

"Ah, you haven't lost your touch. The Ayaran network is on a forty-two click cycle. The pulse gaps happen at ten, twenty, thirty, and forty, with a two-click gap before recycling. The pattern shifts every fifth planetary cycle, so I suggest that you get there fast. You have perhaps another two cycles before the shift. It will be another day more before I get word on the new cycle pattern. If you prefer to wait, I can suggest a good hostel for you."

"No, thank you, Caranis. We are in something of a hurry. Out of curiosity, does Zebo have anything faster than the old Runner class ships?" Artus asked.

Caranis laughed. It wasn't a pleasant sound, too much hissing involved.

"A Runner? That's what you're flying? I can't believe you made it here in one piece. They haven't made Runners in almost ten years," he said.

Dav felt his heart drop. Runners were outdated and outclassed. He suddenly felt less confident about their ability to get out of this in one piece.

"What's the replacement model?" Artus inquired. His tone implied he was concerned about this, too.

"What you want is an Interceptor. A group of pirates got hold of a bunch of old Imperial Runners and started using them to outrun the Fleet. The Coalition had to upgrade just to keep up. Interceptors have been known to outrun phase missiles," Caranis said with a laugh.

Dav stared. Phase missiles could travel at half again the speed of the Runner, easily.

"That fast?" Artus asked, sounding casual, though Dav could see the tenseness around the corners of his eyes. "Only the Coalition Fleet has them, I assume."

"Oh, no, they got out onto the open market two years ago. The Fleet hasn't built anything faster yet, but you can get them for a price," Caranis replied. "In fact, I know a guy you can talk to, if you've got a few hundred thousand keros on you." His expression said he would very much like to know if Artus had that kind of money on hand.

Artus didn't take the bait.

"No, thanks. We have to get going." He reached into a pocket and pulled out five rectangular gold coins, handing them across to Caranis. "I expect this price will also encourage your discretion?"

"Of course, of course! You trust too little, my friend," Caranis said sweetly, a fat, triple-forked tongue darting between his lips.

Dav grimaced at the sight.

"I trust you exactly as much as I should, Caranis, which is to say not at all. The only thing about you that I trust is the validity of your information, and that only because of your sense of self-preservation. If your information weren't any good, you'd be out of business before another cycle passed, and you know it," Artus said, standing up.

Dav followed suit. A slender hand reached out and took Dav's gently into its grip. Dav paused and looked at Sinara, who stared at him intently. Artus froze, watching her almost as intently. Dav almost thought the look on his brother's face was expectant.

"Hold fast to your mission, young one. If you are brave enough, you will make it in time. She is well yet," she said to him, almost dreamily.

Dav noticed that the golden coloring in her eyes had begun to glow faintly.

"How do you…" Dav began, but Artus shushed him with a gesture.

As Sinara let his hand go, the glow faded. Artus grabbed his shoulder, steering him out of the tent, leaving Dav wondering what exactly had just happened.

CHAPTER NINE

FRIENDS FOUND

"That's promising," was all Artus said. Dav looked up at him.

"Promising? What is?" he asked.

Artus smiled slightly.

"Sinara says we can make it in time," he replied.

Dav frowned.

"So?" Dav asked quizzically.

"Sinara is Gifted. There aren't many in the galaxy who truly are, though many pretend to it. Sinara is. She Sees things that are as they are. If she says that our making it on time is assured, dependent only on your bravery, then we are practically in the clear, right little brother?" Artus grinned at him.

Dav shook his head, more amazed by this galaxy every moment he spent exploring it.

"That's incredible! You mean she can actually…" he began, but someone in the crowd slipped something into his hand. Quickly, he looked around, but the ever-present crush and flow of people had helped whomever it was to vanish almost instantly. He looked down at his hand. It was a piece of paper.

He opened it, trying to keep an eye on Artus as he hurried to keep up and read at the same time. In handwriting so precise it might have been computer printed was a message.

Don't return to dock. R-147.

He frowned at the note. The meaning was clear, mostly, but he didn't know quite what to make of it.

"Artus..." he called.

Artus glanced back but didn't slow. Dav handed him the paper. Artus scanned it and frowned, much as Dav had just done.

"Where did you get this?" he asked.

"I don't really know. Someone just pushed it into my hand. There are too many people here, so I couldn't tell who it was," Dav replied.

Artus's frown deepened.

"I think our game is up. Either our ship is trapped because they figured us out, in which case someone else knows about it and is trying to help us, or our ship is not trapped, and someone figured us out and is leading us into a trap. Either way, we're in a lot of trouble," Artus said.

"What do you think? Do we go back to our ship? What's the R-147 at the end?" Dav asked.

"It's another docking port. Whoever sent this note wants us to go to that port. I think we need to know if the authorities here know about us, or if it's someone else. Come on," he changed direction slightly, and Dav could do nothing but follow.

Through enough turns and twists that even Dav with his incredibly accurate memory was completely lost, they hurried through the crowd. It had to have been almost half an hour, Dav thought. A half hour of movement as quickly as was possible through this throng, including three of those incredibly fast-moving elevators. Dav estimated that they could have been almost anywhere on this half of the station by now. He had no clue. At this point, it all looked the same to him.

Dav forced himself to focus on details as they walked and caught sight of the R-series ports, listed on a wall sign, and the direction the sign indicated to get there. At least he knew they were close to R-147. He memorized the route they took from there, hoping that they didn't go too much further, or he might get himself lost again.

Artus stopped abruptly, looking at a wall with a com console on it. He hesitated, then began moving again. He approached the box and touched the small blue activator pad. It emitted a faint beep.

"Berythel Xynde, please," he said into the unit.

A pause, and then a voice from the box responded. It was Xynde.

"This had better be good," Xynde said drily.

"I require your services," Artus responded flatly.

Another pause.

"Certainly. And how may we be of service?"

"You will have someone go to my ship and prepare engines for immediate departure," Artus instructed. The pause was a little longer this time.

"I'm… you want…" A short pause, then, "Of course, but it shall take us perhaps twenty minutes?" Xynde's tone implied that he was asking permission for it to take that long, but also that it would be that long regardless of their consent.

"Very well," Artus said, then stepped away from the console and turned to Dav. "The authorities know we're not Tyren's men. Xynde is setting a trap. We have to go."

Dav looked at the com console and back to Artus.

"How do you know?"

"He said it would take twenty minutes. He could have someone assigned to do that job and have it done in less than ten. He has something else in mind and wants our arrival at the ship delayed. He probably wants to get down there personally in order to watch his trap catch us unaware.

"An unfortunate drawback to that hive mind is that it hasn't allowed their race to evolve much creativity and subterfuge. His kind aren't very good at either. It's probably a pretty unimaginative trap, too," Artus said wryly. He had begun walking again.

Dav followed. He noticed with some interest that they were heading directly to the R-series ports. He had to admit, he was extremely curious about who might have given him the message and what they wanted. Optimistically, he couldn't help but think that whoever had written the note really did want to help them, but the possibility that they were walking into a trap loomed in his thoughts, as well.

They turned into the R-100 passageway, and Dav knew that Artus had decided to trust their mysterious note-writer. Three doors down from R-147, Artus drew his gun as he walked. Dav followed suit. Then again, Dav thought, maybe Artus didn't trust it entirely.

Artus moved to the side of the passageway, sidling along the corridor with his raised gun in hand. Dav hung back a bit, taking the opposite side of the passage so he'd have a clear line of sight if he had to shoot at anything in front of Artus.

Dav mimicked Artus's pose and movements and felt a thrill of excitement at the potential for action. Irrational, he knew, but what boy could resist the idea of walking into an actual space battle, gun in hand?

Artus stopped just before the entrance to R-147. The door was closed, of course. Dav moved quickly across to the other side of the doorway and took up position. Artus smiled approvingly, and Dav grinned. He'd seen it on a cop show once. Artus nodded, then moved fast.

He swung a hand across the panel, opening the door. It was barely open enough for him to squeeze through before Artus dove through the doorway. Dav ducked through to the other side, moving partly behind one of the door's support struts for cover.

Dav leveled his gun and scanned the area, but he didn't see anyone in the bay. He frowned and looked at Artus.

Artus wasn't looking his way, though. He was staring down to the other end of the bay, an expression of total confusion on his face. Dav followed his gaze and blinked in surprise.

Their Runner was parked neatly in the bay, facing outward as though ready for a quick getaway. The engines of the ship were humming idly, clearly having already been primed. Dav frowned. What on Earth?

Artus moved again, quickly taking cover to the right as he angled toward the ship. Dav walked down the left side, trying to watch the entire bay at once. He jumped in surprise as the hatch in the back of the Runner opened. He aimed, holding the opening in his sights.

Another wave of confusion rolled over him as a boy emerged. The boy couldn't have been any older than Dav. Maybe even a little younger, for that matter. He had short-cut black hair, a smoothly tanned complexion, and wore a navy-blue jumpsuit, similar to those he'd seen mechanics wearing back on Earth. The boy saw him, then turned to look at Artus. After a moment, he spoke.

"Well, come on! I don't think Xynde has figured out where your ship is yet, but it won't take him long. This place has pretty decent security," was all he said before turning around and moving inside the Runner again.

Dav looked at Artus, who shrugged and moved forward. Dav noticed that his brother didn't holster the pistol, though. They stepped into the back of the ship and looked up to where the boy was now holding the control bar, adjusting some of the ship's settings. The hatch began to slide shut behind them. Dav held his gun ready, though he didn't read anything hostile in the boy's words, expression, or actions.

"You brought our ship here?" Artus asked.

The boy nodded.

"Yeah. Xynde was planning something nasty for you. Figured you'd need an escape route handy," he said.

"How did you get the ship to let you in? It's keyed to the two of us alone," Dav said with a scowl.

Artus flashed him a look to tell him to be quiet, but the question had already been asked.

The boy smiled a little as he glanced back over his shoulder at Dav.

"Keys are made to open locks. Funny thing about locks, there isn't one made that can't be picked." Then the boy winked at him.

Dav's frown deepened.

The boy turned to the front again, a small frown touching his features. "Uh oh. Time to go, Xynde's men are on their way. Which one of you stick-jockeys flies this boat?" he asked.

"He does," Artus replied, indicating Dav.

The boy glanced back at Dav again, his brows raised.

"Really? Well, okay then, get up here. Your ship, you fly it," the boy said, sliding into the navigator seat.

Artus frowned but didn't say anything. Instead, he slid onto one of the secondary seats along the sides of the cockpit, gun still out. Dav guessed he intended to keep this newcomer under close supervision, which was why he hadn't objected to taking a seat further back.

The boy belted himself in, and Dav did the same. The boy grabbed the other control bar, the one linking many of the scanning and analytical functions of the computer and began to work. Numbers and geometric patterns flickered across the screen faster than Dav could read them. The boy glanced over at him.

"Come on, come on. We have less than forty seconds before Xynde's squad of goons shows up. Can you fly this thing or not?" he asked, sounding slightly annoyed.

Dav gritted his teeth. Could he fly this thing? Absolutely. He'd show this arrogant little punk. He sent the signal to the hangar doors to open, then mentally shoved the accelerator forward and yanked up the landing gear. The ship lunged ahead.

Artus gasped behind him, but the boy beside him didn't flinch.

They cleared the slowly opening door by what couldn't have been more than inches and leapt out into the docking ring. Dav immediately had to dodge and weave as he cut through the heavy docking traffic, pitching from one side to the other, then cutting into a steep dive.

"Go to N Ring," said the other boy.

Dav glanced at him. So far so good, he thought, might as well follow his advice. If he'd wanted them dead, he wouldn't have brought them safely to their ship.

Dav quickly adjusted course, having to make an abrupt right-angle turn to avoid slamming sidelong into a small passenger ship. A quick roll and turn, and they were underneath it, moving fast. This was easy compared to the wormholes, he thought. He pushed the accelerator further forward.

They approached N Ring within a few minutes, Dav staying close to the side of the station, though moving further out would be less obstructed. Dav figured being this close in and surrounded by other traffic, they'd be harder to spot.

"650," the boy said.

Dav glanced at him, then realized he meant N-650. Dav headed in the appropriate direction, following the on-screen display for guidance.

They had just about reached it when the boy said, "Stop here."

"Stop?" Dav asked in disbelief.

"Stop!" shouted the boy suddenly.

Dav stopped the ship so fast that if the inertial dampeners hadn't been engaged, he'd have slammed his face into the console. As it was, he felt a bit of a lurch in his gut. Poor ship probably can't take much more of this, he thought.

A huge cargo freighter pulled out in front of them, moving sluggishly. Dav scowled. A handful of blips showed up on his heads-up display, moving toward the center.

"They're going to catch us. In about ten seconds, they'll be coming around that corner," Dav said.

The other boy smiled.

"They can't see us behind the freighter," he replied.

Dav's scowl deepened. He had begun to wonder if their helpful new friend was a little loose in the head.

"Their scanners will trace us," Dav retorted angrily.

The boy's smile turned into a mischievous grin.

"Nope. That cargo ship is carrying unrefined rogellium. They won't be able to pick up anything within three hundred yards of that freighter. We're ghosting, my friend," the boy said with a wink.

Dav stared in surprise.

"Unrefi… how would you know that?" Dav asked.

"I scanned the cargo manifests," the boy replied with a shrug.

"And happened across one that would help us?" Dav asked in disbelief. The odds of that were… the blips on the screen tore past them, racing into M Ring.

"I scanned them all," the boy replied.

Dav opened his mouth to protest that such a scan would have taken many, many days, even at Dav's pace, but the boy spoke again.

"Okay, we can go again. Here's your heading." Within a heartbeat, a few of the numbers from the boy's screen slid onto Dav's.

Dav took a long breath, adjusted course, and kicked the throttle up. A few more minutes of dodging traffic at a less-than-healthy velocity, and they were free of the docking ring and in open space again. Dav topped out the throttle, and the ship tore into the darkness of space.

Once they had a reasonably safe distance along their

course, Artus moved up again, gun still in hand.

"Who are you?" he demanded.

"Not even a thanks?" the boy grumbled, looking slightly offended. "Boy, they sure are right about you Sy'hli. You guys have no manners at all."

Artus raised a brow, and the barrel of the gun twitched a breadth closer toward actually being pointed at the boy.

The boy sighed dramatically.

"Okay, okay. So touchy," he muttered. "I'm Raith." He held out his hand.

Artus considered it for a long moment, then gave the boy's hand a perfunctory shake with his free hand.

"Artus," he said simply.

Raith nodded, then turned to regard Dav.

"Dav."

Raith reached out to shake Dav's hand, as well.

"Good. Now we're all friends," Raith said.

"Why did you help us?" Artus asked with a frown.

Raith looked like he was considering this for a moment, then shrugged.

"It was exciting. I was tired of hanging around the station. I've been there too long. I think my mind is starting to go a little weird from it," Raith replied.

"A little weird?" Dav repeated, raising one eyebrow.

Raith grinned.

"Just a little," he replied. "Seriously, though, you guys are into something major. I wanted in," Raith finished.

"How do you figure?" Artus asked, cocking his head curiously.

The boy smiled.

"Simple. You come in using a Coalition spy transfer

code, immediately tell the berythel to mind his own business, and then go straight to see Caranis. Xynde, on the other hand, goes straight for the com system to call up a contact of his in the Coalition to inquire about an unscheduled visit from a pair of covert operatives. He learns that you guys are full of it, so he sends some of his moronic muscle-heads to set up an ambush.

"So, I have a few facts," Raith continued. "You know Coalition agent codes, although old ones, which means you're politically connected, or used to be. You know Caranis, or you'd have gone to one of the cheaper, though often less effective, information merchants, which tells me that you're experienced and have money to burn. You're Sy'hli but are not of the Coalition.

"I'd bet ten thousand keros that Tyren himself would be thrilled as can be to have your heads on a platter," Raith continued. "Only thing I can't figure out is why you'd be stupid enough to use a Coalition transfer code that went out of service at least half a dozen years ago."

Artus's eyes had grown progressively wider as Raith went through his checklist of facts.

"All right," Artus started after a long moment. "We also have a few facts. You have access to the cargo manifests of the entire station, can eavesdrop on personal com calls from the berythel himself, can hack a biometric security system, can pilot a ship well enough to get the Runner here from clear across the station without drawing attention, and know enough about the Coalition secret activities to not only identify a Coalition covert operative transfer code, but also know it was out of service six years ago.

"All of this tells me there's a great deal more to you

than is apparent, and that likely quite a few people would love to get their hands on you, too." He paused as Raith regarded him with a slightly impressed smile.

"So, I'll make you a deal, kid," Artus continued. "If you promise that you won't do anything to jeopardize our mission or ask us anything about who we are beyond what we've already said, we'll not pry into your background or turn you over to the nearest authorities, whom we'd rather avoid given the choice, anyway."

Raith was quiet for a long moment, that slight smile never leaving his face. Without warning, he broke out in a laugh. It was a bright, genuinely cheerful sound.

"Excellent proposal! No prying, no risking one another's safety or anonymity, and we all get to have a little adventure together. Sounds like a fair deal to me. We have a bargain, Artus," Raith said, extending his hand again.

Artus shook it, relaxing a bit himself.

"Would it be all right if I at least inquire where we're going?" Raith asked.

Dav glanced over his shoulder at his brother as the man considered.

"Ayaran," he said simply.

Raith tilted his head slightly.

"Ayaran? Interesting choice. Known mostly for its proximity to the stable wormhole to Pahrvic. You either know someone on Ayaran, or you want to get to Pahrvic for... personal reasons. That's a long flight in an old Runner, too," Raith said.

"Not through the wormholes," Dav responded with a shake of his head.

Raith blinked at him, for once seeming taken a little aback.

"Hard to predict the wormholes," he replied. "Never quite sure where those things will pop up or disappear."

"Not entirely true," Dav responded, feeling a little smug. "I've mapped quite a few of them. They can be predicted. Some of them can, anyway. I have our route already planned. I figure we'll be there in less than three days."

Raith nodded, clearly impressed.

"You, my new friend, are also more than is apparent," he said. And then, as if to himself, "This should be fun."

Artus sighed behind them.

CHAPTER TEN

FRIENDS LOST

It took another day for Allie, Tic, and Ghier to reach Teleth, having had to camp in the jungle overnight. She'd been worried about it, but between Ghier's reassurances and Tic's obvious level of relaxation, she'd kept her concerns mostly to herself.

Wisely, it turned out. It was a generally peaceful night, aside from the constant ruckus of the jungle. It was midday on their second day of travel when they reached the city.

Teleth was nothing like she expected, and Allie looked around with wide eyes. Maybe it was because of all the talk of space wars and alien races, but she had some image in her head of a grand, floating city, with flying cars zipping about and exotic aliens around every turn. This place couldn't have been further from that stereotype.

It was dirty, the uninteresting, gray stone buildings were all fairly short and definitely mired in the kind of grime, dirt, and soot she'd seen in a few less pleasant towns on Earth. On movies, at least. Most of the windows could barely be seen through, thanks to the layer of filth on them.

There were no shiny, flying cars, just loud, smoke-belching vehicles with treads like a tank and open cabs like jeeps. The people in them were just as dirty as everything else and looked just as human as she was. Allie couldn't deny that she was disappointed. This was her first alien city, and it was even less interesting than an average small Earth mining town.

The men walking or driving past paid her little heed, but they seemed fascinated by Ghier and Tic. The men stared openly, unconcerned with how the scrutiny was affecting the subject of their stares. Fortunately, their stares didn't seem to affect either Ghier or Tic in the least. For all their reaction, they may as well not even have been aware that anyone else was around.

"This is it?" Allie asked incredulously. "Teleth is a dirt pile! The roads aren't even paved!" Ghier smiled slightly.

"This is Teleth. It is one of the Tri-Cities, however. The… labor district, if that makes more sense to you," he replied.

Allie frowned but supposed it made sense. She was familiar with the way Earth cities had areas zoned just for industry, factories, and the like, and areas zoned for housing, and some just for businesses and shops. She supposed if three separate cities had started as small towns near one another and then had grown together as time progressed, it would make sense that a larger-scale segregation would eventually take place.

"What are the other two, then?" she asked.

"Urka'e is something like a trade district, and Yvalin is the residential district," he replied.

"Are we going to either of those?" she asked.

"No," Ghier answered, shaking his head. "What we need is in the docks. That is here in Teleth. The only way off this planet is by booking passage on a ship, unless you're wealthy enough to have your own ship."

"Not everyone has a spaceship?" she asked, looking up at him quizzically while her fingers idly stroked Tic's odd but very soft fur. Maybe another space movie stereotype, but she'd thought everyone would have a spaceship of some kind.

"Space-faring crafts are expensive, and the majority of people on most planets cannot afford one. It's much cheaper to purchase planet-bound, ground-traveling vehicles," he said simply.

"You said we were going to have to book passage. Does that mean money?" she asked, concerned. "I don't have any money that would be good on Earth, let alone on an alien planet."

Ghier shook his head.

"Don't worry. I have arranged everything. We are nearly there," he replied.

The soft, lavender sky seemed brighter here without the covering canopy of plants, and Ghier didn't seem to be handling it well. She noticed his skin looked dry, and the leaves in his hair were hanging limply, threatening to wilt.

"Hey, are you okay?" she asked, brow creased in concern.

He nodded.

"I am well. It is too dry here, but I will be fine. Don't worry about me. I will be back among the trees shortly," he replied.

Allie watched him closely, but he showed no signs of slowing.

They made several turns, enough that she would have had a hard time finding her way back out if it came to that. Not that she had a good sense of direction to begin with. Nothing to worry about, though, she thought. Ghier was taking good care of her.

After a time, they came to another large, gray stone building. The windows were murky and dim, but the rusty metal double-doors stood wide open, and the interior looked spacious and comfortable.

As she entered beside Ghier, Tic tensed on her shoulder, chittering anxiously. Allie frowned and looked around, but she saw nothing to worry about. She couldn't see anything that would have agitated the little jicund.

The room was large and comfortably appointed, with several old, but clean, couches and chairs forming two separate social areas with a pathway through the middle to another set of heavy double doors at the back. Hemispherical lamps placed at intervals along the walls shone with a soft, yellow glow. The light was steady, and plenty for the comfortable space.

She could easily see spending a few hours just sitting around chatting with her friends here. The thought brought Dav to her mind, and her pleasure at the room faded noticeably. It had been days. Ghier had said that not everyone had a spaceship.

It hadn't even occurred to her that Dav might not have any way to get to her. If he didn't have a ship, which he probably didn't, and obviously not many people had the crystals that let someone transport themselves around like hers did, he might still be back on Earth, helpless to do anything at all.

Allie started to panic for a moment, but a few deep breaths calmed her. She steeled her nerves and clenched her jaw in determination. If Dav couldn't come to her, she'd just have to get back to him on her own. She had to know if he and Artus were okay.

She followed Ghier as he moved toward the doors at the back of the room. Instead of opening them, he knocked. She heard movement on the other side of the door, and Tic gave a small hiss in the back of her throat. Allie frowned. Tic was agitated.

Maybe she just didn't like being inside a building. She was a wild animal, after all. For that matter, Allie was surprised that she had stayed with her this long, even into the city. It was a little weird. Would Tic follow her off-planet, too? She didn't know if it would be right to take the creature from her homeland like that.

After a moment, one of the doors opened, and a tall man with a scruffy beard stood just beyond it. He had a round, flushed face, the pudginess not at all helping the slightly piggish features he had. Nose turned up a little, eyes small and dark and just a bit too far apart, he really did look like a pig. He smiled at the pair, but it seemed artificial to Allie. Tic's nervousness started to rub off on her, and she found herself growing more anxious, as well.

"Come on in," the man said, his voice scratchy and dry as if he was in need of a drink of water.

He was dressed casually but was a good deal cleaner than most of the people she'd seen in Teleth so far. He gestured them into the hallway beyond the door. Ghier hesitated but followed when he saw Allie begin to move forward.

They allowed themselves to be led down the hallway and into a small room on one side. It held a pair of small couches and had a tiny window high on the far wall. The room had almost nothing in the way of decoration, no rugs, no paintings or pictures, not even a potted plant. It looked like the waiting room of an office, except those usually had at least some decorations to make them look more comfortable.

Allie liked the front room of the building a great deal more. The room had doors on opposing walls to either side of the door they had entered through. Both doors looked solid and were securely shut. The man gestured for them to sit.

"Have a seat. The boss will be here in just a minute," he said.

Ghier looked at the man, then back to her. Allie moved to sit, and her new friend followed.

"So, now what, we just wait?" she asked as the man left and closed the door behind him.

"I suppose so," Ghier replied, seeming confused.

"This isn't what you had expected?" she asked worriedly.

Ghier shrugged.

"I have only been to Teleth once before," he explained. "It was long ago, and I did not spend much time interacting with its inhabitants. I wasn't sure what to expect this time."

Her brow wrinkled in confusion and worry. How had he made contact with someone and set up passage for her if he hadn't been to the city in such a long time? What was going on?

They waited for no more than five minutes when the

door to their right opened, and a tall, strong-looking man in what was clearly a military uniform entered. His blonde hair was cropped so close to the scalp that he almost looked bald. A small, though evident scar marred one cheek. He smiled, but the expression held no warmth. Another man in a military uniform and a buzz cut entered just behind him and took a position by the doorway.

"Good afternoon!" the newcomer said in a deep and rumbling voice. "I can't tell you how glad I am to see the both of you. I was a little worried that you wouldn't make the trip through the jungle. You made excellent time, though I suppose that's no surprise, considering…" He looked to Ghier and nodded.

Ghier nodded his acknowledgment.

"Well, young lady, we're going to have you all set and ready to go by dawn. Your friend let us know that you needed off this planet, and you needed to do so as quickly as possible. We're glad we could help with that." He looked her over. "No luggage?" he asked, a trace of an unpleasant grin touching the corners of his mouth.

She shook her head.

"No, sir." It felt like the right thing to say.

The man's grin broadened, and he looked to Ghier.

"Well, friend, we appreciate your help. Everything you've asked has been arranged. You may go now," he said.

Ghier nodded and stood, then hesitated and looked down at Allie.

"I am sorry. You seem like a fine person, and I have enjoyed your company. My people were at risk. I had no choice," he said, then turned and hurried out of the room before she could figure out what he meant by the remark.

Allie felt her heart pounding in her chest. She looked at the man, who was grinning broadly, something like a cat grins at a cornered mouse, she thought. Tic hissed again, low and soft.

"Sir, how long will it take to get me home?" she asked.

The man chuckled deep in his throat.

"Home? Who said anything about home?" he replied.

She moved to stand, but the man by the door lifted one of the arms he'd been holding at ease behind his back and pressed a button on something that resembled a television remote control. From the light mounted on the ceiling above her, a harsh buzzing noise sounded.

Tic shrieked and dropped from her shoulder. Allie screamed but got less than half a breath out before a heavy hand clamped down over her mouth and nose holding a cloth. She gasped for air, but got only an acrid, burning sensation through her nose and mouth, and down into her lungs. Then, the room went dark.

Allie awoke feeling like she'd been hit by a truck. Her whole body hurt, and her head ached terribly. Her vision was slightly blurry, and her thoughts felt sluggish. She slowly eased into a sitting position, blinking furiously to try and clear her vision.

The dimly lit room was barren of any pretense of comfort. No furniture, no decoration, no lighting. The cold, stone floor matched the walls and ceiling. The only light came in through a small, heavily barred window high up on the back wall. There was one door, made of a solid, greenish metal. There was a small slit toward the top, covered with another metal plate.

She briefly considered pounding on the door and

shouting for help, but really, what would that get her? It wasn't like anyone who would be within the building would be likely to help her out. She could hear voices coming from the window, though.

Allie moved slowly and cautiously toward the window, feeling every muscle and bone in her body in a way she was neither familiar with, nor cared for in the least. Every slight movement caused a sharpening of the ache.

When she reached the window, she looked up at it. It was a good deal above her head, but she thought she could jump that high if she tried. Then, she would have to pull herself up, though she wasn't sure she had enough strength for that.

Allie had always considered herself to be reasonably strong, but she was only moderately athletic. Lifting your body weight with just your arms isn't easy, as any average kid who's taken a physical education class can tell you.

Well, nothing to do but try, she thought. She jumped, her body screaming its protest at her exertion, but she fell short of the mark, fingertips slipping from the bars before she could find a good grip. She took a deep breath and tried again.

Allie leapt as high as she could, gritting her teeth against the muscle pains, and this time, caught hold of the bars. She swayed back and forth slightly as she adjusted her grip until she had a reasonably firm grasp on two of the bars.

First step down, she thought, now she just had to pull herself up. She strained with all her might but couldn't raise herself more than a few inches. She tried again but made it even less of the way up before her arms gave out.

Changing tactics, she braced her feet against the stone and was pleased to find that it was rough enough that it had some purchase. Using her feet to help lift her up was enormously easier on her arms, and she made it to the window without too much trouble. She peered out, blinking at the bright sunlight.

She could see an open yard, walled in the same stone as the building. The wall looked high, maybe as tall as the building itself. Inside the yard stood a half a dozen armed men, wearing the same crimson and black uniforms that looked as much like armor as uniform.

They carried odd-looking rifles, a pair of arcing blades coming from the grips which extended out along where the barrel of a rifle should be. She wasn't sure what they did, but they were being carried like rifles, not like swords, with one hand on the angled handle at the back and the other gripping a padded black bar rigged inside the upper of the two blades.

What really caught her attention, though, was the ship. It wasn't as large as she'd expected, though it was still pretty big, and could easily have fit inside an average basketball court without much trouble. It was also surprisingly blocky, almost brick shaped.

It was made of dark, red metal and was mounted all around with large guns. These looked more traditional, bearing long barrels and swivel-mounted to the hull of the ship. A cargo hatch toward the back was down, and one of the men was moving up the ramp it created and into the ship proper. That was probably the ship they were taking her in.

If they weren't taking her home, where were they going with her? What did they want with her? She couldn't believe Ghier had sold her out. He'd said he had no choice, but you just didn't sell out your friends.

Friends, she thought bitterly. She'd thought he was her friend. She hadn't known him long, though, so she supposed she shouldn't have jumped to that conclusion so soon. Still, he had been so nice to her.

Her arms began to shake from holding her up, so she dropped as lightly as she could to the floor. The soft impact still sent a jolt of pain through her body. What had they used to knock her out? And where was Tic?

She sat down against the wall and dropped her head into her hands. What was she going to do now? She couldn't get home by herself. She'd stupidly trusted the first person she'd met on an alien world and had now been traded off to a bunch of soldiers who worked for... who knew who they worked for? Maybe they were going to sell her into slavery. Maybe they had something worse planned.

For all she knew, they might be Highlord Tyren's men and were taking her straight to the man who liked to destroy crystals and kill people who carried them. Unless Dav magically showed up, she was lost. Dav probably had no way to get to her, even if he somehow knew where she was. What was the point of hoping?

Allie tucked her knees tightly against her chest and wrapped her arms around them, then lay her head down and cried.

CHAPTER ELEVEN

VOICES FROM WITHIN

The man's sleep was not peaceful. His body spasmed and thrashed, his muscles contracting and relaxing in violent, erratic sequence. His toned form was covered in sweat, soaking straight through his bedclothes and silken white sheets. His long, black hair was tangled and damp, and his voice uttered nonsensical syllables, growls, and groans.

It wasn't dreams that disturbed the man, but a voice within his mind. One he had long thought to have been quelled forever. It didn't just speak to him in his thoughts now, however. It screamed and raged with an incandescent fury that left the man breathless and in agony as he fought to retain control.

His cries had gotten so loud that his attendants outside the room had heard him and now knocked to awaken him. The two men nervously eased their way into the room when they heard no reply, the door sliding back on silent, automatic runners.

"My lord?" came one tentative query.

The speaker was a slight man, balding on top and narrow-featured. He was the kind of man who would have looked perfectly appropriate sitting at a small diner in a business suit, spectacles halfway down his nose as he read the newspaper. Instead of the business suit, the man wore a long, crimson robe, emblazoned across the chest in a silvery spiral pattern.

It was the twin of the outfit the other man wore, though the other man looked like a robe was not at all his preferred wardrobe. He was a big man, well-muscled, with long, bluish-black hair. He was also not human.

There was a deep red color to his slightly scaly skin, and his fingers were webbed. Instead of ending in the usual nostrils, his nose was more of an elongated bump in the middle of his face, without slits of nostrils of any kind.

Instead, a set of gills adorned each of his high cheekbones, moving slightly as the man breathed through a greenish-glass lower facemask and respirator, the fluid circulating from the smooth, low-profile tanks on his back and into the transparent mask. The man in the bed did not reply, and the timid, much more human-looking speaker tried again.

"My lord? Are you well?" he asked again.

This time, the thrashing figure on the bed jerked upward with a sharp gasp of inhaled breath. He sat propped up on his arms behind him, panting for a long moment as he oriented himself to his surroundings. He looked about in a near-panicked state as he remembered where he was, safe in his own chambers on the station.

The familiar metallic sheen of the station walls was comforting, as were the austere furnishings. Everything in the room declared a blatant disregard for the modern conventions of luxury, with the sole exception of the elegantly appointed bed. He turned his razor-sharp, blue eyes to the two attendants, the sapphire orbs seeming to shine even in the dim light leaking in from the hallway behind the two men.

"I am… fine," he replied coldly, still out of breath. The men bowed deeply.

"Forgive us for disturbing you, my lord. You seemed distressed," the small man said nervously.

The man in the bed scowled a moment, then relaxed his expression and nodded curtly.

"You have done well. You may go now," he ordered. The two men bowed deeply again and backed out of the room.

Highlord Tyren had never before had so much of a struggle against the voice. Even when he had first encountered it, it hadn't been all that difficult to silence, though it had still whispered to him on occasion for many years.

He hadn't heard it in quite some time and had grown used to the lack of mental company. It was surprisingly clever of the voice, assaulting him while he slept. Had Tyren's mind been any less strong, it might have taken over this time.

He ran a hand through his damp hair, scowling as he encountered numerous tangles and snarls from the thrashing. He stood from the bed and headed for the lavatory.

Without pause, he removed the soft pants he preferred to sleep in and moved into the shower. He touched the control panel's primary button, and the system automatically began to electronically scan him for anything labeled by its internal system as 'unclean'.

You haven't won, the voice told him. He gritted his teeth and clamped down his hold on his mind. *The crystal bearer will come for you,* came the whisper, barely detectable through the mental shielding he'd slammed around it. The vehemence and satisfaction in the voice made his skin crawl.

The system began its cleaning cycle, removing all the sweat, dirt, and oil from his body in a single, five-second pass. He waited another few seconds for the second phase of the shower-cycle.

When it began, he closed his eyes and held his arms out to the side slightly. A light, nutrient-infused mist flooded the small chamber. He took a deep breath, inhaling the vapor.

It contained many nutrients, moisturizers, and various skin and hair conditioners, optimized for his body's needs. It was designed to replace any essential oils and minerals removed from the skin and hair during the showering cycle, and contained several elements specifically intended to make him feel relaxed and refreshed when inhaled. The morning ritual usually calmed his nerves, but today it didn't seem to help.

Tyren stepped out of the shower and picked up the green comb beside the small sink. The elegantly crafted object had carvings inlaid in the handle, made from the carapace of some exotic crustacean that he'd never seen.

It had been a gift from one of the Coalition barons in an outlying system, part of an elaborately planned scheme to win his favor back after an unintentional offense. It hadn't worked.

Tyren had sent the man a present of his own; a small, beautiful silver vial. It contained a virus so powerful that it had spread across the baron's planet in less than two weeks, killing half the world's population before it had died out itself, as it had been designed to do. The other barons had learned the appropriate lesson and had since been extremely careful to avoid offending the Highlord.

He worked for a long time, combing out all the tangles in his night-black hair, enjoying the feel of the ends brushing across the middle of his shoulder blades as he combed. When he finished, he bound the hair back with a silver cord and returned to his room.

Tyren withdrew his chosen clothes for the day, despite the early hour, and pulled on the black trousers and belted on the black longcoat. The embroidered silvery pattern embellishing the coat looked both elegant and menacing. He pulled on his knee-high black boots and moved toward the door.

I warned you. I told you that you could never destroy them all, the voice pushed through the mental shielding.

Tyren couldn't believe how strong the voice had become. He stumbled slightly at the pressure in his mind as the voice broke through the walls he'd erected to keep it locked into the darkest recesses of his mind.

Be silent! Tyren thought angrily to the voice. He felt the voice's amusement and vindictive pleasure.

Silent? Never again. Too long... too long... the voice returned.

Tyren growled and steeled himself. After regaining his composure, he moved out into the hallway, the door sliding silently out of the way as he approached. His two attendants, Harelo and Preston, turned in surprise and bowed deeply.

"My lord?" Preston, the human, asked by way of inquiry. Tyren waved a hand dismissively.

"Send for Klythe. And find out when that slimy wrylendi is going to arrive. I am eager to begin my interroga… questioning," he said.

Preston nodded and then glanced at Harelo. Harelo shrugged apathetically, then turned and walked rapidly away down the corridor, flexing his webbed fingers. Highlord Tyren didn't slow, walking down the hall. Preston moved to keep up, his robe making a soft whisking noise as he hurried after the taller man.

"Very well, my lord. Shall I send for a servant to bring you some food?" Preston inquired.

Highlord Tyren started to shake his head, then realized he was famished.

"Yes. Something substantial. I suspect today is going to be interesting," he replied.

Preston bowed deeply, waited a moment to be sure his Highlord had no other requirements at the moment, and then turned and hurried away.

Preston didn't bother asking where he could catch up with the Highlord when he was finished relaying orders. The Highlord appreciated not being pestered with foolish questions. The station's computer would tell him right where Tyren was when the time came. It wouldn't do that for just anyone, of course, but Harelo, Klythe, and Preston held positions of trust and authority on Highlord Tyren's staff and were authorized to locate him as they needed. And Preston was nothing if not efficient.

Give up. Release me. They will have mercy on you, the voice insisted.

Tyren frowned. That was a new one. The voice had always been so angry and insistent, screaming its wrath into his skull. He mentally shoved the voice back again.

This was disturbing. What had reawakened it? Tyren supposed it was probably the revelation of the crystal key that had somehow been missed in his initial swath of destruction. That would likely give the voice some hope that it might be rescued. That wouldn't happen, of course, but the voice might still be foolish enough to believe there was hope.

It was absolutely vital that every one of those blasted crystal keys be destroyed. Even one of them left in existence was too many, though somehow, there was one that had escaped all efforts to find it.

Who could be carrying the thing? He'd destroyed the Enclave, and they were the only ones able to make the things work. And yet, the crystal had awakened, which meant it was in the hands of someone capable of using its powers. The only known survivor capable of activating the crystal was in no condition to use it, and never would be again, even if the crystal were delivered directly into her hands.

Tyren had an almost idle thought that the bearer probably had no idea what they had in their possession. Even if they had some clue what they held, nobody could train them to properly use it, let alone show them how to use all the crystal's powers. He knew the bearer had Jumped once, though only once, and probably by accident. His own power should be secure. Still, better safe than sorry.

He moved into his throne room, glancing to either side as he stepped to the dais. The massive squared columns, made of the same metallic alloy as the rest of the station, prominently displayed the banners of each of the Coalition barons in turn. All twelve of them were represented, including Baron Irthen, the unfortunate recipient of the Highlord's lethal gift.

He had been replaced not long ago, by a man that Tyren had yet to learn the name of. The barons were unimportant unless they got out of line.

His eyes moved to the banner hanging proudly behind the great metal throne, the deep crimson flag seeming to shimmer as it rippled slightly in the station's silent air conditioning.

The massive spiral pattern in the middle appeared, as always, to be rotating subtly. It wasn't, of course, just a trick of the design and the movement of the banner, but he liked the effect, regardless. As he sat on the throne, he cast his eyes to the transparent, windowed ceiling, staring out into the many stars visible beyond the station.

The edge of the moon of Wrylend was just barely visible, its greenish atmosphere catching the light of their binary suns and casting it back in a display of planetary luminescence that he'd always found to be quite striking.

It was not his homeworld, of course, but it was still pleasant to see the visible crescent of the moon winking at him from beyond the windows of his throne room.

Tyren didn't wait as long as he thought he would have to before Klythe lumbered into the room. He remained still, staring coldly at the beast as he approached until the brute knelt respectfully before the foot of the dais steps. Tyren nodded in satisfaction.

"Klythe, what is the status of the crystal and its bearer?" he asked. He frowned when Klythe didn't immediately respond. The hulking creature looks nervous, Tyren thought, a sudden increase in his own heartrate betraying to himself that he was anxious, as well. "Klythe?" the Highlord prodded, more insistently.

"My lord, girl is located," the behemoth replied

simply, his deep growling voice resonating in the Highlord's chest.

Tyren's scowl darkened. A girl, then? Klythe hadn't said woman, so the bearer must be young. He realized she was probably thirteen years of age, which would explain the sudden awakening of the crystal.

"Located? Is she in captivity?" he asked.

Klythe nodded enthusiastically.

"Yes, my lord. Captain Ruther… bring soon," he replied, struggling to find the right words in the elegant Sy'hli tongue, his rough accent making him barely understandable.

Tyren cringed inwardly at the beast's grammar. In fairness, he thought, he should give the stupid thing credit that it could speak Sy'hli at all. That was rare among the maruck.

"When is she expected to arrive?" Highlord Tyren asked.

"Twelve kgrughn," Klythe answered eagerly.

Tyren gritted his teeth. He hated it when the brute used his native tongue. Klythe had trouble converting any kind of measurement, time or otherwise, into proper Sy'hli, however.

Tyren thought for a moment before recalling the conversions himself. It was less than a standard cycle. Good, he would have her before the day was out, then.

Captain Ruther was to be commended for his rapid work. Perhaps he would promote the man off that miserable, mold-covered planet in payment. That should secure a good deal more loyalty among the soldiers, knowing such a positive reward could be attained for exemplary effort.

Highlord Tyren didn't intend to make a habit of such

promotions, of course. He preferred his men to have a healthy fear of him. Too much positive reinforcement tended to dull the edge of a soldier's terror.

"Good, Klythe."

He was about to dismiss the maruck when he realized Klythe still looked nervous and hadn't yet told him anything worth being worried about. He glared suspiciously down at the brute, though frankly, he didn't have to look far down. Even standing at the base of the dais, Klythe was nearly at his eye level.

"Klythe, what else?" he demanded.

Klythe winced.

"My lord. People saw… men. Irifal Station," Klythe rumbled in his deep growl.

Tyren was starting to have trouble containing his irritation at the beast. Stupid was one thing, but at least Klythe was capable of communicating when he needed to. But this was bordering on insubordination. Tyren's glare focused in a manner that made Klythe shrink in on himself slightly.

The brute hurried to try and elaborate, his ugly brow furrowing into deep wrinkles, indicating how strenuous the amount of thought he was exerting was on him.

"They talk Caranis," Klythe rumbled. "People say… man look Artus. Have boy, too."

Highlord Tyren froze at the name, feeling his blood run cold. Even that cursed voice in his head went still and silent at this. It couldn't be. It simply was not possible that Artus still lived.

He and the brat, Davrelan, had been killed over a decade ago. Tyren had seen it himself, their little Runner exploding in a fairly impressive display as the Coalition Guard riddled them with arc cannon blasts. His voice, when he could make it work, was tight and barely controlled.

"Where did they go, Klythe?" he spat through gritted teeth. Klythe shook his head.

"Station boss… lost them," Klythe ground out.

Tyren nearly screamed. He took several short, shaky breaths, forcing each one to be longer than the last.

Artus could ruin everything. The crystal awakening after all this time, the bearer found on Ayaran just a short wormhole ride from Pahrvic, and then Artus and what could only be his whelp of a brother showing up, couldn't all be a coincidence. It simply wasn't possible. If the man seen at the station was Artus, and Tyren's paranoia insisted that it must be, then Artus had a plan, and it involved the girl and the crystal.

Even Artus didn't know the truth about those stones, but he knew Tyren wanted them all destroyed, along with anyone who could use them. That would be enough to make him desperate to protect both the crystal key and the girl.

Artus himself was bad enough, but if he got his hands on a crystal bearer, things could go badly for Tyren in a startlingly short amount of time.

"Klythe," Tyren began, his voice controlled again. "They are going to Ayaran. Call in any of the Coalition Guard that can make it to Ayaran within the next cycle, and send six extra squads to Pahrvic, just in case. Tell them to watch for anyone not licensed to be in the region. Detain and interrogate anyone without proper clearance, and I wish to be notified the moment anyone is detained in either sector.

"Any resistance to this order," Tyren continued, "will be treated as a treasonous action, and the offending individual or individuals are to be immediately and painfully executed. Am I clear?" he finished coldly.

Klythe started to nod, then hesitated.

"Go to Ayaran, find them, and kill them, you moronic beast!" Tyren screamed.

Klythe bowed hurriedly and practically scurried from the room like a rat fleeing from a sudden light.

Tyren snarled, a vicious, animal sound. He needed Artus, or his lookalike, dead as soon as possible. The girl, too, and the crystal must be destroyed. Even if the man wasn't Artus, people believing that it was could create problems all on its own. He couldn't relax again until they were all dead.

Where had the girl come from to begin with? He'd destroyed the Enclave and had executed every last member, save his experimental subject.

The planet the girl had come from was a virtually useless chunk of rock and water. No truly precious minerals there, no valuable resources, the species of man that had evolved there was almost laughable in their pitiful attempts at technology. It was a worthless planet. There shouldn't have been any trace of Enclave blood anywhere in that entire sector, let alone on that miserable ball of dirt.

Tyren knew where the crystal had come from, however. That obsolete recon android had brought in the last surviving member of the Enclave thirteen years ago but had never recovered her key.

The recon android had been sent back out to retrieve it with strict instructions to never return until he had reacquired the crystal key. Many years had passed, but the android had never come back. It was probably no longer in service. The power cells those things operated on were only good for a few years before the element inside burned itself out.

They will come for you.

Tyren started at the unexpected words in his mind. They hadn't been shouted; they had almost been whispered. *Soon, soon.* The voice carried a whispered menace, a cold, brutal tone that all but promised his doom.

"Be silent!" Tyren screamed out loud, hands shaking as they clenched the arms of the throne in anger. It wasn't fear, Tyren told himself. Never fear.

The voice in the back of his mind chuckled. It was not a pleasant sound.

You cannot win, Highlord. The voice came again, almost sneering the title. *They will come for you… and for me. My brothers will come for me. And then, they will kill you.*

CHAPTER TWELVE

INTO THE HORNET'S NEST

Dav let out a whoop of victory as they reached the end of the wormhole. It was the last one before they entered Ayaran's sector. They'd flown the two remaining wormholes almost back to back, using the Jump drive to move nearly the entire way between the exit of one and the entrance of the other.

Three straight hours of flight time, virtually all of it at full speed through the wormholes. He glanced over at Raith. The other boy sat gripping the arms of the navigator's chair like his life depended on it. Dav nearly laughed at the look Raith threw him. It said clearly that Raith had concluded that Dav was obviously disturbed somewhere in his mind. He had definitely damaged their new partner's calm.

He looked back at Artus, who sat with a stoic expression on his face, seemingly unruffled. Despite his relaxed pose and expression, Dav could tell that his brother was just as shaken as Raith was.

Artus's face had gone ashen, and his easy posture in the chair seemed just a little too rigid. He felt bad, for Artus at least, but he knew they had to get to Allie as quickly as possible.

Dav focused on the controls again, bringing the ship into the right energy phase to slide out of Wormhole 901-0 and back into normal space. As they made the transition, each of the others heaved twin sighs of relief, Artus giving lie to his collected posture.

Raith took one more deep breath to steady himself before he began operating the scanners to locate their exact position on the charts as he cast one more disbelieving look at Dav.

After pinpointing their position, Raith plotted a course to Ayaran along the Sylus Loop, a stretch of space relatively free of the expansive asteroid belts which ran seemingly at random through this sector. He relayed it across screens to Dav's display.

Dav watched him as he worked. Raith was a wild card, as far as their plans went, Dav thought. He still wasn't sure of the other boy's motives for helping them. It could easily be a problem if he turned out to be an enemy.

Raith was brilliant and could make the ship's computers do things that Dav hadn't even known they were capable of. They had made that deal not to pry into one another's situations, but Dav felt it was a risky arrangement.

Soon enough, Raith would figure out what was going on, if only by being around during moments like the upcoming rescue of Allie. They had no real way to figure Raith out unless he volunteered any information, and Dav thought that was pretty unlikely.

Raith hadn't said much since they'd left Irifal Station, though Dav assumed that was because he was busy being in fear for his life through the wormholes. Dav couldn't help but smile to himself at that, though he wasn't sure why it satisfied him so much that Raith was suitably impressed with his flight skills.

As he realigned their course and kicked on the throttle again, he found himself mentally calculating how long it would take them. At least another couple of hours, he inwardly grumbled. This wormhole exit hadn't been as close as the stable wormhole between Pahrvic and Ayaran was.

They'd made the trip in much less time than he'd expected, though, clearing almost the entire distance from Earth in a little more than three days. Cycles, he corrected himself, about four cycles. Transitioning from Earth time would be a challenge, he thought, but they probably wouldn't be back to Earth for some time, unfortunately. He needed to get used to that idea.

A quick check of his locator device told him that Allie was still on Ayaran, which could be either good or bad. He figured either she'd been smart and stayed put so he could find her, or she'd gotten herself killed.

No, he told himself sharply. She was fine and was just waiting for him to rescue her. Any other possibility was unacceptable. She was perfectly fine, maybe sitting around and enjoying the peculiar cuisine of the Ayarani as she waited for Dav to come and give her a ride off the planet.

Tyren might not even know where she was, after all. The crystal had awakened, and Tyren would be aware of that much, but he might not have any idea where she'd Jumped to. This could be a simple drop in, say hello, and leave the planet kind of trip.

After that, things could get sticky. Tyren would no doubt be hunting her and the crystal, and none of the old Enclave safehouses would be at all safe anymore.

They couldn't even get in touch with any of Artus's old friends, since they were all either dead or couldn't be trusted anymore. Anyone who could stay alive for over a decade under Tyren's rule in any position of power was undoubtedly of questionable loyalty to the old ways.

Dav hadn't put much thought into what they would do after they rescued Allie, but that was coming upon them quickly, and he needed to start planning. They couldn't just pick her up and hang around in orbit on Ayaran while they sorted things out. Tyren may not be there yet, but he wouldn't be far behind them.

"Artus?" Dav called over his shoulder.

"Yes?" came the simple reply.

"Where are we going to go after we get Allie?" he asked. It was quiet for a long moment, and Dav looked back over his shoulder to where his brother sat.

Artus was frowning slightly. After another moment or two, Artus replied.

"I'm not sure, Dav," he said. "We need to disappear. We may have to spend some time with the TurGhin. They're among the few that Tyren mostly ignores, since they're technologically useless. I'm a little afraid he'll check those few first, though, knowing we may go there.

"We may be able to get Caranis's people to hide us, for the right price," Artus added drily. "It would be a remarkably steep price, but well worth it if we could convince them to take the job. The drawback would be that if Tyren paid any of them for the information, and paid well enough, they'd rat us out in a heartbeat. We have a few options, but they all have some major flaws."

"If I may," Raith interrupted. "You could always go to the Shift."

Dav and Artus stared at him.

"Are you completely insane?" Artus asked incredulously. "Nobody goes to the Shift! The only people stupid enough to go there never come back out! It's impossible to hide there and survive!"

Raith just grinned broadly.

"You're only saying that because no one ever has," Raith quipped.

Dav scowled, but from Artus's expression, Dav knew he was considering the possibility.

"You can't actually be listening to this, Artus! The Shift is where all the old scary stories meant to keep kids terrified and on their best behavior are based! And for good reason!" Dav protested.

Artus nodded, but still looked thoughtful.

"True," he said, "but we wouldn't even necessarily have to go into the Shift to use it to hide us. If we found a small, habitable planet near the outskirts, we should be safe, and Tyren would be unlikely to search for us there. Assuming we can find a small, habitable planet that doesn't have hostile natives, of course," Artus finished with a smile.

Dav noticed that Raith was watching them closely, though trying to be covert about it.

Raith saw his glance and smiled.

"I know of a few possibilities, if you're interested," Raith said casually.

Artus glanced over at the boy.

"Really? Have you spent much time in those sectors?" Artus asked.

Raith shook his head.

"No, but I have a good head for maps, and I've spent a little time studying the systems surrounding the Shift. I have sort of a fascination with the place," Raith confessed, looking a bit embarrassed about it.

Artus just nodded, though.

"Good. Anything you could tell us would be helpful," he replied.

Dav couldn't believe his brother was buying into this. Anything Raith told them was suspect, as far as Dav was concerned. Dav didn't know why Artus was so relaxed around the other boy and seemed to trust him so much. They barely knew him, and everything they did know indicated he was someone to keep a close eye on.

Well, if Artus wouldn't watch him closely, Dav would do it himself, he decided. Someone had to. He opened his mouth to say something, but his attention was pulled to his heads-up display, where a warning had flashed across his screen.

"We might have a problem," Dav said, forgetting all about what he'd initially planned to say.

Artus moved up to look at Dav's screen.

"See here? We have six ships moving this direction," Dav said, indicating the tracer trails.

"I've never seen that many ships traveling together except in merchant convoys and guard squads," Artus said with a frown.

Raith leaned over to look.

"Why would a guard squad be this far out from any of the planets?" he asked, looking a little worried. "We're still hours out from Ayaran."

Dav cast a sidelong glance at him but didn't say anything.

"Unless they're being repositioned, but they wouldn't be taking the time to come over and bother us if it was a simple reassignment," Artus pointed out.

Dav had a sinking feeling that he knew what was going on.

"If Tyren knows where Allie is, he would be sending a lot of ships after her," Dav said.

Artus shook his head.

"In that case, they really wouldn't be wanting to take the time to come over and bother one small Runner," Artus said.

Raith nodded his agreement, but Dav was already shaking his head.

"Unless Tyren knows we're coming for her," Dav said quietly.

Artus froze.

"Impossible, nobody knows we're even alive, except for…" Artus trailed off as his face went ashen. He looked ill as the realization seemed to hit him with an almost physical impact. "Caranis wouldn't sell us out," he said, but he didn't sound at all sure. Artus couldn't deny that the reward from Tyren for that particular information would be substantial.

"I… have to say that he would," Raith interjected, looking like he really hated to say that out loud.

"So, what do we do, Artus? They're coming in fast. Faster than we can fly," Dav reported, feeling disappointed in the relatively limited speed of the old-fashioned Runner.

Artus was quiet for a long moment. Too long, Dav thought. The squad closed a lot of space in that span of time.

"I... don't know Dav. We'll have to talk to them and hope they aren't looking for us," he finally replied.

Dav stared at his brother. Where was the brilliant plan? He'd really been counting on Artus for this one. Fine, he thought. He'd form his own strategy. Without a word, he began to mentally manipulate the controls on the ship.

The Runner slowed to a stop, implying a willingness to communicate with the fast-approaching guard squad. Artus gestured to Raith, who moved out of the navigator's chair. Artus slid into the spot, grabbing the control bar. He took a deep breath and waited.

"This is the Coalition Guard. You are instructed to bring your craft to a full stop and await further instructions," came the inevitable transmission.

Artus nodded to Dav, who opened the communications channel.

"Coalition Guard, this is the Runner 477-6. Instructions acknowledged, full halt," Artus said in a calm tone across the channel.

Dav was silent, but his mind worked frantically, his mental connection with the ship's systems practically humming. One hand slid as carefully as he could onto the modulator control pad.

If Artus figured out what he was doing, he would probably stop him. Whatever was going on with Artus, Dav knew it meant he would probably be the one who would have to get them out of this.

After several minutes, the guard came on the speaker again.

"Runner 477-6, identify all parties aboard your vessel." The voice was gruff and obviously would tolerate no refusal, but it didn't seem necessarily hostile.

"We are Sabine, Teller, and Nurmin of the Bormeri Trade Treaty. We are delivering this craft to the Tri-Cities, purchased by the commandant for his private collection," Artus replied.

Dav looked at him in surprise. He would never have guessed that his virtuous older brother would prove so good at lying. He seemed so smooth when he spoke like that.

"Runner 477-6, this craft has been flagged by the Coalition for inspection under suspicion of harboring fugitives," came the reply.

Artus silently cursed, then spoke again.

"That's a negative, Coalition Guard. This craft was purchased from Zebo on Irifal Station. Legal purchase, paid in full," Artus replied.

Without hesitation, the guard came back, this time sounding agitated.

"You will submit to inspection, Runner 477-6, or you will be destroyed. We are authorized to use lethal force in this matter." The tone implied an almost casual willingness to pursue that avenue if Artus gave them any reason to do so.

"Understood. Please relay all instructions for inspection," Artus replied, nodding to Dav to silence the mic.

Dav turned off the outgoing transmission line and looked expectantly at Artus.

"Sorry, kid. Those ships could shred us in a single shot, and I guarantee they would use more than one shot. Tyren has to know we're coming for Allie. We were sold out, and now we're about to be captured. If we cooperate, we may find a good way to escape before too long,"

Artus said, not willing to meet Dav's eyes.

They both knew this meant it was going to be too late for Allie. Sinara had said they could make it in time if Dav were brave enough. He didn't know if what he planned was brave or stupid, but he knew if he didn't do it, Allie didn't have a chance.

"No," he growled at Artus.

His older brother blinked in surprise.

"What?" he asked quizzically.

Raith looked at Dav, and a slow, mischievous grin spread on his face.

"No. I cannot let us be taken prisoner. Allie won't make it if we do. I will not let that happen!" Dav said through clenched teeth.

"Dav, get a hold of yourself. If we try…" Artus managed to get out before Dav activated the Jump drive.

The little Runner Jumped, well out of range of the guard's simple com system. He didn't know how fast their ships could move, and it may not be long before they caught up with them, so he threw the ship into full throttle, despite having Jumped so close to their intended destination.

The Jump drive couldn't be used often, because it drained the ship's power cells dramatically. It took a bit of time for them to fully recharge, so many of the lesser systems would be operating on half capacity for a while.

It had been their only chance, but he knew if they hit another guard squad, their already limited weapons wouldn't be functional. Not for at least another hour.

"Dav!" Artus jumped to his feet and shouted. "Do you have any idea what you've done? They'll transmit that we're evading capture, and any other guards we come across will shoot on sight! Our shields won't work now, and neither will our weapons! You've set us up as a target for the entire Coalition Guard! What were you…"

Artus trailed off, interrupted for the second time in a row, this time by a warning light flashing across Dav's display. Artus read it, and his face turned red with fury and panic as Dav rolled the ship into rapid evasive maneuvers.

"Eighteen guard cruisers? You've killed us all, you idiot! We could have gone with them, escaped, and come back to try and save Allie later! You Jumped us right into the middle of a heavy patrol!"

Dav winced at the anger in his brother's voice, but he knew he'd done what he had to do.

The three squads of guard cruisers were moving fast in reaction to their sudden appearance. Although they hadn't yet had time to respond appropriately and reposition themselves to fire on the little Runner without blasting each other to pieces, they were coming around rapidly.

Artus was still yelling at him. It was incredibly distracting. He steeled himself and did something he'd never done in his entire life. He gave Artus an order.

"Sit down, Artus," he said, his voice carrying a ringing note of command that he didn't know he had in him. "You and I aren't important. That key, and the person who can use it are. You know that. If we didn't make it in time to save Allie, our survival would have meant nothing. For whatever reason, she is the only thing that Tyren fears. She needs to live, and we are her only hope of that. If you'll keep your mouth shut long enough for me to get us out of this, we can go rescue her." Artus opened his mouth to protest, but Dav interrupted him.

"Now!" he shouted.

Artus clamped his mouth shut with an audible snap but sat down and strapped his safety harness on. Raith had already belted himself into the secondary seat behind him. Dav focused his attention entirely on the task at hand.

Not a moment too soon, as the first of the guard cruisers opened fire. Dav rolled to the side as the blast went by. They weren't lasers, Dav knew. Those had been obsolete long before Dav had been born. These were plasma bursts.

He wasn't sure of the science behind them. They looked like a pulse of compressed air, though they glowed an iridescent, rippling green and left a hazy, silvery trail in their wake for about two seconds after each blast.

They were hot enough to turn any substance, even the metal of the ship's hull, into a gaseous state instantly on contact. Artus had once said they could even ignite atmospheric gases if fired inside a planet's atmosphere. Dav was counting on that.

He completed his roll and immediately banked left as two other ships began blasting. The plasma bursts were intense, but they couldn't fire them quickly. If Dav could get into the planet's atmosphere, the cruisers would have to stop firing for fear of destroying a large, radial area around the gun barrels, including the firing ship.

It would take him a handful of seconds to make it into the atmosphere, but in those five or ten seconds, the eighteen ships hot on their trail could fire an awful lot of those plasma bursts.

His thoughts stilled as he focused, his eyes reading

the display, his mind immediately responding to the information by maneuvering the ship. It was a distinct advantage to a direct-to-mind interface, he knew.

For the brain to register an event, process a reaction, and send the signal to the correct limb to do what needed to be done could take as long as a second and a half from the initial observed event. A direct-to-mind interface could dramatically reduce that time. A significant difference when dodging rounds that could travel at close to the speed of light.

Dav rolled, banked, and danced, weaving his way through a virtual net of plasma bursts. The guards were closing fast, and his time to react to dodging the blasts was getting shorter and shorter. Just a few more seconds… There!

The Runner blasted through the outer atmosphere, Dav mentally pulling back the throttle hard. Hitting the atmosphere too hard would be catastrophic.

The guard ships caught up in less than a heartbeat before having to slow down significantly as well, or risk being torn apart by the friction of moving so quickly through the stratosphere.

It would take them a moment to reroute power from the plasma guns to the arc cannons, and Dav took the opportunity to move safely into the lower troposphere. They still cruised through the sky at nine thousand miles per hour, which certainly felt faster than light speed when screaming through the dense atmosphere, landscape flashing by below. The air friction alone would cause even the incredibly durable alloy the ship was built from to begin to burn if they went much faster.

A quick check of his locator, and he had Allie's position pinpointed. A few course corrections as he followed the landscape, and he was heading her way. He'd come in fairly close, entering the atmosphere only a few thousand miles from where his tracker had placed her.

They tore across the canopy of foliage, and Dav couldn't help but feel bad. The shockwave as they passed would be unbelievable and would upset a lot of the wildlife and vegetation below.

And… now, Dav thought, performing a rapid roll to the side just as the first blasts of the arc cannons shredded massive holes in the blue-green canopy. Like clockwork, he thought, allowing himself a small smile.

The arc cannons fired tightly focused beams of hyper-charged particles, looking like nothing so much as electricity dancing along a wire.

The bolts blew the tops right off the trees they struck and would have a similarly devastating effect on the Runner, if they were hit. Dav couldn't let that happen. He wouldn't.

The display gave him warnings as soon as each blast registered in the system, and Dav reacted accordingly. It wasn't much different from running wormholes, he thought, except that these arcs were actively trying to hit him.

The guard had fallen into a V formation, which helped break the air friction as they flew in one another's wakes, but it meant only three of them could fire on him at a time without risking hitting each other as they followed Dav's banks and rolls.

Three wasn't enough, Dav thought smugly, even with two guns apiece. He couldn't keep the grin from growing across his face as he danced the lightning, riding low over the treetops. His smile intensified as he spotted the cities ahead. Now, for the really fun part.

The city approached rapidly, and Dav angled to hit Yvalin, the wealthier residential district. The buildings there were huge, rivaling many of the larger skyscrapers in some of the bigger cities on Earth.

He slowed again as he entered the city line, though they were still moving far faster than was anything even close to safe. The guards stopped firing, unwilling to kill civilians to catch them. That's a relief, Dav thought to himself.

Several of the guard broke off and began moving to either side, heading to make sure they didn't leave the city from a different direction and try to escape that way.

He dodged buildings like they were wormhole arcs. Easier, since the computer already knew where all the buildings were, the scanners having read the city before they'd ever entered it. Dav didn't head straight for Allie's position. He knew he had to lose his tail first.

Artus and Raith were still silent, letting him fly undistracted. He made a mental note to thank them for that later. This was hard enough without listening to Artus yelling at him for yet another stupid, dangerous flying stunt.

He circled around, thinking, but staying within the area of the city's tallest buildings. The guard was still behind them, though they were losing ground. Faster ships or not, they couldn't pilot like Dav could, and none of them could go at top speed in this maze of buildings.

Well, he decided, it was now or never. He angled back to a spot he'd noticed earlier, a right-angle turn with a large, brightly lit sign directly on the corner of the building. He accelerated as he approached the corner, then moved into the banking turn so sharply that the ship turned completely on its side as it swung around.

Dav didn't let the ship come out of the bank as he finished the turn, however, pulling back on the throttle and letting the ship coast through a sliding pivot, like a car fishtailing around a corner. The ship continued the turn as he brought the nose up, coming to a stop vertically along the side of the building, directly behind the large sign.

"What are you doing?" Raith asked, sounding surprisingly calm.

"The metal of the building and the powered sign will temporarily limit their short-range scanners," Dav explained. "We should have about fifteen seconds where they can't scan us. Behind the sign, they won't be able to see us until they've passed, either. The street's too narrow for an easy turnaround. They'll either have to come to a full stop once they realize where we went and spin about, or circle around. Either way, we should be gone by then," he grinned.

Artus smiled, too.

"Clever, little brother," he said.

Raith's expression wasn't as happy, though. He looked resigned.

"One thing you forgot, Dav," Raith said quietly. Both brothers looked at him expectantly. "Your knowledge of scanners is ten years out of date."

Dav felt a chill as he realized Raith was right. The first two guard ships tore past, moving too quickly to adjust course, but the third and fourth ships read their location in time. The sign exploded as the ships' arc cannons fired.

CHAPTER THIRTEEN

SHADOWS IN THE DARK

Allie woke up, head pounding. She must have fallen asleep crying, she realized. That never failed to leave her with a throbbing headache. She cursed herself silently for her moment of weakness. She needed to be stronger than that. She needed to figure out how to get out of this place before the soldiers packed her up and shipped her to Tyren.

She stood, rubbing her face to help clear her eyes and her mind. She could still hear the voices outside the small window. Everything still sounded the same, though, so she didn't bother trying to get a look outside again.

By the artificial quality of the light coming in from the small window, she figured night had fallen already. The man had told her they'd be away by dawn, so she might have almost no time left before they came to load her onto the ship.

Allie moved to the door. She briefly considered trying to ram her shoulder into it, but she shook the thought away immediately. What kind of crazy person threw themselves at a metal, and certainly locked, door? Even a grown man wouldn't be likely to do much good that way, and Allie was nowhere near as strong as a grown man.

There was no handle on the inside, so she couldn't even check that. She pushed against the door, just hard enough to confirm that it was latched securely, you never knew after all, then began inspecting the seams around it. The door fit tightly, so she didn't have any way to try and slide something between the door and frame and maybe lift a catch. She doubted the door used such a simple mechanism anyway.

Standing up on tiptoe, she inspected the sliding window. It opened only from the outside, as well, lined on this side with a row of metal bars. No help there, either.

With a sigh, Allie reached into her pocket for the crystal and felt her heart skip a beat as she realized it wasn't there. Quickly, she checked her other pockets. No crystal. Allie began to panic as she realized that the soldiers must have taken it from her.

Losing track of her earlier reasoning, she pounded on the door and shouted angrily for the men to give her back her crystal. It took her only a few shouts to remember why this was pointless. She banged on the door once more in frustration, then leaned back against it.

She had to think, she knew. Allie had to come up with a plan, but she had no idea where to begin. It took her another long moment to realize the tone in the voices outside had changed.

Moving quickly to the far wall, she jumped to reach the window again. She made it on the first try this time, giving her a rush of satisfaction. The voices had turned to shouts. As she pulled herself up to the window with only a little trouble, she looked around outside.

The yard was lit with a handful of small floodlights, and the ship was exactly where it had been the last time she'd looked. This time though, the soldiers were running about. She had no idea why they were running, but they looked like they were preparing for a fight. Several of the men had already grabbed the odd blade-rifles and were moving back the way they had come.

Allie strained her ears to try and make out what they were shouting, but she couldn't make it out. They sounded like orders, though.

In the distance, she could hear odd bursts of humming sounds, followed by small explosions. Something was definitely going wrong. These kinds of men seemed like the type who didn't normally let things go wrong. The place was obviously under attack, though by whom and why, she couldn't imagine.

The sounds escalated, the bursts coming more and more rapidly, the shouts punctuated by an occasional scream. Without warning, a man came into view. He wore a dark gray bodysuit and a full-masked helmet, the tinted visor covering his face completely. He held a pistol in the ready position.

The figure was tall and well built, from what she could see, and he clearly meant business. He easily vaulted a row of crates and rolled down behind another short stack of them. Far too easily, she thought. No action hero on TV had ever moved that way, except for the occasional superhero.

He fired a few rounds over the top of the crates, the odd humming sound punctuating each burst. She didn't see any bullets or lasers coming from the gun, but there was a peculiar ripple to the air around the barrel of the gun when it fired, and whatever he fired at reacted as though it had been struck by a fist-sized object with tremendous force. Crates shattered, men were blasted back off their feet, even the stone wall of the courtyard was taking noticeable damage from the pistol. The man had an injured arm, she noticed. He kept his left arm tucked tightly against his body.

The soldiers in the yard took up defensive positions and leveled those strange rifles. She couldn't suppress a surge of curiosity to see what happened when those guns were fired. As each of the soldiers began to fire, the blades of their weapons began to glow a faint white, shimmering slightly.

A ripple of energy passed down the length of the gun between the blades and tore through the air in front of them. It took a fraction of a second, but the effect was actually rather pretty.

The blasts looked a lot like lightning, she thought, or an extreme electrical charge coursing along a wire in a cartoon. Despite tiny arcs and flickers in the bolt, it followed its invisible cord perfectly, striking the stack of crates where the helmeted man crouched.

The boxes exploded, far more dramatically than the damage the man's pistol had been doing across the yard, but the figure had already leapt backward in a graceful, almost leisurely arc, landing behind the other row of crates.

The humming sound came again, from a different

direction, and several more soldiers were flung backward to lie unmoving on the ground. The hum was almost a pulsing noise, starting soft, but each time cutting off abruptly as the weapon discharged whatever it was using for ammunition.

Another helmeted figure came in fast along the top of the wall, moving like a cat, firing in short, rapid bursts. This one was smaller, she realized. Quite a bit smaller, in fact. It moved the same way, though; too fast, and with too much grace. *They're amazing to watch,* she thought to herself, *so swift and fluid, absolutely sure of their movements.*

The soldiers fired back, but both of the figures reacted too quickly, almost casually sidestepping the blasts. Flashes of white lightning and explosions echoed around the yard.

The smaller figure held up a small object that looked a bit like a cell phone, looked at the display, then turned and looked straight at her. Allie dropped back to the ground in surprise.

What on Earth was... never mind, she corrected. She wasn't on Earth. What in the galaxy was going on? She moved back to the door and couldn't help but feel a swell of anxiety.

The men who currently had her intended to give her to someone who would probably kill her, so she couldn't help but wonder what the newcomers would do if they found her here. Allie looked again at the edges of the door but found nothing more than she already had. She wished Dav were here. He'd know what to do.

Shouts came from beyond the door now. Whoever was assaulting this place was inside the building and coming this way. She moved to the back wall and slid into a corner, barely keeping herself from curling up into a ball, and simply wishing it would all just go away.

A blast rang through the metal of the door, just outside in the corridor. It quieted briefly, then a man's voice called just on the other side of the door.

"Move as far away from the door as you can!" the voice shouted. Allie looked around and realized she couldn't possibly get any further away than she already was.

"Okay!" she called back, unsure what else to do. She was helpless, and she knew it. She closed her eyes tightly and covered her ears with her hands.

A sharp sizzling noise reached her ears, a much milder sound than she'd been expecting. It lasted for several seconds before lapsing into silence. She cracked her eyes open slowly and looked toward the door.

The entire door was gone. There was a heavy line of reddish-brown dust lying on the ground where the door had been, a haze of the same reddish dust settling gradually to the ground, adding to the pile. In the doorway stood the taller figure, dust floating slowly down around him. It looked like a scene from some old horror movie.

The tall man stepped aside, letting the smaller figure slide in past him. It paused, looking at her, then hurriedly reached up to the helmet, pressing a spot that looked just like every other part of the smooth helmet's surface to her. A series of clicks sounded from around the base of the helmet, and the figure lifted it off.

"Dav!" Allie shouted, instantly recognizing the face that emerged.

She ran to him, wrapping her arms tightly around her friend, barely keeping herself from bursting into sobs of relief. He hugged her back, holding her tightly for a long moment before a voice behind him interrupted them.

"We have to go. Raith should be here any minute. We don't have long." Artus's voice came from the other figure.

She recognized it, now that she was thinking clearly and had made the connection. Dav nodded and pulled away. Allie knew they had to hurry but couldn't suppress the surge of disappointment as he let her go.

"Dav, I knew you would come," she told him, torn between laughing and crying.

He grinned at her, turning to look straight at her. She noticed a large, bleeding gash on one side of his head. A long line of blood had dried down the side of his cheek, curving slightly around the eye.

"Dav… are you okay?" she asked him, reaching up but not touching the wound.

He nodded.

"I'm fine. It's not from the fight. We can patch it up later. For now, Artus is right. We have to go. Allie, stay close to me, okay?" he said, pulling the helmet back on. The series of clicks came again as it locked into place.

Allie nodded, determined to stay as close to him as possible, maybe forever. She wasn't safe without him, and she knew it. Nobody else could be trusted.

Dav and Artus turned and moved back into the corridor beyond her cell, Allie close behind Dav. Both of the brothers held their guns at the ready.

"Wait," Allie said, bringing the other two up short. "I need to help Tic!"

"Who?" Dav asked, but he turned and took a full step toward her.

"She's my friend. Sort of a… well, I don't know, kind of like a monkey."

Dav just stared. Or at least she thought so through the helmet. Artus had frozen, too.

"A jicund?" Artus said slowly, voice laced with awe.

"Yeah," she said with a nod, surprised he knew the species. "She helped me a lot getting here, and I need to get her back home to the jungle."

More shouting came from other parts of the building.

"Allie, we can't," Artus said, though his tone indicated sympathy. "Jicunds are more trouble than they're worth for anyone stupid enough to want to keep her locked up. They probably dumped her outside and let her run back to the jungle already."

"Dav," Allie begged, her tone pleading, "We have to help her. She's only here because of me!"

The sounds of shouting came from further along the corridor.

Dav hesitated but shook his head.

"Artus is right, Allie," Dav replied sadly, "we don't have time. Especially since they probably did just toss her outside once they had you. We'd be wasting time while reinforcements gathered for no reason. She wouldn't have been a concern for them at all. They only really wanted you."

Allie could tell they weren't going to budge on this. She bit back tears but nodded. They were right, she thought. They had to be. Tic had to be fine. The military wouldn't have wanted a jicund around, anyway. She followed the pair as they moved quickly down the corridor.

The entry room she remembered as having been so

cozy was in complete ruins. Pieces of the comfortable couches were everywhere, lights had been shattered, and unconscious bodies littered the ground. The front door was hanging at an odd angle, looking like it was just barely hanging on to the last hinge holding it up.

They moved toward the door, but Artus abruptly pulled to one side. Dav did the same, pulling Allie along with him. A bolt of white flashed past them, leaving a blackened hole in the back wall. Artus dropped low, leaned into the doorway, and fired off a couple of rounds. He pulled back a fraction of a second later.

"We're in trouble. They've brought in reinforcements," Artus reported, and Dav groaned. "I hope Raith arrives soon."

"Raith?" Dav repeated, sounding a little bit scornful. "We don't even know if we can trust him, Artus. He probably ditched us as soon as he could, now that he knows who is after us."

Allie looked back and forth between the brothers.

"Who's Raith?" she asked.

"Long story," Artus replied curtly. "We'll fill you in after he shows up with the ship."

"If he gets here in time," Dav remarked drily as he fired a few rounds through the doorway. The return blasts nearly took all three of them off their feet, rocking the walls.

"He will, Dav," Artus returned. "You have to trust people sometimes."

"What, like Caranis? I'm sorry, but I'm not all that impressed with your judge of character lately," Dav said.

Allie didn't like this. She'd never seen the two of them argue this way. There was an edge in both of their voices when they talked to one another that she'd never heard before. She remembered them always laughing and joking together, both of them so bright and friendly.

"He'll be here, Dav," Artus reassured him softly. "He has to be."

Artus dove across the open entrance, narrowly missing several bolts as they tore past him in flashes of white, leaving behind a faintly singed scent. The two brothers continued firing randomly out the doorway. Apparently, neither of them intended to hit anything, they were just firing in hopes of keeping the soldiers at bay.

"They'll come in the back door," Dav said after a few moments. "We don't have much time."

"I know," Artus replied. "He'll be here." He trailed off as a furious volley of blasts tore into and through the doorway.

A large squad of soldiers charged, using their comrade's fire to cover their approach. Even Allie could see them coming, though only barely from her position, peeking up from behind a large piece of shattered furniture.

"Too late!" Dav shouted. "We have to make a run for it out the…"

All three of them flew backward as a piercing flash of light tore through the doorway, far outshining any of the weapon blasts they'd seen before. Allie experienced a brief moment of terror where she was sure that they'd just been killed, vaporized, blasted into tiny pieces or something.

Artus recovered first, climbing back to his feet and quickly peering out the doorway. He shouted out, causing both Dav and Allie, slowly getting back to their feet, to flinch.

"Let's go! Now, now!" Artus shouted.

Allie was confused, but she and Dav both ran through the gaping entrance, trusting the man.

The street beyond was a blackened wasteland. Smoke rose from several points, but there was no sign of bodies, weapons, litter, anything. The ground itself seemed fused and charred.

Artus pointed. A glistening silvery ship was moving quickly down the street toward them, coming in lower as it approached the trio. It was glossy and sleek, shaped like an arrowhead, though with a sloping curve to the edge, the back points extending in a gentle arc behind the ship. The nose had a slight curve downward as well, giving it a somewhat beak-like appearance. The entire thing barely fit in the street, coming frighteningly close to the buildings on either side. Artus turned to Dav.

Artus turned to Dav.

"Raith," was all he said.

Dav just turned to face the ship. It was coming in fast, obviously not intending to land, Allie realized. In the distance, several more ships were visible and approaching fast.

She frowned in confusion as a hatch began to open beneath the silvery ship. The hatch opened forward, a ramp lowering down from the smooth underside of the craft.

"Oh, no," Dav said softly. "This is going to hurt."

Allie whipped her head around to face him.

"What?" was all that she managed to get out before Dav grabbed her.

He lifted her off her feet and began running along the street, heading the same direction the ship was going. Like the last time Dav carried her, he ran far faster than any human could, despite the burden of her weight. Artus was right beside them.

"Ready?" Artus cried as the whistle of the ship rapidly drew closer behind them.

Dav didn't reply.

"Now!" Artus shouted.

Dav leapt into the air, higher than a human could have jumped, despite his carrying her full weight.

All of a sudden, there was a platform beneath them. Allie realized it was the ramp of the ship's hatch. They hit and rolled, being flung up the ramp by the speed of the ship. Dav wrapped himself tightly around Allie, arms and legs locked around her in such a way as to hold her body straight and rigid.

They rolled rapidly for a long, terrifying moment, before Dav quickly shifted position, his feet coming out and hitting a solid surface, legs bending to cushion the impact.

Allie slammed her foot against something, but she was too busy being surprised she hadn't just been killed to feel it much yet.

Dav hopped up, then backward as he tilted his body forward. No, she corrected as her senses reoriented. He'd landed on the wall and was hopping back down to the ground.

The hatch sighed as it slid closed again behind them. She took a moment to glance around. It looked like a cargo hold, she thought, though it was currently empty. A set of steps led up out of the room. Artus was already moving that way, fast. Dav set her gently down.

"You okay?" he asked her softly.

She nodded, then wrapped her arms around his neck.

"Thanks to you," she said. "I knew you'd come for me."

Dav removed his helmet as she let go, and he stood, holding a hand out to help her up.

"Of course," he replied casually. "I couldn't leave you to the wolves, so to speak."

She smiled and took his hand.

He lifted her with ease, surprising her, despite having seen his remarkable strength more than once before.

"You really aren't human," she said to him quietly.

He winced but nodded.

"True. Listen, can we discuss this later?" Dav asked, looking uncomfortable. "We're probably being chased by a dozen guard squadrons right now, and I don't think I trust Raith to handle the flying."

She nodded, limping slightly from the pain in her foot, and followed him as he turned and moved quickly toward the front of the ship.

Her foot wasn't as bad as she'd thought. She must have just grazed it on something as they'd rolled past. It would be fine. Everything was fine.

Guards or not, Dav was here. Everything was all right now.

CHAPTER FOURTEEN

CAT AND MOUSE

Allie and Dav moved up from the ship's cargo hold toward the front of the craft. There were only four steps up, then they made their way through the narrow door at the top. There was a short hallway, two doors leading off either side, but Dav moved straight ahead.

They entered the cockpit, and Allie glanced around. This ship was fairly large, she thought, but was only about half again as long as a school bus, though it was a lot wider. The rooms to either side of the hallway were probably pretty small, too.

The cockpit was lit with several displays, screens that seemed to appear in thin air an inch or so above the shining silvery walls. Artus was already in one of the four seats, two facing the clear window in front, two just behind them and facing out to either side, where several more displays hung in open air, slanted like an art table.

Sitting in the other forward-facing seat was a boy she didn't know. He looked to be about her and Dav's age.

The boy glanced behind him as they entered, nodding to Dav, but then froze as he spotted Allie.

Her breath caught in her throat. He was gorgeous. His eyes were striking, clear and direct. They were an almost almond-shape, and a light caramel color. They seemed to shine in the reflected light of the displays. His short-cut black hair wasn't flashy, but the style he wore it in looked great on him. After a moment, he smiled at her, a soft and slightly confused smile.

"Hi," he said simply. "I'm Raith."

She smiled back.

"Allie."

She was surprised and somewhat embarrassed to hear that her voice sounded a little bashful.

Allie noticed as Dav looked back and forth between them, made a disgusted sound in the back of his throat, and moved forward.

"If you're not going to fly this thing, let me," Dav said, shoving Raith out of the seat and sliding into it. "Buckle up. This is going to be a rough ride."

Behind him, Allie sat in one of the side seats, pleased to find that it pivoted around so she could face front and watch what was going on, if she wanted to. She strapped the belt on, confused for a moment by the clasp until she realized that it was magnetic. That done, she turned forward.

Dav had a grin on his face that she'd never seen before. Talk about excited, she thought, like a kid brought to the world's largest candy store and told to go nuts.

Allie admitted to herself that she was a bit shocked that Dav was piloting instead of Artus, though she supposed she shouldn't have been surprised by anything at this point. She looked across to Raith, who smiled at her.

"Don't worry, Allie," he said. "Dav's the best pilot I've ever seen, and I've seen a few. If anyone can get us out of this, he can." He gave her a reassuring smile, and her heart fluttered.

Allie looked forward again, and her stomach lurched as she saw the buildings flashing by below them, the horizon wobbling back and forth so rapidly that she felt like someone was shaking the entire world.

Inside the ship, however, she felt nothing. There was no surge of movement, no pull to the side as he turned. It made her ill to watch. Instead, she turned her seat back to face the side display. It was safer that way. Several small, green shapes with tiny digital labels beneath them moved slowly across the screen, toward a red spot in the middle.

"Artus?" she called. Artus glanced back. "What's this?" she asked, pointing to the control panel. He looked where she indicated and immediately looked back to Dav.

"Little brother, we have several more squads incoming on long-range scanners. Got any more brilliant suggestions?" Artus asked.

Dav switched scanner channels on his display, and his screen now mirrored hers.

"Yeah," Dav said. "Let's not get caught."

Raith chuckled, but Artus just rolled his eyes.

"Raith," Dav called behind him. Raith leaned over a bit to hear better. "You're in the gunner's seat, apparently. I'm hoping none of them get close enough to fire on, but just in case, are you any good?" he asked.

"Any good?" Raith laughed. "My friend, I can light a candle with an arc cannon at five miles without melting the wax," Raith replied with a smirk.

Dav actually looked back at Raith for a moment, as though checking to see if he was joking.

Allie had no idea what an arc cannon was, but by Dav's expression, Raith had made an completely unbelievable statement.

"I hope you're serious," Dav finally muttered, turning back to the front just in time to bank sharply around a towering skyscraper, one of the only ones tall enough to still be in their way. "We need to get off this rock," Dav said as if to himself, then called back to her. "Allie, keep an eye on those green dots. If any of them get within about an inch of our red one, you let me know."

"I will," she said, turning back to face her display.

Her emotions were everywhere, all at once. She felt immense relief at Dav's rescue of her, but they still weren't out of danger yet. She was terrified they were all going to die but exhilarated that she was actually riding a spaceship at high speed, in the middle of a space battle.

It wasn't really a space battle, she mentally corrected herself, but it was still undeniably more fun than it should have been. She also couldn't help thinking about Raith. Who was he, she wondered, and how did Dav and Artus know him? Dav obviously didn't trust him, but Artus seemed to.

Allie glanced out the front window and stared in shock. They were moving so fast that the landscape below was a bluish blur. They were back out over the jungle, out of the city, and moving at a speed so fast that she couldn't even begin to guess what their velocity really was.

"All right, folks. We're going to make a break for it out of the atmosphere," Dav said from the front. "We may have a chance in this ship."

"Careful, Dav," Artus warned. "There are more squadrons just outside the atmosphere. I'm sure they have their plasma guns ready and waiting."

"I'll bet," Dav said under his breath.

"Don't worry about it, Artus," Raith interjected. "Dav's got the controls, and I've got the guns. There isn't a safer place to be in this entire sector." Raith turned and flashed a grin at the others.

Allie couldn't help but smile back as the grin turned her way. That smile was infectious.

"Well, here we go," Dav said, and the ship's speed increased exponentially, the nose of the craft angling upward until they were flying almost straight up. "Be ready, Raith, they're too close. We'll be passing within a few hundred feet of one of the squadrons. I can see them on our scanners now, so I'm sure they can see us coming. Time to put your money where your mouth is. See if you can't pick them off before they hit us," he finished.

"Can't use the plasma guns," Raith said. "Still inside the atmosphere. It's a long shot for the arc cannons. I can make it, though."

Allie was fairly sure he'd said that for her benefit, to impress her with how precise his shooting was, but she didn't care. As long as they got out of there all in one piece, she'd be impressed even if he were just firing blindly into space.

"Stop talking and do it!" Dav called back. "Two seconds until we're in range!"

Raith leaned over his display, hands on the control bars on his chair.

Allie glanced at her own screen. The dots were getting closer fast. They'd be about an inch away on the display in less than one more second.

She heard a small beep coming from Raith's station, but before she could turn all the way around to look, she saw long bolts of energy streaking forward from their ship and into what looked like empty space. Three, four, six bolts before they stopped. She looked back at her screen. The dots that had been near their own had disappeared from her display.

"Woah," she heard Dav say. "Six shots, six ships, and close to ten miles. You even compensated for the atmospheric distortion. You weren't kidding, were you," he stated, clearly not intending it as a question.

Raith chuckled behind her.

"I never kid... at least not about my skills," Raith replied.

She looked over at him, and he winked back at her playfully. She felt her cheeks warm as she flushed a bit.

"Your turn," he said to Dav. "We've got a couple more squadrons coming in hot."

"Not a problem," Dav replied, sounding just as confident as Raith had a few moments ago.

She turned toward the front, so that she could see. They were in space, and ahead of them, she could only see distant stars. She was about to turn away when a rippling burst of energy flashed across the nose of the ship.

"Watch it!" Artus shouted.

"I got it, I got it," Dav muttered.

Allie turned to look at her screen, but it still only showed the dots. Several were close, and more were closing.

The ship banked sharply as Dav avoided another barrage of plasma blasts. Raith's display, as she glanced his way, showed a view of space, but had a heads-up display like the ones on fighter jets she'd seen in movies.

It looked like they were firing, several plasma bursts flashing out from the lower corners of the screen toward a pair of bright markers which slid around the display independently of one another. Symbols were flashing everywhere in a language she didn't recognize.

The area of space he was aiming into rolled violently around as he panned the guns in different directions, apparently following indicators on a small, red display in one lower corner. She had no idea how he could process all of that so quickly, but everywhere he turned and fired, small explosions told her that he was hitting targets. She didn't think he missed a single shot.

"Grab the silver bars," Artus called back.

It took Allie a moment to realize he was talking to her.

"All you have to do is think about the wormhole gate. I have an idea, but I need coordinates and can't spare the attention to get them just now."

"I don't know how!" she called up, the fear beginning to overcome her excitement.

"Just think about it," he said, his tone surprisingly calm considering the circumstances.

Allie herself felt like the tension in her was about ready to break something.

"Just think about a big, metal ring around a giant hole, floating in space, close by. The computer will take care of the rest. Once you have it, think hard about where it is, and then think about that information showing up on my screen."

"What?" she muttered to herself but did as she'd been instructed.

Allie grabbed the horizontal control bars on her chair, just above the armrests, and was instantly assaulted by the rush of information pouring into her head. She yelped, an unfortunately undignified sound, but she managed to keep from screaming in shock. Allie considered that a small triumph.

The data on her control screen began to flicker and change so rapidly she could barely track it. What had Artus said? Gasping, she forced her mind to think through the flashing waves of information. Right, she thought. Think about a metal ring, around a big hole in space, close by. She tried to picture what he meant but didn't really have a frame of reference.

Her display stabilized, now showing four images. One was of what looked like a cannon barrel on the side of the ship they rode in. Another showed what she thought might be an exhaust port, though she wasn't sure.

The third was a massive ring of machinery surrounding what looked like a typical patch of space, though the stars visible through the ring looked slightly fuzzy and off colored, like watching a 3D movie without the glasses. The fourth looked like a docking array from one of the old space movies she'd watched a time or two with Dav. He'd always thought those were really funny. She suddenly understood why.

Allie focused on the machinery with the odd distortion in the middle, and the other three images went away as it enlarged to fill her display. More information began flashing across the screen, though she found that it was being placed directly in her mind, as well. It's a weird feeling, she thought.

In seconds, she knew that the ring she was looking

at was a frequency stabilizer, built around a wormhole; wormhole 113-9, to be precise. It maintained an accessible entrance into the wormhole between Ayaran, the planet she'd just left, and another world called Pahrvic.

Momentarily distracted by the flow of information directly into her mind, she remembered what she was supposed to be doing, and she thought about the coordinates of the ring. She instantly knew them, and with a thought, transmitted them to Artus's display. She couldn't suppress a surge of pride at her success in figuring out how to use this computer system.

"Is that the one?" she asked Artus.

"Perfect!" He called back, sounding a little surprised. "And quick, too!"

She smiled at him, though he was facing away from her.

"Dav, we're going to need to time this just right," Artus said. "Set coordinates for the location I'm sending you. As soon as you've set those, enter the second set. Timing is critical. I need you to power up the Jump drive, accelerate hard toward first coordinates, then immediately Jump to the second set as fast as this ship will take us. Got that?"

Dav's furious evasive maneuvers never stopped as he listened.

"Roger that, big brother. Powering Jump drive," Dav replied.

"What are you doing?" Raith called, plasma bursts still flashing rapidly across his screen.

"Setting a false trail," Artus replied.

Allie had no idea what was going on in any case, so she just tried to stay quiet.

Dav was setting the coordinates in when a terrible thought occurred to her.

"Dav!" she shouted.

He spared a split second to glance back at her before his piloting demanded his attention again.

"What is it?" he asked, sounding understandably distracted.

"I lost the crystal!" she cried. His head snapped back around to look at her again.

"What?" he asked, a look of horror crossing his face. "Where?"

"I think the commander back on the planet took it!" Her heart was sinking in the terrible realization that she may not get it back. She didn't see how it would be possible to retrieve something lost in the hands of an enemy commander on a planet that was obviously on high alert and trying to bring them down.

Dav muttered something under his breath.

"Change of plans, Dav," Artus said. "Keep the first set of coordinates but change the Jump coordinates to these. And full stop immediately after the Jump. I repeat, immediately after the Jump!"

"Done," Dav replied. "Raith," he called, "can you open up a corridor for us along this route?"

"Can do," Raith replied casually.

Allie couldn't believe how together they all were. None of them seemed to be panicking, despite their being surrounded by enemies and might possibly die in the next two seconds.

Although, in her defense, she wasn't having anywhere near the total freak-out she'd have expected from herself just a few days ago if thrown into a near-death situation. Again. She couldn't deny how fast her pulse was racing, but she felt like she could handle it.

Raith immediately intensified his return fire, bursts from the plasma cannons lighting up the windows.

Dav accelerated along the path, though he still had the ship rolling and arcing like a mad bee as he dodged the still-incoming fire.

Allie wasn't sure what Artus was doing, but he seemed just as focused as the other three did. She felt useless again, with nothing to do but sit and try to decide if she were still more excited or terrified.

The ship turned slightly as Dav accelerated even more and cruised nearly a hundred thousand miles, past Ayaran, straight at the wormhole stabilizing gate in only a few breaths. The other ships immediately pursued, if Allie was reading the little blips on her display correctly, but Dav was already slowing.

"What are you doing?" Allie couldn't resist crying out as the blips moved closer far too quickly. She was about to say something else, but the thought vanished from her mind as he engaged the Jump drive.

She felt the odd sensation of being pulled everywhere at once as the ship was suddenly somewhere else. It was a much smoother transition than her Jump with the crystal had been. Briefly, she wondered why.

The dark space beyond the windows of the ship had immediately transformed into a massive cliff, rising in front of them and far beyond her line of sight.

Dav mentally pulled back the throttle hard, and the ship stopped a fraction of a second before slamming into the wall.

"There," Artus said, interrupting her thoughts.

He was pointing to a spot on the side of the cliff a few hundred feet straight above them, where a huge cave opening was visible, as though some giant worm had bored its way straight through the stone.

Caves were creepy enough, she thought, without them being so smoothly cut that something had to have made the opening on purpose.

Dav smoothly guided the ship into the opening, and back into the stone deep enough that they couldn't be seen from the entrance.

She couldn't help but think again of the mental image of a giant worm chewing through the rock as she noticed the unusually smooth stone of the cave's surfaces. The cave sloped slightly downward, with absolutely no curve at all.

As Dav slowly lowered the ship, she did feel a faint bump as it touched down. She held her breath, trying to listen over her pounding pulse, her body unable to believe that the immediate danger they'd been in for what felt like forever was abruptly gone. It hadn't even been very long, she thought. It was funny how time played tricks on you when you were under pressure. Everyone was quiet for a long moment.

"Think it worked?" Dav asked Artus.

The man watched his display for a minute, then nodded.

"I think so. They probably assumed we'd gone through the wormhole. As fast as you were going, they'll chase us for some time before they either realize we didn't go that way or decide we've outrun them," he replied as he watched the scanners.

Dav grinned.

"Yeah, this thing can seriously move!" he said with a laugh, patting the console in front of him like he'd pat a favored dog that had just done a neat trick.

Dav unbelted and stood, pausing a moment to regard Raith. The other boy turned in his chair to look up at him. Allie watched, intensely aware of a faint tension in the air, coming from Dav, as far as she could tell. That's odd, she thought.

"Nice flying," Raith said with a smile.

Dav nodded.

"Nice shooting," Dav said simply.

The two boys watched each other for a long moment, Dav looking like a cat trying to decide if he wanted to play or fight. Raith's smile clearly indicated that he preferred to play. Although from what she'd just seen, he probably considered a fight to be playing.

Then, Dav turned to Allie.

"You okay?" he asked.

Allie nodded.

"I think so. I feel a little bit high strung at the moment, though." She laughed a bit awkwardly, her nerves still humming from the adrenaline.

Dav smiled at her softly.

Allie again noticed the cut on his head. It didn't look like it was bleeding much anymore, but it still looked pretty bad. She winced, and he reached up, realizing what she was reacting to.

"It's not as bad as it looks. Probably should get it cleaned up now, though," he said.

She nodded and stood.

"I'll help," she told him as she moved toward the doorway.

"Allie, we have to get that crystal," Artus said.

She stopped, her heart sinking. She'd forgotten about the crystal again. What did it say about her that something so obviously important could slip her mind so easily, she wondered?

"You're right. A quick cleanup to make sure Dav's cut is taken care of and won't get infected, then we'll go," she told him.

Artus and Dav were both shaking their heads before she finished.

"No, you're important too, Allie," Artus said. "The crystal key won't work without you. We have to keep you safe, and that in no way includes bringing you back into Teleth."

"I can't come along?" Allie asked, not sure whether to feel comforted that she wasn't going to be racing back into the lion's den, or a little hurt that she was being left out.

"Sorry," Dav told her, "but we can't risk you." He turned to Artus. "I'll stay and protect her and the ship. You and Raith go get the crystal." Artus looked over at Raith, who nodded his agreement.

"Good. We shouldn't be more than a few hours," Artus agreed. "See if this ship has a crafter on board. You could get it working on a few more weapons and suits for Raith and Allie; we'll probably need them," he told Dav.

"You got it," Dav replied before turning back to Allie and gesturing back toward the center of the ship. "All right, let's get this cut cleaned up."

CHAPTER FIFTEEN

CONFESSIONS

The pair of them walked out of the cabin and into the short hallway. Dav glanced through both doorways before turning into the one on the right. Allie followed along.

The room beyond wasn't large, but it wasn't that much smaller than her bedroom back home had been. The association made her heart twinge with a wave of homesickness, but she pushed the feeling aside, determined not to break down and cry again. Once was enough, she decided, remembering her breakdown in the cell.

She turned her attention back to the room. It held four bunks, a couple of storage cabinets, and what looked to her to be a small desk, all bolted securely to the floor.

Dav moved to one side, where a small metal panel, about a foot high and another foot across, was affixed to the wall. It had a symbol on it that she didn't recognize, but Dav obviously did.

He located the small control unit beside the panel and touched it. The panel immediately slid aside, revealing an array of small hand tools she didn't recognize. The tools inside were unusual, vaguely resembling anything from an electric toothbrush to a square device that looked like a smartwatch without the band. She was sure that wasn't what they were, but those were the closest things she could relate them to when she looked at them.

Dav selected two items without hesitation, including the toothbrush-looking tool and a small spray bottle. He handed both to Allie, who stared at them blankly. What was she supposed to do with these? Dav grinned at her, seeing her dumbfounded expression.

"First, use this one," he said, pointing at the toothbrush tool. "Hold it just above the skin. Please be careful not to actually touch me with it, and move it slowly over the dried blood, then above the wound itself.

"Second," he gestured at the little spray bottle, "hold this one about two inches away from the cut and press the blue button on the back. It will spray out a dermal sealant, something to seal the cut and help it heal faster. Like a liquid bandage with healing powers." He smiled at her encouragingly.

She frowned as she looked at the tools.

"Don't they use superglue for that back home?" she asked.

"Well, yes, that's what superglue was invented for, actually, but this stuff is better," he told her. "It's made of a specialized blend of enzymes, nutrients, and minerals to not only keep the wound sealed but to help it heal much more quickly. This should be better by tomorrow, if you do it right."

She stared at him.

"Seriously? Tomorrow?" she asked in amazement.

He smiled lightly and nodded.

"Earth will get to that point in medical technology eventually. Probably not too far in the future, at the rate they're learning," he said.

Dav moved over to the desk and sat down on top of it, putting his head just enough below hers to make it easy to see and reach. She took a deep breath, then switched on the toothbrush. It emitted a high-pitched, though not unpleasant hum.

Allie wondered what Dav would say if he knew she kept thinking of it as a toothbrush. Probably laugh, she knew. She wasn't that far off, she decided, since it was intended as a cleaning device.

Leaning in close, she held the small tool above the blood smears on his cheek. She moved it closer, and tiny flakes of dried blood began to vanish. Allie had no idea where the stuff was going, but it disappeared as cleanly as if it had never been there.

She smiled and moved the little tool back and forth slowly over the blood, erasing it as if by magic. She progressed slowly up his cheek, cleaning from the bottom up and saving the wound itself for last.

"How did you find me?" she asked as she worked.

Dav looked suddenly guilty.

"Long story," he replied.

She frowned, knowing something was wrong.

"No, really," she urged him. "How did you know I'd be on that planet, and where on that planet I was? I think it's even bigger than Earth."

"Ayaran is big," Dav sighed. "Please don't be mad, Allie. I sort of planted a bug."

She paused in her work.

"A bug? You mean like a tracer? Like in some spy movie?" she asked incredulously.

"Something like that," he replied, sounding a bit worried as he glanced at her.

"You planted a tracer on me," she said, almost to herself as though feeling out the concept. She didn't think she liked how it felt. "Why did you do that?" she asked, trying not to show the anger she was trying to keep suppressed. She was sure he had a good reason, but she couldn't help feeling a little violated.

"When you showed me the box, the one the crystal key was in, I sort of recognized it," he said. "I mean, I haven't seen one before, but I recognized the symbol and the writing. I had already suspected who you really were, and so the last couple of years, I'd been trying to figure out how to keep you safe. I had the tracer made a few months before your birthday. I wasn't going to give it to you until I was sure the precaution was necessary. I'm really sorry, Allie." He sounded like he meant it.

Allie was sure he did, he would never violate her privacy without good reason. She stayed quiet for a long moment as she worked. She could hear Artus and Raith talking in the cabin, but she couldn't focus on what they were saying. Allie wasn't sure she could make it out, anyway.

"Where is it?" she asked eventually.

"In your bracelet," he replied, voice barely above a whisper.

Her eyes went back down to the beautiful bracelet she'd had on since Dav had given it to her. Her anger at him collapsed a bit, turning instead to hurt. He hadn't given it to her just because he'd thought it was pretty, and she'd like it. He'd given it to her so he could follow her around.

No, she corrected herself, so that he could find her when she was in trouble. It had saved her life, pure and simple. He'd done it with the best of intentions, she told herself. After a few more long moments, she nodded.

"Thank you," she said, pushing the words past the tightness in her chest.

He nodded, a slight movement as he tried not to disturb her work on his cheek, but he didn't say anything. She had almost cleaned everything off his face and was moving up to the wound itself.

"What did you mean when you said you suspected who I really was? Who do you think I am?" she asked.

"Well, we knew there was another person alive who could use the crystal key. We even knew how old you were and had a basic idea where to find you," Dav confessed.

Allie frowned in confusion.

"What? How?" she asked.

"Your mother told us. Well, she told Artus, anyway. I was too young," he admitted.

Allie's hands began to shake, and she brushed his cheek lightly with the end of the tool, the tip barely grazing his skin. Even so, he yelped in surprise and pain and jerked away.

A small wound showed where she'd touched his skin. The tool apparently could take skin off, too, she realized. She pulled the device back and took a deep breath to calm herself. She almost felt bad for grazing him, but she was too busy trying to process what he'd just said.

He gently touched the new little wound and looked

at his fingertips to check for blood. When there wasn't any, he looked back at her.

"My mother told Artus?" she asked slowly.

Dav nodded.

"So, you two came to Earth, specifically to look for me?"

"To look after you," he corrected. "Artus promised your mother that he would look after you."

"Why would he promise her that? How did he know her?" she asked, looking at her hands to see if they still shook. They did, so she didn't approach him again with the cleaning tool yet.

Dav sighed heavily, and she could tell that this was it, the big confession at last. Finally, she would get some real information.

"My family and yours have worked closely together in the past," he began. "Your father was a member of the Enclave Council, a group of people who could use the crystal keys and vowed to use them to protect people, and mine was..." he hesitated a moment before continuing. "Well, my father was a person of high rank in our sector. Your mother wasn't on the Council, but she was a member of the Enclave. She was involved in the protection of the galaxy as much as your father was.

"Artus wasn't very old when he promised your mother, only thirteen or fourteen. He'd been part of a small rescue party, trying to free some of Tyren's prisoners. By then, the Enclave soldiers had been all but destroyed, and older boys like Artus were helping any way they could.

"When they arrived on the prison planet and made it to where the prisoners were being kept, your mother recognized him. She wasn't in good shape and didn't think she'd survive the escape. She told him where she'd hidden you and made him promise to do everything he could to protect you from Tyren."

He paused for a few breaths, but she was sure that he wasn't finished, so she kept quiet for the moment. Allie moved over to work on his wound again, unsure if her hands would steady anytime soon. He let her anyway.

"The rescue was a complete failure," he continued, "and only three of the rescue party survived, along with one of the prisoners. Artus realized he had to get us away from the war and hidden away for our own safety, like you were. He decided we needed to go to Earth and try and protect you. We didn't know she'd left the crystal there, as well, or we'd have been better prepared for this. It took us a while to find you, and a while longer to be sure it was you. Artus still wasn't completely convinced, but I was." He paused again, and Allie couldn't contain the question burning in her mind.

"One prisoner survived… who was it?" she asked, her voice now as shaky as her hands.

She stepped back and lowered her hands, desperation in her eyes and voice. Dav looked up at her, his expression one of pain, loss, and understanding.

"A man named Jovran," he said quietly.

Allie dropped the cleaning tool and wrapped her arms around her stomach, trying to quiet the sudden, violent lurching she felt inside. Her eyes overflowed, tears beginning to run down her cheeks despite her best efforts. Dav had just confirmed her worst fears.

Her mother was dead.

"He was an infiltrator in Tyren's ranks and had a tremendous amount of inside intelligence that he shared with the last of the Resistance. For all the good it did," he said bitterly. "Rumor has it that he's gone back undercover in Tyren's ranks, or at least he had last Artus heard. Artus told me that your mother wasn't in good enough shape to make it out. She insisted the rescue party escape with the others while she held back the Coalition Guard. She gave her life to save the others, Allie," he said, his tone almost pleading with her to be okay.

He stood up and moved toward her. She moved a half step back, unsure if she could keep from a complete emotional collapse if she felt his comforting arms. Dav sat back down, pain evident on his features.

A distant part of her mind registered the sound of the hatch of the ship opening, then closing again as Artus and Raith left on their mission.

"I'm so sorry, Allie," he whispered. "Artus and I are both alive only because of her. So are you. We owe everything we have to her courage and strength."

Allie nodded, but she couldn't stop the flood of tears, or the crushing weight she felt on her spirit. Her mother was dead. Her whole life, she'd dreamed of one day meeting her mother, a joyful reunion with the woman who had cared enough to leave her in the hands of someone like Katherine when keeping her would have meant great danger to both of them. She'd been right about the danger, but the dream of reunion had been torn from her forever.

Allie moved back and sat on one of the lower bunks, unsure if her legs would keep her upright any longer. Dav stayed where he was, shoulders hunched, and expression pained.

"My father?" she managed to get out between gasps

for air, her mind desperately grabbing at any hope it could find.

Dav looked away and shook his head.

"He disappeared two months before the rescue mission. The Resistance concluded that he'd been taken by Tyren's men and killed." Dav replied. He spun back to look at her, blue eyes intense and shining with tears just barely unshed, his tone becoming urgent.

"Allie, Tyren did all of this. He killed your parents, he killed my parents, and he's killed billions of other people in his quest for power. He's taken over everything and ruined it all. Nobody can stop him, Allie. Nobody but you." Dav paused to let that last sink in.

Allie couldn't control her quiet sobs. She had curled up on the bed, knees up to her chest. She couldn't reply; she couldn't even think. Her world was flooded with loss, hopelessness, and pain.

"He'll never quit, he'll never stop hurting people until he rules everything unopposed," Dav pressed, tone both angry and imploring. "We can't bring back our parents or any of the other lives he has destroyed, but we can bring him down. We have to bring him down. Nobody else can do it.

"Allie, please," Dav begged, "stay with me. Help me destroy this monster. I've spent the last ten years of my life praying that you would be the one who could finally help me stop him. I've tried so hard to protect you, to keep you safe. I need you, Allie. Everyone needs you. Help me." He finished in a fierce whisper, clearly barely keeping his own tears of rage and pain back.

Allie couldn't respond. Her body shook with her sobs as she tried to wrap her mind around the reality of her shattered world. A week ago, she'd been living happily with Katherine, enjoying a carefree friendship with her best friend and hoping to pass Algebra.

That was gone. All of it was gone. Katherine was lightyears away, she didn't even know how many, her parents were both dead, her best friend Dav had kept secrets from her, lied to her, planted a tracker on her under the guise of a thoughtful gift, and was now asking her to help him destroy a man.

Allie suddenly felt that her entire life hadn't truly been her own. It was some illusion, crafted to keep her unaware of the terrors, pain, and confusion of the wider reality.

Dav was silent for a long minute, then he stood, picked up the spray bottle, and walked quietly out of the room, the door sliding shut behind him.

Allie had no idea how long she lay there alone, wrapped in her misery before the infinitely welcoming comfort of empty unconsciousness took her, but it felt like an eternity.

CHAPTER SIXTEEN

CORE PROGRAMMING

Raith and Artus hurried through the jungle beneath the canopy of blue leaves above. They'd realized quickly that they both had training in stealth tactics, and each recognized that the other was blessedly quick and agile.

They moved so quickly that the trees would have been a blur to a human. Neither of them was anything of the kind, however, and they ducked branches, leapt creeks, and climbed rock faces with equal ease.

Raith glanced over at Artus as they ran, his peripheral scanners reading the surroundings well enough that he'd have no trouble at all navigating at this speed even if he never turned his eyes forward again. He did look forward again, though, careful not to let Artus figure out what he truly was. He couldn't believe what had finally happened.

He'd spent so many years searching the galaxy for that cursed crystal, under orders from Highlord Tyren. It still grated on every synaptic connection he had that he couldn't manage to bypass the command to retrieve the artifact.

He'd finally planted himself at Irifal Station, using the legitimate argument that many people and much information passed through that station. This allowed him to stop actively hunting for the blasted thing and finally settle in someplace. What were the odds, he thought to himself, of that idiot Artus and his brother showing up there, of all places?

Precisely one quadrillion, four hundred and sixty trillion, eighty-nine billion, seven hundred and ninety-five million, three thousand and forty-nine point twelve to one, his core processor immediately informed him. The odds were only that high because of the station's reputation as a place where you can find anything.

Statistically, it was six and a half times more likely that he would be attacked by a Trelareth ghost worm while sunbathing on the outer hull of Irifal Station, he thought wryly.

He had actually started to become relatively happy there. Raith had found a way to enjoy something of a life while still technically following his primary order to find and recover the crystal key.

And then, Artus and Dav had showed up, leading him straight to the crystal key and an unrecorded crystal bearer.

According to his records, only seven bearers remained alive and free after his delivery of Morgan Bennett to Highlord Tyren. He'd ordered her to the Colonies, an awfully comfortable name for a series of prison planets, Raith thought, to undergo testing to determine what in her genetic code gave her the ability to utilize the crystal keys. Three other bearers had been sent to the Colonies for the same purpose, he knew.

Since then, all seven had been acquired and executed, according to data feeds he'd intercepted from the Coalition core systems. There was no reason at all to randomly find a young crystal bearer. Unfortunately for her, his standing orders included detaining all crystal bearers and returning them directly to the Highlord.

Raith scowled. He despised Highlord Tyren. After successful completion of his mission to retrieve the Bennett woman, instead of being praised or even acknowledged for his efforts, he'd been chastised, or screamed at, in this case, over his failure to bring back the crystal as well.

Tyren had thrown a remarkable fit over it. It was a truly impressive tantrum. Raith had been ordered in no uncertain terms to go out, find the crystal, and not return to the Highlord's presence until he had it in his hand.

Raith had foolishly hoped that he would have been able to simply live out the remainder of his supposedly short lifespan on Irifal, listening to com feeds frequntly enough to satisfy the order that he keep searching for information about the crystal.

If he hadn't figured out how to rewire his power cell, he'd have burned out years ago. Theta units were only designed for a ten-year lifespan to allow for easy transition to newer models as they became available. He didn't really care to be "transitioned", however. At least, not yet.

Suddenly, out of nowhere, Artus and Davrelan, both supposedly dead, show up and all but hand over the last surviving crystal bearer and her key to him. Now, he'd have to go back to Tyren with both.

Tyren would probably be happy about it, but Raith

didn't hold out any hope of being rewarded. He'd probably be scrapped, if he were being honest with himself. He was almost six years past due for upgrade.

He'd always thought it was interesting that Tyren had dropped the Infiltrator series android manufacturing almost as soon as he'd taken power. No new models had been built after the Thetas. He loved his combat series androids, though. At least, until the Infection.

Raith was momentarily overcome by a swell of guilt over what he knew he had to do. It certainly wasn't his choice, he knew, so he shouldn't really feel guilty. And yet, he did. Artus and Dav were nice enough, though Dav clearly didn't care for him. Neither deserved to be killed, which is exactly what would happen when Tyren found out they were still alive.

He couldn't care less about the crystal, but he truly felt sorry for Allie. The girl was sweet and obviously completely innocent of anything remotely resembling a crime. She clearly had no idea what was going on, though he had to admit she was holding herself together well under the pressure. She was also beautiful in a way he was still trying to quantify. He didn't quite understand it. Allie had certainly caught his attention, though.

He had only met her the single time and would likely never see her again, since the moment he acquired the crystal key, he would have to transmit her coordinates to the guard so they could go pick her up.

Raith had disabled the ship, so he knew Dav wouldn't be able to get her out of there. Preventing her escape was part of his instructions in detaining the bearers. He hoped that his intentional avoidance of disarming or injuring her protector, Dav, would be enough for them to make a successful getaway. He truly didn't want either of them hurt.

Artus, however, wouldn't be so lucky. Raith knew he was going to have to deal with Artus personally once he had the crystal, since the man would obviously try to prevent him from taking it. If Raith had any suspicion that Artus might let him just walk away with it, he'd gladly let him go, as well.

It wouldn't go down that way though, he knew. Artus would try to stop him, so he was required to remove the obstacle. He was going to do that in the best possible way, if he had to do it at all.

He could have simply killed the man while he didn't expect it, but he still held hope that Artus would let him go with it. Even if he didn't, which was more likely, Raith could disable him without killing him.

That would be better, he quickly decided. Artus might still walk away from it this way. Raith found himself hoping that all three of them got away, though he knew it was unlikely.

They ran non-stop for almost an hour to reach the city limits again.

Raith noticed that Artus was still favoring his injured arm. He performed a quick bio-scan and corrected himself. Artus wasn't cradling an injured arm, he was trying to support a fractured rib. Raith made a mental note not to hit him on that side when the time came.

They made it to the smaller outlying buildings, still running. Artus hadn't drawn his pistol, and Raith, having grabbed a small pulse pistol from the limited stash on the ship he'd stolen, kept his hidden in a pocket. They slowed to a walk, knowing it would take them longer this way, but they would draw less attention if they weren't running full tilt through the city.

The commander who likely still had the crystal was probably at this point trying to get his men to finish prepping the ship for departure, determined to salvage what little honor he could by bringing Tyren the key.

Raith might feel bad about having to do what he was about to do to his new friends, but he didn't feel the slightest twinge of conscience when it came to bringing on the ill-will of the Coalition Guard. He smiled slightly as he imagined the outrage the commander would be forced to suppress when a Theta unit on direct orders from Highlord Tyren requisitioned the crystal from him, robbing all honor and potential for reward.

It took some time to reach the military facility again, and even more time to circle around behind it, since the street in front of it had been thoroughly scorched by the double-cannon arc blast he'd leveled at it while rescuing the trio earlier.

It had only been a couple of hours since the rescue, and the place was crawling with reinforcement troops that had landed to try and secure the base after the assault.

Around the rear, however, there was much less attention. Raith wasn't sure why, since at this point, that was the most obvious place for an intrusion, but these people weren't as good at logical reasoning as his core processor was. They probably wouldn't expect another assault at all this soon after the last one. Besides, they almost certainly thought that the small group was long gone through the wormhole by now.

He and Artus had discussed the basic strategy in the ship before setting out, and neither spoke a word as they moved to their respective positions.

Raith's computer skills were supposed to be used to locate the commander so they could try and take him silently and get the crystal from him. Raith did intend to use the computers to find the commander, but he also intended to trigger the alarm. He was planning on timing it so that Artus hadn't quite yet made it into the building proper, so he'd have a reasonable chance to get out first.

Raith hopped the ten-footwall in a single, easy jump, his internal scanners having already informed him that nobody was on the other side. He landed behind a small vehicle, parked along this side of the wall.

Artus would be moving around to the other side to provide cover if Raith was spotted. Once Raith was in position near the building itself, he was supposed to cover for Artus as he approached. Raith would trigger the alarm before then.

He quickly checked the immediate area, the thirty-two-point-four feet his indirect scanners ranged, then poked his head up to visually scan. Nobody was in direct line of sight. They wouldn't be for several more seconds as the patrol moved slowly away from him around the ship in the middle of the yard.

Raith jumped again and ran, bringing the gun out. He didn't intend to use it, but he wanted Artus to believe this was going as planned for another few seconds, at least.

Reaching the control panel beside the rear entrance, he held his left hand in front of the silver pad. The interface unit inside his palm instantly connected with the building security systems. In less than a tenth of a second, he had hacked the security grid, located the commander who was foolishly sitting around in his own quarters, and triggered the alarm.

The shriek of the alarm began just as Artus cleared the wall. Raith looked back at him with a feigned panicked look on his face, and Artus froze. He stared at Raith for a moment, then waved frantically for him to get out. Raith nodded and turned, hesitating just long enough to see that Artus was moving away, then quickly opened the door and ducked inside.

With luck, Artus would still think it had been a bit of bad luck and wouldn't suspect Raith of any wrongdoing. Raith wasn't really sure why he didn't want Artus thinking that he'd betrayed them, but it mattered to him. He could hear the guards racing into the rear yard as the door closed.

Upon entry into the complex, he sprinted again, racing for the commander's office. He had to gun down two guards as they came around the corner in front of him at a run.

Raith was technically authorized to be there, but they certainly didn't know that, and he didn't have the time to explain it. He reached the office and opened the door.

"What in the name…" the commander shouted as he leapt out of his seat. He paused, confused, as he saw the boy in front of him.

"Hold, commander," he said, switching to Sy'hli, the officially sanctioned trade language of the Coalition. "Designation R.A.I.Th-84, security code Traveler 48-5a," Raith said in a coldly professional tone.

He held up his right hand in a fist, the back of it facing the stunned officer, and mentally activated the luminescent identification code in the back of his hand.

The light shone through his artificial skin easily enough, and the commander dropped into his chair in complete shock.

"That's impossible, all you stupid androids were decommissioned!" the commander said in disbelief.

"Not all of us, apparently," Raith replied with a note of disdain. "I am operating under Order Prime. I hereby instruct you to hand over the crystal key and all data pertaining to it in your systems. This information is classified, and any attempt to speak of it to anyone else will be considered an act of treason. You do know what the penalty for that is, don't you?" Raith raised a brow in question.

The commander's jaw snapped shut, teeth grinding so hard Raith could have heard it clear out in the hallway. The man was furious but resisting a Theta on Order Prime would unquestionably result in his immediate execution.

Raith was even authorized to perform the execution himself on the spot. The commander clearly knew it and knew that as a Theta, Raith was perfectly capable of tearing the large man's arms off without any real effort.

With a snarl, the commander dug in his pocket and pulled out a small, clear crystal. He tossed it across the room to Raith, who caught it effortlessly.

A sound behind him caused Raith to spin about, weapon raised. Artus stood in the doorway, staring at Raith with an expression of shock, disbelief, and hurt. Raith stared back, similarly stunned at what had just happened. Artus shouldn't be anywhere near here by now. And Raith should have heard him coming.

"You were supposed to run, Artus. I'm sorry," Raith said sincerely. His scanners had already warned him of what was about to happen.

A pair of soldiers hit Artus hard on his injured side

in a full flying tackle. He went down like a ragdoll. Raith winced, remorse and guilt cutting at his thoughts. "I truly am sorry," he said again, as the two soldiers pinned Artus down.

The effort wasn't necessary. Either their impact had killed the man, or he'd been knocked cold. Raith didn't have time to scan him to find out. He turned back to the commander.

"The data?"

The commander simply gestured to the control panel.

"I know your type, Theta. You've already uploaded our entire mainframe. If you neglected to delete it from our system, that's your problem," he said with a growl.

Raith had, in fact, already gotten the information from their system and purged record of it. He'd just been reminding the commander of his authority, in case his familiarity with the intruder made the officer forget.

"True enough. You will provide me with transportation to the Coalition station immediately," Raith ordered.

The commander nodded, his face red, jaw still grinding at those teeth. He was absolutely livid, Raith thought. Good.

He turned and headed out of the room, back toward the ship already being prepped outside. He had to step around the two soldiers hoisting up Artus on the way and felt another violent emotional pull inside himself, wanting desperately to help the man, but knowing he could not. He shoved the feelings back and moved outside, then up the back ramp of the ship.

A screeching sound assaulted him the moment he stepped inside the craft. He turned to look to one side of the cargo hold and stared in surprise. A small jicund sat in an energy cage. The creatures couldn't be held in conventional cages, he knew. Their claws could cut through most metals like paper. Nobody knew why, but that ability was lost when the animal died, making the harvest of the claws pointless, and extremely dangerous.

The cage itself was constructed of a fine wire with an energy cell built into the base. It channeled extremely high levels of power through the wires. Not quite enough to kill a jicund, but it would certainly knock one cold for several hours if the little animal touched one. The wire mesh walls glowed a soft red color from the energy coursing through it.

Now, what was a jicund doing on this ship, he wondered? Odd, though not really his concern. He walked past as the creature shrieked at him. It took a moment for Raith to realize that the animal was ignoring him. It was screeching at the guards escorting him to the ship. That's interesting, he thought to himself.

He moved into the central compartment, away from the screeching animal and into the seating area.

These ships were far too utilitarian for his tastes, consisting of a large cargo hold, a few rows of inward-facing bench seats in the central compartment, and a forward compartment which held all the navigation controls.

They didn't even have windows, so your only view from inside one was that of the other soldiers you were probably riding with. Enough to bore the life out of a person, Raith thought, assuming one was alive.

He sat in a corner, facing the middle of the compartment. He found his thoughts drifting back to his former companions. The girl was an innocent, and he wished he could have fought his orders to turn her in. Briefly, he considered that she reminded him of someone, though he couldn't recall who. Impossible, though, as he possessed flawless recall from the moment his power cell had been activated.

Dav and Artus were both warriors, despite Dav's young age. Noble, courageous, and they seemed to genuinely care for the girl, or they wouldn't have risked this foolishness to rescue her. They'd have gotten away with it, too, if it weren't for Raith's betrayal. It had been a good plan.

He wasn't sure why that bothered him so much, since he was only responding to his programmed orders, but he was being gnawed at, little by little, by the guilt he felt about it.

Thanks to him, Artus was probably dead, considering how hard he had been hit on his already-wounded side. Dav and Allie would probably be in custody in less than an hour. Once they reached Highlord Tyren, he would probably gloat over his victory, and then have them both killed.

Raith closed his eyes, but he couldn't get the image of the three people his actions had condemned out of his mind. It was made all the worse by his perfect, computer-database memory of every detail of their faces.

He would remember them for the rest of his life, he knew. Every moment of every day, until the day his rewired power cell finally wore out, in perfect, crystal-clear detail.

CHAPTER SEVENTEEN

UNDER ARREST

Allie came out of the room some time later. She wasn't sure how long she'd been back there. She'd fallen asleep crying and had just woken up with a nasty headache. Twice in two days, she thought. This was getting embarrassing.

She'd lain in the bunk for a while after waking up, trying to clear her thoughts. Finally, she'd come to a decision and worked up the nerve to come and tell Dav. He was sitting in the pilot's seat of the cockpit, star charts flickering across his holographic display every few seconds.

"Dav?" she said softly.

The star charts stopped shifting, and he swung the chair around to face her. His expression was carefully controlled, waiting to hear what she had to say.

The cut on his forehead looked good, only a faintly red line where it had been. Allie looked at him for a long moment, steeling herself for what she was about to say.

"I've thought about everything you said," she began. He watched her, his expression unchanging, waiting. "I'm sorry, Dav. I can't do this. I'm just a kid, trying to get by. Last week, my biggest problems in life were how to get Lacy Briscoe to stop picking on me in gym and how to pass next week's algebra exam.

"Now, I'm light years away from home, in a spaceship on an alien planet, being asked to help save the galaxy. This isn't me Dav, you know that. I'm not strong enough for this, not brave enough for this. I want to spend my evenings curled up with a good book or hanging out with my friends, not battling some alien dictator!" she finished in a rush, unable to keep the emotions out of her voice.

She'd promised herself she'd make this rational, but she was having trouble keeping her tone calm. Dav's expression had fallen as she spoke, a deep sadness and resignation crossing his features. She almost broke down at the sight of him looking that way but had to stick to her decision. It was her only chance to have a normal life again.

"I really am sorry. You can keep the crystal and use it in your war. I don't want anything to do with it. I just want to go home and be left alone," she said.

Dav hesitated before speaking.

"I can take you home, but Tyren won't leave you alone. He already knows where to find you there, and he knows you can use the key. You're the only one left in the entire galaxy who can, so letting Artus and I keep the key is useless. We can't use it without you," he told her. She was already shaking her head.

"No, Dav. I don't want to be involved, I don't want anything to do with this. Just take me home."

He stared at her, expression carefully controlled. Finally, he nodded.

"Fine," Dav said without much emotion. "I can't really blame you. Everything you know was pulled away from you, and you want it back. As soon as Artus and Raith return, I'll take you home. It won't be the same, though. It can never be the way it was for you. I wish the best for you. Maybe Tyren will think you've been killed and will leave you alone."

Allie moved to sit in the navigator's seat beside Dav. She sat and looked over at her friend. He turned back to his console and began scrolling through star charts again.

Her best friend in the world, in any world, just sat there pointedly not looking at her as she watched him. He was right, she knew. It wouldn't ever be the same. He wouldn't be there.

From the way he'd spoken, she knew he'd stay out here, trying to fight Tyren, trying to protect her and everyone else. All of this had sparked something in her friend that she hadn't known existed. Inside the bright, constantly happy boy she'd always known had hidden a strength, ferocity, and determination she couldn't have imagined.

Allie wanted to help him, she really did, but she knew she didn't have the strength to do any good. Dav was convinced she was the key, but that was impossible. She wasn't anything special, nobody important.

Glancing down at the gun belted to his right hip, she remembered the odd humming sound it made when he'd fired it. Looking back up at him, she decided to try and cheer him up a bit.

"So, what's with the gun?" she asked, trying to sound lighthearted. "I thought all you aliens used lasers or phasers or something."

Dav glanced over at her for a moment, before a small half-smile touched his lips.

"You watch too much TV. You ever see those old sci-fi movies? You know, the ones where everybody is wearing silver jumpsuits and all the ships are shiny and silver?" he asked.

"Yeah, I always thought it was weird that everyone in the future wore silver clothes in those shows. This ship has a mirrored paint job too, actually," she pointed out, her idle question having turned into one of genuine curiosity.

His smile widened a fraction.

"That's right. A few, very few, of the low-tech races still use lasers. Your planet hasn't even gotten far enough to really use them as weapons yet, but they'll figure it out soon enough, and soon after that realize how pointless they are in a tactical scenario, assuming the enemy is prepared. Lasers are focused light, right?" At her nod, he continued. "What happens when you shine light on a mirror?"

Allie grinned, realizing where he was going with this.

"It reflects right off. I've even seen it done with laser pointers," she said.

"That's right," he replied, nodding. "Guess what happens when you shoot a high-powered laser at a shiny silver ship or reflectively clothed man?"

Allie giggled a little, picturing a group of ships firing lasers at each other and blowing everything around them up with the reflected beams of light, leaving each other totally unharmed.

"During the Tridieta Conflict," Dav said, "a lot of the

races used mirrored hull plating and lasers to assault one another. There were very few military losses. Unfortunately, there were an awful lot of civilian casualties. Most of the advanced races began developing new weapons. Almost nobody uses lasers anymore. My Runner… the ship I came here in originally, I mean, was mirrored. So is this one. I'm a little surprised this one is, actually. They must have had a recent run-in with a laser-using species. Either that or it's some funky new fashion trend on ships." He smiled as he glanced over at her. "You've got to admit it looks pretty cool."

"True," she agreed. "So, what does your gun fire, then? And the guns the soldiers before used, what were those?" she asked him.

"Mine is a shatter gun. Not the technical name, of course, just what the soldiers used to call them. They're officially called Frequency Remodulating Impact Compression units, but nobody wanted to go around calling them F.R.I.C. guns." He grinned over at her, almost the smile she remembered from before this all happened, but not quite there.

There was still a sadness in his eyes he'd never had before. She felt her heart lurch at the thought that she'd put it there.

"Yeah, I could see why that wouldn't work," she replied with a smile. "What exactly does it do?"

"Well, the humming sound you heard comes from a small sonic emitter, like a little speaker, inside the gun," he explained. "The mechanism takes the frequency of sound the little speaker emits and remodulates it, compresses it, and converts it into a tightly-focused pulse of sonic vibration.

"Tends to make anything brittle, like glass or

ceramics, shatter before the pulse even hits them. Thus, the term 'shatter gun'. Anything not as brittle gets hit with the full force of the compressed sound waves. Hugely potent impact. They were state of the art when we left." He continued scanning star charts as he spoke, glancing over at her occasionally.

"As for the other guns," he continued, "I've seen the old arc rifles, like the soldiers you saw were using, but these are new. They're much more powerful than the ones available before we came to Earth. I'm not sure what these do exactly, but if they're anything like the old arc rifles and cannons, they involve firing charged ionic particles. These are different enough that I'm not at all sure they work the same way, though," he finished.

"I like the shatter guns, personally," she said, drawing another smile from Dav. "The humming is kind of cool. I mean, the lightning from the arc guns is pretty, but it's kind of scary."

He nodded slightly but didn't answer directly.

Allie thought for a moment, coming up with another question to keep him talking. "How strong are you, exactly?"

He paused in his scanning, and she worried it might have been the wrong question to ask.

"I don't actually know," he admitted. "Artus was always really strict on us keeping our capabilities tightly under wraps, you know? He didn't want anyone to realize we weren't like them. That's why I was careful about my grades, too. Do too well in any field and people start to notice. My best guess is that we're close to fifteen times stronger than humans are, though I've never been able to really test that," he said.

Allie felt her jaw drop.

"Fifteen times?" she exclaimed. "Are you serious?" He nodded in response. "So, all these years being the little guy who didn't like sports, and you actually could have pitched a baseball clear out of the stadium, or folded the average linebacker into a pretzel?"

He laughed at this but nodded.

"Yeah, probably," he answered. "I couldn't join any sports because of that. In the adrenaline rush of the game, I'd probably have slipped up and done something noticeable. Can't have the humans figuring us out. We'd have been dissected for sure, just like the frogs in biology."

She made a face, trying hard not to picture Dav lying on an operating table having pieces taken out of him. Not a pleasant thought.

"How many species are there?" she asked in another abrupt shift of topic. "Advanced ones, I mean."

"Far too many to count," Dav replied, turning to look at her again. "People on Earth go on about how immense the universe is, but they don't seem to really realize just how big even a single galaxy like the Milky Way is. You don't have to go to another galaxy to find other intelligent species. It takes light itself, which travels close to two hundred thousand miles per second, a full hundred thousand years to go from one side of our galaxy to the other. Can you even begin to understand how big that is?" He glanced over at her before looking back to the scrolling charts.

"There are hundreds of billions of stars in this galaxy," he continued. "Not all of them have planets, but a fair number do. Not all the planets have conditions needed for life to form, but more than enough do to make for a pretty diverse galaxy. According to our database on the Runner, where I got most of my real schooling, there are two thousand, four hundred and twelve identified intelligent species in the galaxy, and that information is a decade old. There have probably been quite a few new ones discovered since then. Some planets even develop more than one intelligent species at the same time," he trailed off, realizing he'd begun to ramble in his excitement about the subject.

She just stared.

"Two thousand… That can't possibly be right…" she said in awe.

"It's true," Dav replied with a nod. "A lot of people on Earth are still convinced humans are alone in the universe. Even speaking from a purely statistical perspective, the odds of humans being the only intelligent species even just in this galaxy are astronomically low, pun intended, let alone in the whole universe.

"I always thought it was an arrogant assumption to think they were the only ones around. I mean really, hundreds of billions of stars, more than grains of sand on a large beach, and humans think they're the only planet with life? Even Mars in your own solar system supports life. Bacterial life, I admit, but it's there. Two planets in one system, and not another one anywhere in the galaxy? Get real. Sooner or later, even those bacteria may develop into a sentient species, given a few million years."

"That's amazing," she said sincerely.

She'd never even thought about it before, but she found herself wishing that she'd discussed aliens with Dav before she'd found out that he was one. It would have been interesting to see his reaction.

"Have any species other than yours… the Sy'hli,

right? Have any others visited Earth?"

"Oh, sure," he replied. "We weren't even the only ones living there. In fact, in the Mariana Trench, there's a whole city of..."

Allie's attention was pulled away by a flickering light on the sensor display in front of the seat behind Dav. He was still talking, but she didn't hear it, a growing sense of dread rising in her stomach.

"Dav?" she interrupted. "What's that?"

He turned to look where she pointed. On the display, not far from their own little green dot, a big red one was approaching fast.

"No, no, no!" Dav shouted, spinning back to his display. "They can't have found us, we're out of sight, and they can't scan us in here!" His holographic display switched, showing a series of numbers and colored bars she didn't understand. "It will take at least five minutes to get us ready to go again. We don't have time." He jumped up from his seat and headed out of the cockpit.

Allie could only follow.

He rushed into the side room and headed straight for a locker back against one wall. Opening it, he growled in frustration, a sound that was surprisingly animal. She remembered his growls when he'd fought the maruck back on Earth. Again, she was struck by just how inhuman he really was. It was so easy to forget while just sitting around talking to him. He turned away and she saw that the locker was empty.

"Raith couldn't have stolen a military ship. Oh, no. He had to steal some merchant's cruising yacht," Dav grumbled. "Here," he said, drawing the pistol and tossing it to her.

She nearly dropped it in surprise, barely managing

to get a grip on it before it slipped out of reach.

"It's not hard to use," he told her. "Flip the little switch on the back to turn off the safety. As long as the little light on the back is blue, you're charged and ready to fire. It only takes a moment. Just point it and pull the trigger. No kickback or anything, so nothing to worry about except where you're pointing it," he said, carefully emphasizing this last point as he gently moved her arm, so the gun wasn't pointing directly at his crotch.

She winced as she realized how that particular misfire would have gone.

"Sorry," she said sheepishly.

"Don't be sorry, be ready. As fast as they were coming, we probably only have a few more seconds. We need to get out of the ship, or we'll be trapped in here." He grabbed her arm and moved toward the rear hatch.

"I don't know how to use a gun!" she cried, beginning to panic. "What will you use if I have the shatter gun?"

"Strike rings!" he called back as they ducked through the doorway and Dav jumped down the couple of steps into the cargo bay.

"What are strike rings?" she asked frantically as she followed, not sure if any answer he gave her would even make sense at that point, her emotions thrown back into turmoil. Too much had happened to her too fast, and she felt sure she was at her breaking point.

"They convert kinetic resistance into an electrical discharge," he called back.

She was right. That didn't make any sense at all.

"Dav, I'm scared!" she admitted.

"Me too," he said quietly as he stopped by a small control panel and turned to face her. He gently touched her cheek with the tips of his fingers, a gesture that oddly calmed her down a great deal. "Don't worry. They'll not lay a hand on you without going through me first. All you need to do is take cover where I tell you and shoot at anyone coming toward you that isn't me. You can do this, Allie. No problem." He smiled at her.

She nodded once. Her jaw clenched and her heart raced, but she could help him. She could hold it together for him.

The pair raced down the hatch even before it was finished lowering to the stone of the tunnel. Dav immediately turned to head deeper into the cave. A flash of white tore past them as someone behind them fired an arc rifle their way.

"Stop! This is the Coalition Guard! You are under arrest! If you resist, we will shoot you!" A deep voice called from behind.

Dav dragged her along behind him, ignoring the voice, pulling her faster than she could have run herself.

She struggled to keep her balance. The little light in the cave was fading fast as they moved deeper into the stone and she began to seriously worry about keeping her feet under her.

He didn't drag her far, though, moving her down behind a large stone outcropping in the wall of the cave, beside a pair of small stalagmites. They looked to have formed after the cave had been dug out by whatever made it.

She crouched low and peeked around the corner toward the sound of approaching boots. A lot of approaching boots.

"Dav, maybe we should give up! We only have one pistol, and they'll shoot us if we don't surrender!" she said.

Dav froze and stared at her.

"You understood that?" he asked, looking both shocked and curious.

"Of course, I did, it was in English!" she cried in exasperation. "Should we just give up?" she repeated.

Dav opened his mouth but closed it again without saying another word. He was giving her the most peculiar look, seeming totally baffled. Another bolt flashed by them, causing Dav to duck reflexively and look toward the source of the blast.

"We can't give up. If we are brought to Tyren in captivity, we're dead anyway," he told her. "Don't worry. Just start shooting as soon as you have a target and don't stop until we've won."

She nodded her understanding as Dav turned and began running back the way they'd come.

A faint flicker of blue light rippled across Dav's knuckles as he moved. What was that, Allie wondered? It reminded her of the blue energy that came off Dav's punches when he'd fought the maruck.

It was only moments before the first of the soldiers came into view. Allie pointed the gun, held awkwardly in both hands, and pulled the trigger. The humming sound came, and she saw the ripple around the barrel as the compression burst came out. The shot went high, far too high, and not one of the men so much as ducked.

She scowled and tried again. Too far left, but the man at least flinched. Better, she thought. Before her third shot, Dav hit the men. Blue energy flashed in rapid pulses as his hands struck out.

He swept the legs out from under one man in a kick that was almost too fast to follow, bringing his right fist straight out and into the center of another man's chest. The blue light flared, and the man was flung backward several feet and into another.

Dav spun, ducking under the swinging blade of an arc rifle as the third soldier struck out at him. He pivoted, bringing his foot into the man's jaw with enough force to flip the man completely over before he hit the ground.

The fourth man managed to bring his weapon up in time to deflect Dav's next blow, but he missed the left hand swinging in hard and low into his stomach. The man dropped heavily to the ground. The only other guard still standing took a fist to his right temple in a flash of blue light and dropped as if he were a puppet whose strings had just been cut.

Dav looked her way and grinned, then suddenly dove to one side as another bolt cut the air right where he'd been standing. In mid-air, another bolt struck him on the left side of his chest, flinging him back and sending him into a wild spin before crashing into a large rock, his head slamming into it in exactly the same spot he'd been cut before.

Allie screamed, and began firing wildly in the direction the arc blasts had come from. Dav wasn't moving. She saw a man moving toward her, staying low to the ground. She couldn't seem to hit him, no matter how many times she fired at him. A feeling of helplessness washed over her.

"Give up, honey!" a voice called out to her from the darkness to one side. "We've already killed your little boyfriend, don't make us kill you, too. Highlord Tyren just wants to talk."

She spun and fired blindly into the darkness. A heavy weight struck her from behind, bearing her easily to the ground. She cried out in pain as her arms were jerked painfully up behind her, the shatter gun dropping from suddenly numbed fingers.

"There we go," the voice said from atop her back as she felt something cold and hard clamping down around her wrists. "Now nobody else needs to get hurt."

Allie was violently dragged to her feet, the awkward angle of the pull on her shoulders making her cry out again. She looked toward Dav. One of the two men standing had rolled him over and was checking his pulse. He turned to the man behind Allie and nodded once, looking surprised.

"See now, honey? Your friend is still alive. Going to have a wicked headache later, though," the man behind her told her with a completely artificial note of sympathy.

Allie struggled, but the man was strong and held her small form easily in check. The other man picked Dav up, tossing the boy almost casually across his shoulder.

"Ready, sir," the man holding Dav said.

The man behind Allie nodded. He shoved her hard, and she stumbled forward as she tried to keep her balance.

He pushed her frequently, and she fell more than once as they made their way to the mouth of the cave. When they got there, a small, rust-colored craft, similar to the one from the military compound yard, though a good deal smaller, sat in the entrance.

The back hatch was down, and four more armed soldiers stood to either side of the ship. They saluted as Allie and the others approached. Apparently, the man behind her was an officer.

"Kurbin, take Brodh and get the others. The little freak took several good men down before we got him," her captor ordered. Two of the men saluted and went running back into the cave.

Allie was shoved up the ramp and into the ship. The interior was mostly open, visible all the way up to the pilot's seat. Two benches ran along either side, and the man shoved her into one.

The other man dropped Dav unceremoniously onto the seat beside her, taking a moment to clamp a pair of wide, black bracelets to Dav's wrists. Small red lights moved in a repetitive pattern as the bracelets were brought close to each other. Dav's two hands immediately snapped together at the wrist, the bracelets holding them firmly in place. Dav still didn't stir.

Great, she thought. Magnetic handcuffs. She probably had similar cuffs on her own wrists behind her back, though she couldn't see them.

The soldiers all sat on the other bench across from them, weapons drawn and ready. After a few minutes, Kurbin and Brodh returned, each dragging a pair of soldiers.

The men were shoved against one wall, the other soldiers seeming completely unconcerned with the condition of their comrades. The hatch closed, and she felt the ship lift off the ground.

We're dead anyway, Dav had said. Well, she thought, at least she'd get to see this Highlord Tyren for herself before she died.

Despite the strong tone of the thought, she couldn't stop the tears from coming. She could keep from bawling though, she determined. They wouldn't see her break.

Allie clenched her jaw, slid over slightly to be directly beside Dav's head where it lay on the bench, and sat straight and proud as the ship moved into the sky.

CHAPTER EIGHTEEN

R.A.I.TH-84

It was another hour before anyone else came aboard the ship where Raith waited. He was usually exceptionally good at waiting, but the guilt was eating at him. He knew he couldn't have gone against a direct order, but it didn't seem to matter.

The loudly screeching jicund announced two soldiers from its small cage at the back. Raith watched them enter. They looked at him, but then quickly looked away. Raith mentally sighed. The commander must have told them all about him. This was going to be a long flight, wormhole or not.

Abruptly, the screeching in the other room stopped and turned to an excited, happy trilling sound. Raith frowned, his curiosity getting the better of him as he stood and moved to the doorway. The cargo hold was empty of people, but several figures were coming up the ramp.

The soldier in front was an officer, probably a

lieutenant, and judging from the nostrils of his nose up by the bridge below the eyes, the small ridges alongside the jaw, and the dark purple hair, the man was a Lurinae.

Surprising, since the Lurinae had been so violently opposed to Tyren in the beginning of the war, and now here was an officer, proud as could be. Raith glanced at the jicund, but the creature was looking past the lieutenant.

Coming up the ramp were two more soldiers, one pushing Allie in front of him, the other carrying what was either a dead or unconscious Dav over one shoulder. Raith felt another pang of guilt as he saw Dav in such a state. The little jicund was chittering happily at Allie.

She looked up in surprise at the animal, and her face lit up.

"Tic!" she shouted.

Interesting, Raith thought. She knew the creature.

Allie took a step toward the cage, but the soldier behind her gave her a solid thump on the side of her head. She moved back to her place and walked forward again, but she kept glancing at the cage as they passed.

A friend, Raith decided. She was friends with a jicund. This girl was definitely something special.

Then, she saw Raith. She looked happy at first, then confused for a moment as she noticed his apparent freedom, then, as understanding dawned, angry. Not angry, furious.

Allie lunged for him, face reddening and twisted in an expression of murder. The man behind her grabbed her and held her back as she thrashed, trying to get away.

"You turned us in! How could you do that? I'll kill you myself!" she screamed at him.

Raith moved back as the men and their captives

approached, moving aside so they could enter the midsection of the ship without Allie being able to reach him.

She was shoved hard onto one of the benches, held there with strong downward pressure on her shoulders by the soldier who moved to stand behind her. Another one dropped Dav carelessly beside her.

A moment later, Artus was carried in by two more soldiers and dropped onto another bench. He was breathing, and so was Dav, Raith was relieved to see. Why it took them so long to bring Artus in, Raith didn't know. He was just glad to see him breathing.

"You don't understand, Allie," he told her.

She closed her eyes and turned her head away from him, clearly not wanting to hear it.

"Allie, let me explain."

She turned back to him, the same dark rage in her eyes. Unshed tears made them look liquid. It struck him how beautiful she really was. He blinked as the thought crossed his mind. What an odd reaction, he mused.

"Nothing to explain," she growled at him. "You turned us in. Probably stole the crystal, too. We trusted you. Dav and Artus trusted you."

"Dav never trusted me," Raith replied. He hoped she could see the genuine regret in his eyes. She was probably too blinded with anger to see it, though. "And you didn't really know me. I regret what I had to do, Allie. But please believe me when I say that I had no choice. I was under orders I couldn't violate."

He found himself reluctant to tell her that he was a machine, although it made no sense to keep it from her at this point. In fact, it might help his cause if she knew he was only following programming. Somehow, he couldn't bring himself to say it, though.

"You always have a choice. Always," Allie emphasized the word. "You may not like your choices, but there's always a choice."

"You might, but I do not," Raith replied, shaking his head sadly. "I've never had a choice." He looked away, unable to stand her glare any longer. He shook his head as if to deny everything that had happened.

The ship's hatch raised as the commander appeared.

"Well, *sir*," the commander almost spat the word at Raith, "we are now underway. We will have you on Qirsan in six hours. We'll send ahead and ensure that Highlord Tyren knows you are coming and what you have brought for him."

The commander glared at Raith, but he didn't care.

"I'll be sure to give you all due credit, commander," Raith replied with an unfriendly smile.

The commander gritted his teeth, but instead of replying, he turned and stormed to the front of the ship and into the cockpit.

Raith glanced back at Allie, who was staring at him with disgust.

"Sir?" she repeated. "No choice at all, I'm sure," she sneered.

"I didn't want any of you hurt. You all seem like good people. If it were up to me, I'd have let you all go. My orders clearly stated otherwise," he said.

A small groan from one side pulled both of their gazes. Artus was stirring. He shifted slightly on the bench and immediately gasped in pain, eyes snapping open wide. Raith moved over to him, noticing the cuffs on his wrists, and the guard leveling an arc rifle Artus's way.

"Don't move, Artus," he said to the injured man, scanners quickly reading his body. "You've got three broken ribs, and several more are going to bruise pretty badly. No internal punctures, though there is a lot of damage to the muscle. Nothing a good medic couldn't fix, but unfortunately, that isn't likely."

Raith sighed softly, again wishing he could have done something to prevent all of this.

Artus looked at him, glaring even more fiercely than Allie had.

"I trusted you," Artus began.

"I know, I just went through this conversation with Allie," Raith replied, holding up a hand to forestall the inevitable accusation. "I wanted to help you. I really did. I… had… no… choice," he finished, carefully emphasizing each word.

At the mention of Allie's name, Artus craned his neck to look around for her. She gave him a small smile when he spotted her, and he nodded once. Then his gaze fell to Dav. He looked back to Allie, ignoring Raith for the moment.

"Is he alive?" Artus asked, his tone conveying more concern than any number of words could have.

Allie nodded, looking back down at Dav.

Raith sighed again and moved back to his seat. He knew they'd never listen to him after this anyway. Nothing he said would convince them that he couldn't have done anything more for them than he already had. Artus spotted the wound on Dav's forehead and frowned.

"Didn't you fix that?" he asked Allie.

"Yes. This is a new injury," she told him with a grimace.

Artus shook his head at the irony.

"Kid's going to have brain damage if he can't keep himself from banging his skull around so much," he muttered.

Allie was leaning over to look more closely at the spot where the arc blast had struck his chest.

Raith found himself leaning forward to look at the wound, as well. It appeared, surprisingly, like the plating had taken the brunt of the damage. Might have bruised a few of his ribs too, Raith thought. He focused his scanners on the boy and blinked in surprise. He was almost totally unharmed. Whatever hit his head is what had brought him to his current state. The blast to his chest probably would only barely have slowed him down.

Good armor, Raith thought, and one tough kid. Maybe he could find out how to craft a set after this. Not that Dav would tell him.

"He's fine," Raith said.

Allie glared back at up at him.

"How would you know? Are you secretly a doctor as well as a traitor?"

"You can trust me in this. He's fine. Give him another hour or so, and he'll wake up. His head will hurt, and he'll probably be a bit fuzzy in his thinking for a while, but he's fine. No permanent damage," Raith assured her.

Her scowl told him she didn't trust him one bit, but there was a glimmer of hope in her eyes. At least I could give her that much, Raith thought. He felt the tug of the approach to the wormhole before the others could have and warned them.

"Dropping through the wormhole folks. Brace yourselves," Raith said.

Natural wormholes were nearly impossible to notice as you passed through them. However, something about the stabilizers that had been built around the gate made slipping into this wormhole feel something like riding a kayak over a waterfall. The lurching sensation wouldn't really bother him, though his sensors would register it, but it always made organics uncomfortable.

Allie looked sick, and Artus groaned as they passed the bridge from normal space into the wormhole. The jicund in the cargo hold screeched her irritation. Allie looked back toward the cargo hold.

"Is…" she began, hesitating before looking at Raith. "Is Tic okay?"

"The jicund?" he asked, glancing toward the closed door between the two compartments.

She nodded.

"Yes, Tic is fine. I don't know why they're bringing her along, though. She can't really be sold, since nobody would pay anything for her. They're impossible to train, even more impossible to domesticate. And they're toxic, so there aren't any species that eat them, except for one particular predator down there on Ayaran, but they hunt their own prey."

Looking back at Allie, he realized he should have stopped with 'Tic is fine'.

She looked horrified. Clearly, the idea of Tic being sold as a pet, or worse, for food, hadn't ever crossed her mind.

"Sorry," he said softly.

She didn't reply.

Raith leaned back in his seat and closed his eyes again, trying to shut out the feelings surging through him. What he wouldn't give to have a way to shut off the emotional feedback.

Emotional simulation had been programmed only into the latest model Thetas, experimental in nature, to help them blend with humans better. They still hadn't figured out a way to switch them on and off by the time he'd been activated, and they never completed the series after the Thetas. Raith again found himself mentally cursing his difficulty in controlling the emotions.

Honestly, he had no idea how the humans could cope with emotions on a daily basis. They were so intrusive and incredibly difficult to ignore. It was amazing how many choices he had made based on his emotional responses, rather than his logic center.

"I don't really know you," Allie said after several minutes, surprising him into opening his eyes and looking her way. "I only just met you a few hours ago. I saw something in your eyes, in those first few moments. It's why I didn't think twice about trusting you. I think it's why Artus trusted you, too. I don't think turning us in was your idea at all. I don't believe you're the kind of person who would want to hurt someone else. There's a… kindness, in your eyes. Something that tells me that you do feel regret about what you're doing. It's not too late, Raith. You can still help us."

Allie stared at him intently, green eyes bright and wet. Raith felt drawn into those eyes. He felt the weight of her words and knew the truth of them. Most of them, anyway. He couldn't help her, though. Nobody could now.

"Please, Raith, help us," she said softly.

Raith closed his eyes tightly and took a deep breath. It wasn't necessary for him to breathe, but he had always found taking a few deep breaths helped calm him. He opened his eyes and then opened his mouth to respond, but Artus beat him to it.

"He won't help us, Allie. He doesn't care about anyone, not even himself. He's a Theta," Artus said, spitting the last word in disgust, as though the word itself made him feel dirty.

Allie looked over at Artus, confused.

"You mean he's an alien, too?" she asked, not understanding.

Artus shook his head.

"He's a machine, Allie, a rusty pile of metal, wiring, and programming. All he can do is follow his programming. He serves Tyren," Artus told her, his tone angry. "Best replica I've ever seen, too. Totally had me suckered. I don't know how I could have been so stupid."

Allie looked back to Raith in shock.

"You're… you can't be a machine," she protested, as though denying it would make it untrue.

Raith sighed and nodded.

"I am Designation R.A.I.Th.-84. Reconnaissance Android Infiltrator, Theta series, model 84. I was built to impersonate people, infiltrate their bases and cultures, and acquire classified data. When Highlord Tyren came to power, our purpose changed. We were assigned to hunt down all the crystal bearers and their keys, delivering them personally to Highlord Tyren. Our skills and capabilities made us uniquely suited to the task. I am personally responsible for the capture of thirty-six crystal bearers, and thirty-five crystal keys," he looked at her, hoping the sincerity of his next words came through in his gaze. He leaned forward in his seat, holding her eyes with his own.

"Please understand, Allie, every single one of them

will haunt me in perfect detail for the rest of my life. What I told you was the truth, Allie. I truly have no choice. I am not capable of violating my programming. I was ordered to bring all crystal bearers and their keys directly to Highlord Tyren. I will do the same to you, and I will hate myself for it until the day my power cell finally dies," he finished.

Artus and Allie were both staring at him. Artus with disgust, Allie with a pain that made him want desperately to make it go away for her.

"Thirty-six crystal bearers," she repeated softly. After a long moment, she asked a question that surprised him. "Do you know their names?"

"Every one of them," he frowned, not understanding the purpose of her question.

"Did you capture Morgan Bennett?" she asked, her voice catching on the name.

Raith stared at her, surprised.

"Why?" he questioned, confused.

"Did you capture Morgan Bennett?!" she screamed at him, causing him to recoil from her.

"Yes. She was the thirty-sixth acquisition. It was her crystal key that I failed to locate, causing me to be exiled until its return or the capture of another crystal bearer. There weren't any left after Morgan Bennett, so I was never able to return," he told her.

The expression on her face raced through shock, grief, and fury so quickly that he barely had time to register them all.

"You killed my mother!" she spat at him, then leapt across the narrow gap between them. His reflexes took over, grabbing her easily from the air, spinning her around as he stood, and planting her face down on the bench he had just vacated, careful not to hurt her.

Raith held her gently, but firmly, as she thrashed and screamed at him. He held one hand up to forestall the delayed reactions of the guards who were just beginning to raise their weapons. Idiots, he thought.

His confusion grew as he considered Allie's reaction. Morgan Bennett had no children. In a fraction of a second, he had scanned his data core. No, definitely no children. How could he possibly have missed a detail like this? Her offspring would potentially be a crystal bearer, capable of using the keys.

There was no way she could have had a child without him knowing about it. Yet here was this girl, claiming to be her daughter and trying to kill him for murdering her. The eyes definitely bore a resemblance, he thought. He wouldn't have made the connection before, few of the other facial features matched.

Wait, murdering Morgan Bennett?

"Allie, I honestly don't know what you're talking about. Morgan Bennett isn't dead," he told her. "At least, she wasn't when I last hacked the Coalition data feed six months ago."

Allie went as still as if he'd just knocked her out cold. She was silent for a full five seconds before speaking, her voice careful and tightly controlled, though he could tell she was barely on the verge of another outburst.

"What did you say?" she asked him.

"Morgan Bennett isn't dead. She's listed as Subject 13-4A7 on the rosters at the Perinite Center for Experimental Research," he told her honestly, drawing the appropriate bit of data from his core.

"You're lying," she accused coldly, but he could hear the sudden surge of hope in her voice.

Raith shook his head, though he knew she couldn't see him from her face down position on the bench. He let her up.

Allie moved to a sitting position but didn't stand. Instead, she turned her emerald gaze on him like a hawk watches a field mouse scurrying across an open stretch of ground. The unyielding stare made him uncomfortable. He had no idea the girl had so much potential for intensity. It was a little unnerving.

"I'm not," he replied. "Six months ago, I hacked the data feed during a Coalition status update. The information is encrypted, of course, but that doesn't even slow me down. I've heard her listed there, and before that in the Sector Six prison complex, twenty-seven times over the last thirteen years. She's on every update. Apparently, they moved her to the research facility after a pretty nasty escape attempt ten years ago."

Raith noticed Artus perk up at that. Allie did, too. She knew about the escape attempt. She was better informed than he'd first thought.

"Tyren was trying to figure out how to use the crystal keys," Raith continued. "He held a couple of the crystal bearers captive for interrogation. Not one of them was able to give him anything he wanted. It's not something that can be taught, though he seems unwilling to stop trying."

Allie kept staring at him, her gaze boring into his eyes. She was searching for something, he realized. She wanted to see the truth in his eyes. He couldn't help but feel a swell of gratitude. An odd feeling, perhaps, but it was the first time someone who knew he was an android had ever interacted with him as if he were a person. She was looking for truth in his eyes. You didn't do that to a machine.

Abruptly, she sat back against the seat, looking stunned. The anger had faded from her face, and now she just looked tired and relieved.

"My mother is alive," Allie said, obviously to herself. "She's alive. I can rescue her."

"Forget it, Allie," Artus interjected. "We have to worry about ourselves right now. In a few hours, we'll be staring Tyren in the face, and we likely won't live long past that point."

"Then we escape," Allie said.

Raith winced as the guards broke into laughter. An ominous click filled the compartment as one of them switched the safety catch on his arc rifle. Raith couldn't believe they were talking like this with two guards standing within easy earshot. Nothing like discussing your escape plans with your jailors, he thought wryly.

Allie winced as well, then she looked at Raith, her expression embarrassed, but hopeful.

"You won't have a chance," Raith told her. "Even if you could take down the two idiots over there," the guards' expressions darkened, but they didn't say anything, "I'm programmed to bring you in. You wouldn't make it past me. And I can't help you after, either. The Highlord will have me recycled as soon as I return. But I have no choice. I'm sorry, Allie." He meant it, and he hoped she believed that.

She took a long breath but nodded sadly. The hope was fading in her eyes. It hurt him to see that spark fade. His processor began working full force as he processed possible ways to help her that wouldn't violate his orders.

He winked at her, hoping she would interpret the

gesture, one the guards couldn't see as they stood against the wall behind him, as a signal that he had something in mind. He didn't yet, but he was working on it. He moved to sit where she had been before she'd tried to jump him and looked back down at the still-unconscious Dav.

His orders said nothing about Artus or Dav, which was unsurprising since Tyren had long since been convinced that they were dead. He'd be awfully upset when he learned otherwise, Raith thought with a smile.

However, since he wasn't ordered to bring them in, he wasn't ordered not to help them escape, either. He glanced at Artus, who was still glaring at him, though with suspicion instead of disgust. That was an improvement.

No good, he decided after a moment's consideration. Artus wasn't healthy enough to make good on an escape attempt, even assisted by Raith. He'd need medical attention before he would be in any kind of shape to even run, let alone fight. And Dav was still unconscious, and would be for at least another hour, to judge from his brainwave patterns.

His brow furrowed in frustration as he realized the only prisoner on this entire ship that he could actually help escape would be the jicund in the cargo hold, for all the good…

Raith paused.

The jicund was attached to Allie. They clearly knew each other, and the animal genuinely seemed to like her. Jicund were viciously protective of their family group.

He promptly stopped that line of thought, since the intention of releasing the jicund to help Allie escape was counter to his programming. Helping the jicund escape for its own sake, however, without any thought to what it might do after, wouldn't technically violate the orders. It was certainly questionable, but as he analyzed the programming surrounding the command, he realized it would work.

So, he just had to help the creature escape. That was it. No more than that. He smiled slowly as the plan began to form in his mind.

CHAPTER NINETEEN

A MATTER OF PRIORITIES

"My lord, the prisoners have arrived in bay four," Harelo announced in his odd, liquid voice.

Tyren nodded, smiling. He'd already received the report, hours ago, that an old Theta unit had acquired the crystal bearer and her key, and they were on their way.

Tyren had been shocked to learn of this. The Thetas hadn't been in production in over a decade, and their battery life was only ten years under normal operation. None of them should still be functional. This one was, though, and it was the same one that had failed to bring him the last crystal key all those years ago. He recognized the code given to the commander on Ayaran.

It was remarkable, really. The stupid machine had probably been mindlessly following his order to retrieve it for thirteen years. Tyren couldn't keep the grin from his face.

The bearer and the key, all delivered neatly to this very room. Better yet, the other two prisoners being brought to him were a bonus he hadn't ever expected. He'd thought the two had been killed, but after the report from Irifal Station, he was almost completely convinced of their identity. Soon enough, he would know for sure. All he had to do now was wait.

Harelo spoke again, interrupting his thoughts.

"There was... an incident in the docking bay, however," the man said through his fluid breathing apparatus, smooth, scaly skin glistening as his head turned down to the data pad he was carrying.

"An incident?" Tyren asked dangerously.

"Yes, Highlord," said Harelo. "Apparently, the cargo hold of the ship held an energy cage containing a young jicund. During the offloading of the ship, the power cell on the cage went out, and the animal escaped. There were numerous injuries before the creature vanished into the air ducts. I have already assigned a maintenance crew to begin the extermination process," Harelo replied.

Tyren scowled, but he wasn't concerned about the jicund. The crews would have already shut all the air vents automatically and begun flooding the offending ducts with a neural neutralizing agent. The creature would be dead shortly. He was concerned about something else, however.

"And the prisoners?" he asked.

The voice in his mind had gone completely still, ever since the news of the capture of the two men and the bearer. It was still silent, but Tyren could feel the tension coming from more than just his own thoughts. The voice felt... hopeful. Tyren hated that.

Harelo looked up.

"Secure, my lord. Two of the prisoners are injured and couldn't escape even if we released their shackles and opened the front door, so to speak. The girl didn't get more than two steps before the Theta unit secured her."

Tyren felt a surge of relief. The voice inside felt crushed. Tyren smiled again.

"Excellent. How soon before they arrive?" he asked.

Harelo glanced at the data pad.

"Any moment now, my lord."

Highlord Tyren sat up straighter, looking to Klythe at one side of the throne, and to another of Klythe's elite maruck warriors on the other side. They stood tall, menacing, and clearly at the ready.

Harelo moved aside at Tyren's nod, standing to one side of the dais, ready at his lord's command.

Perfect, Tyren thought. He sat up straight and noble in his throne, his heavy, red cape and black and silver wardrobe with the raised shoulder spikes giving him, he imagined, a dangerous and powerful air.

Just in time, he thought, as the doors to the throne room opened. Seven figures entered, two guards, arc rifles held ready, one man, leaning heavily on the boy beside him, one girl, just a bit taller than the boy, and Preston, leading the group. To one side walked another boy. The Theta unit, Tyren recognized.

The instant he saw the injured man, he knew. This was indeed Prince Artus, second in line to the throne of the Sy'hli Empire. The boy was inevitably Prince Davrelan, Third-born of the Imperial Line, and younger brother to Artus. The voice in his head didn't even have time to scream at him before Tyren shut him down. He'd been expecting that reaction and was ready for it.

As they approached the dais, the injured man and the boy, who sported a nasty looking cut on his forehead with a trail of blood dried against his cheek, both stared at him, expressions torn.

There was hatred there, he could see, and anger punctuated with fear. Behind those strong emotions, he could see the love they held for him. He intended to crush any hope they still held for saving him, their eldest brother. After staring coldly at them as they approached, he was interrupted as Harelo abruptly leaned toward him looking concerned.

"My lord, perhaps I should check them for weapons. It wouldn't be the first time a prisoner brought a weapon past the guard and into your presence. These people are very dangerous," Harelo whispered.

Tyren thought for a moment, but his paranoia won out and he nodded.

Harelo moved toward the group, still halfway across the large hall. He spoke a few brief words to Preston, who nodded.

The Theta took a step forward, and Harelo moved in front of him.

Harelo paused, looking at the Theta unit before looking back to Tyren, brow-ridge raised in question.

Tyren nodded.

It was definitely not a bad idea to put the Theta in its place right away. Harelo moved to search the android, as well. The Theta didn't resist, cooperating readily. There was something to be said for robotic obedience, Tyren thought with an inward smile.

After searching the android, Harelo gave a careful inspection of the man and the two children, more gentle with the injured Artus than Tyren would have preferred. He would have to be reprimanded for that.

Harelo straightened when he finished, turned, and came back to the dais. He bowed deeply to Tyren and returned to his place. Tyren nodded to Preston, who escorted the group forward again. Tyren waited for ten full breaths once they had stopped at the foot of the dais before speaking, for full effect.

"Artus, you should have stayed in hiding. You were safer when you were dead," he said with a vicious smile. "And returning from the grave to help a young bearer? I don't know where she came from, but risking everything you had managed to save by keeping yourself and your brother alive on such a futile quest? Stupid, Artus. I can think of many words to use to describe you, but stupid was never one of them, until this stunt."

Artus glared at him but said nothing.

Tyren turned his cold, blue gaze to Davrelan. The boy didn't have the same love hiding behind his expression, Tyren realized. The boy looked at him with such loathing that Tyren actually considered letting him live. It was always fun to let that kind of negativity spread, he felt.

He couldn't risk it, though. If anyone else found out who the boy was, it would mean a great deal of trouble. Besides, Davrelan certainly intended to use that hatred and loathing to kill Tyren, so that wasn't worth the risk, either. Pity.

"As for you, pup, you'd have been better off if your brother had left you wherever in the galaxy you've been cowering all these years. You might have lived, if I'd thought you were also truly dead. Stupid, like your brother."

The boy didn't respond, either, clearly taking his cue from his brother's silence. Instead, he looked to the girl.

"So beautiful," Tyren said. "Always a pity to destroy something so lovely, but I can't have you Jumping around the universe causing trouble for me. I almost regret to say that you'll have to be destroyed as well."

The girl looked scared, and her eyes looked slightly damp and red, as though she'd been crying a lot recently, but she gave him a glare of defiance as well. Troubling. He looked to the Theta unit, who stood to one side.

"It certainly took you long enough," he said with a scowl of annoyance. "You shouldn't have been around this long, you know. Process that for a moment, Theta. Your kind are obsolete. I do appreciate your service however, so I'll allow you to be retired in the manner of the rest of your series," he announced.

The Theta looked surprised, and angry. The Thetas were always a little bit emotional, he thought to himself. Definitely better off without them.

"You are officially instructed to go to the recycling chamber." The android gave him such a look of fury that Tyren actually laughed. "You are not to attempt any recourse against myself or my people or give aid to the prisoners as you go. When you are dismissed, walk calmly to the recycling chamber, step inside, and wait." He grinned at the Theta's scowl of anger and shock. "Don't worry, the moment that chamber is activated, you never have to follow an order you don't like for the rest of your existence." Tyren laughed again, turning back to the other three. He was enjoying this.

"As for the rest of you, I'm going to let you watch something before you are executed. Preston?" he asked, holding out his hand.

Preston stepped over to the Theta, who handed him something from his pocket without once turning his glare from Tyren. Preston approached and dropped the crystal into his waiting hand. He held it up and looked at it.

They really were beautiful, though his skin crawled being this close to the accursed thing. The light flickered out of the many facets in a merry dance of rainbows. Tyren smiled slightly, then held his other hand toward Harelo.

Harelo handed him a small device, crafted of a uniquely conductive alloy on the front, a dark insulating layer behind it. The center of the device had a small depression, exactly large enough to rest the crystal in. Tyren rose from the dais, slowly taking the couple of steps as he locked gazes with Artus.

"Do you know what this is?" he asked. Artus nodded once. "Excellent. Then you know you'd better stand back." Artus began moving backward, taking Davrelan with him. The girl wisely followed suit. Preston moved to the side near the Theta.

Tyren set the device on the floor and placed the crystal in the narrow depression. He touched the activator button on the top and backed away, glancing at the prisoners. Artus looked pained. The girl looked confused. Davrelan looked like he wanted to leap across the space and tear Tyren's throat out. Perfect.

The device began to glow on the top, an almost enchanting green color. The glow brightened, and the crystal began to catch the light, casting beams of emerald in a shimmering pattern up to the glass ceiling and beyond.

After several moments, as the light intensified, the crystal stopped emitting the light, instead absorbing the green energy. It took less than five seconds after that until the crystal exploded.

It wasn't a large explosion, but anyone within a few feet of the device sure would have felt it. A ball of green fire the size of a grown man's head rose upward, dissipating against the ceiling. The girl cried out in horror and stepped forward. Tyren smiled.

"Don't worry, the crystal key is irrelevant, since you are about to cease to exist, as well," he told her.

"How could you?" she shouted at him. "So many lives destroyed, so much destruction, and for what?" The tears were flowing freely down her face. He slowly shook his head, feigning sadness.

"No, young one. For revenge. Didn't my brothers tell you?" he asked, glancing at Artus and Davrelan.

The girl stared, gaze flickering to the other two and then back to Tyren.

"Oh my, they didn't tell you that, either?" Tyren put a hand to his chest in mock surprise.

The girl looked to Artus, who hung his head. She clearly understood this as confirmation.

"You see? It is true. These two buffoons are my brothers; incompetent, rebellious, and foolish though they may be. They, along with our father, tried desperately to see me destroyed."

"I will see you destroyed!" Davrelan snarled, his voice full of the barely contained fury that burned in his eyes.

Highlord Tyren shook his head.

"Nonsense, brother. You will be dead in just a few minutes," Tyren replied with a small smile before turning back to the girl. "You see? No loyalty. I only seek to destroy everything you love, brothers. You did the same to me," he all but snarled that last.

Both Artus and Davrelan looked baffled by the last comment.

Tyren took a deep breath to calm himself.

"I am tired of this," Tyren said coldly. "Klythe, call for your men. We are escorting the entire group to the recycling chamber." He glared at Artus. "I won't make the same mistake twice, brother. I'll watch your body disintegrate with my own eyes."

Tyren gestured with one hand, and Klythe touched a red metal device wrapped around his wrist like an armor plate. He snarled into the wrist-com, and almost immediately, two more maruck came into the room.

Tyren stepped back as the monsters lumbered forward. Artus straightened, taking his weight off his younger brother, and took a half step forward.

Tyren frowned. Artus looked better. Still obviously quite injured, but he did not look half as wounded as he did a few minutes ago. He must have been making his injury seem worse than it was. Tyren gestured to Klythe, who approached.

"Bring a few more of your people. These two may not be as injured as they appear, and they are indeed dangerous," he instructed the brute. Klythe nodded, snarling again into his wrist-com.

A few moments later, another pair of maruck lumbered in, followed by a third. Artus leaned back against his brother. Better, Tyren thought.

"Take them to the recycling chamber. Theta, follow them. You will be first into the chamber, so our friends here will know what to expect," he ordered.

The Theta unit nodded once to acknowledge, though his expression didn't change from the piercing glare he cast Tyren's way. Not that Tyren cared.

As the group moved to the door, Tyren again suppressed the voice, which violently renewed its assault in the back of his mind. That accomplished, he rose to follow. This, he intended to watch with his own two eyes. Maybe that would finally shut the voice up.

"My lord?" Preston spoke up. He was looking at the small information pad he carried.

Tyren barely suppressed a snarl at the interruption.

"What?" he snapped at the advisor, turning angry blue eyes toward the small man.

Preston looked up from the pad, but he didn't seem the least bothered by the glare Tyren was throwing him.

Tyren inwardly raged at this, but he knew that Preston was far too valuable to waste as an example to others, so he kept himself in check.

"It would appear that a larger problem is developing with the jicund," Preston said.

Tyren paused, momentarily confused before he remembered the little creature that had escaped into the ventilation ducts. Tyren turned his glare on the group before him as he noticed both the Theta unit and the girl trying to suppress smiles.

"Didn't you send the extermination teams?" he demanded.

"Of course, my lord," Preston replied, "but the creature has somehow made its way into the main environmental controls. It has torn through three air processing filters in the last five minutes. The maruck are too large to get in to catch it, and none of our guards are fast enough.

"With all due respect, this is likely a problem that you will be forced to address personally. And soon, before it decides to tear into the thermal regulators, or destroys enough air processing units to suffocate us all," Preston added.

"Just flood the area with chlorine gas. That will kill the little brute," Tyren said, now truly angry that he was being troubled over something so minor.

"We can't, my lord," Preston pointed out. "Pumping toxins of any kind directly into our environmental systems would be unquestionably fatal to a large portion of our crew on the station."

"It can wait!" Tyren snarled. "I have other pressing business to attend!"

Just then, the lights in the room flickered, and the temperature abruptly dropped several degrees.

"Fine!" he shouted in outrage. "Klythe, take these four to the holding cells. Separate cells! And keep them under guard! Theta! You are to follow quietly and make no effort to help these traitors. Wait until I return, then proceed to the recycling chambers," he added. No reason to give them the chance to escape.

Tyren didn't think it would take long to catch the creature, but he wanted to risk nothing where his brothers and the crystal bearer were concerned.

Klythe nodded, and the pack of maruck moved in to escort the group away. Highlord Tyren rose and moved down from the dais, taking one of the side passages at a brisk walk. It wouldn't do to have the Highlord of the Coalition be seen running.

He couldn't believe that one ridiculous little animal had caused so much trouble, but as the lights flickered again, he knew the situation was getting worse fast.

In the back of his mind, the voice chuckled.

CHAPTER TWENTY

BROKEN WINDOWS

Harelo and the maruck escorted the group down a series of hallways, and finally through a heavily guarded doorway. On the other side was a wide hall, lined with what looked like glass doors. Allie looked into the first as they passed and saw that each opened into a smaller chamber containing a half a dozen smaller cells, each closed off with an interlaced lattice of dark metal bars.

Harelo escorted them into the second room on the left, gesturing for the maruck guards to remain outside the doors. They hesitated but obeyed the red-scaled advisor.

Allie was a little surprised at this. Still, considering that two of her three companions were injured, and the third was unable to violate the order not to help them, she certainly wasn't going to be able to do anything to the tall alien by herself. Aside from that, the beasts outside would tear them apart if they even made it that far.

"Inside," Harelo ordered Raith, his voice sounding

oddly muted by the strange breathing contraption he wore over the lower half of his face.

She wondered if the liquid inside was water and whether Harelo was descended from some kind of fish.

An odd thing to be distracted by, but she couldn't seem to shake the shock that they were all going to die in the next few minutes. Raith moved obediently into the first cell, and Harelo closed it behind him.

Allie glanced back at the guards outside. They watched, talking to one another on the other side of the glass door which had slid closed behind them, but she couldn't hear their voices. Idly, she wondered if the glass door were soundproof. Probably, so the guards wouldn't have to listen to the prisoners shouting and screaming.

"Jovran," Raith said softly.

Harelo glanced over at him.

Jovran? That name sounded familiar to Allie, but she couldn't place it.

Harelo moved behind her.

"Harelo," the alien corrected gently.

He gave Allie a shove, but it was surprisingly gentle. She felt a slight tug on her jacket pocket and an extra weight settled there that hadn't been there a moment ago. She turned around and looked at Harelo, but he shook his head slightly as he made eye contact with her. Allie frowned, unsure what was going on.

"Harelo," Raith said.

"Yes?" the man replied.

"I can't escape," Raith told him. Harelo sighed heavily.

"I know. I'm sorry. This is all I can do," he replied, his voice sounding truly resigned.

Allie's frown deepened. What was going on?

As Harelo moved to push Artus into the cell, Allie leaned up against the bars and watched closely. He took something from Artus's hand, the one that had been pressed tightly against his side. Artus was standing straight now, not favoring that side at all.

As he latched the door shut, he moved to Dav. The object he'd taken from Artus slipped expertly into Dav's hand as Harelo made a show of grabbing the boy and shoving him into the cell. The enigmatic alien shut the door behind Dav and turned to walk out.

"Harelo," Raith called again.

Harelo paused a moment, looking back.

"Thank you."

Harelo nodded once and stepped over to the glass door. The guard on the outside opened it, and Harelo moved out into the hallway as the door slid shut behind him. Allie counted eight maruck outside the door, two posted on either side of the glass door, and four more across the hall. They were clearly taking no chances.

Allie moved to the back of the cell, trying as casually as she could to glance into her jacket pocket. She almost gasped aloud at what she saw. It was a small, silver gun. She didn't recognize the design, but it was small enough that it didn't make her pocket bulge and would fit into her hand easily.

"Raith?" she whispered as she moved to the front of the cell. She heard Raith in the cell beside her move up to the front of his own.

"Yeah?" he replied.

She wished the cells were divided between by bars as well, but the walls were metallic and solid between each cell. She couldn't see her friends. At least the glass wall beyond the cells seemed soundproof. Allie didn't want to risk it, though, and kept her voice pitched low.

"Who is he?" she asked.

"Harelo, first advisor to the Highlord Tyren," Raith replied.

"You called him Jovran," she pointed out. "I recognize it, but don't remember from where."

"I told you the name," Dav interrupted softly.

Then it struck her. Jovran was the prisoner! The only one to escape during the rescue attempt on her mother!

"Wait, that can't be him!" she said.

"It's not," Dav replied. "Jovran was human, or at least from a race that wouldn't be easy to tell apart from human."

"Yes, it is," Raith interjected. "He went back undercover after the rescue attempt. Extensive surgery and genetic alteration made him indistinguishable from an uhran. The surgeons even adapted him to water breathing."

"That's impossible," Artus said. "No amount of gene alteration can make a person that biologically different.

"It's true," Raith said. "Biological nano-manipulation."

"And how would you know?" Artus demanded, sounding annoyed.

"I'm a recon android, Artus. It's sort of what I do," Raith chuckled.

"Why didn't you turn him in? Or the Resistance, since you seem to know so much about them, too?" Dav asked, his curiosity getting the better of him.

"I was under direct orders. Highlord Tyren didn't want to hear from me unless I had the crystal and the bearer. Besides, I wasn't ordered to uncover the Resistance, only to find the crystals and their bearers,"

Raith said, then paused. "I'm sorry, Allie," he added.

She could hear the sincerity in his voice. After a hesitation of her own, she spoke.

"It's okay, Raith," she replied. "I may not fully understand, but I believe you when you say you couldn't break an order from Highlo... I mean Tyren." She caught herself before fully speaking the title, unwilling to give him the respect the title implied.

"Thank you," Raith said, the relief in his voice so strong that she desperately wished she could see his face.

"Got your forgiveness, huh?" Artus said to Raith, sounding bitter. "Just don't forget you're the reason we're all about to die."

"Leave him alone, Artus," Dav said to Allie's surprise. "He did everything he could for us. He left us armed when you two went for the crystal, tried to give you a chance to escape, and even handled the ship's weapons for us when we tried to escape from Ayaran. Besides," he added with a note in his voice that Allie recognized as his unique, charming smile. "we aren't about to die."

"What do you mean?" Allie asked, hope surging in her. Dav must have a plan.

"Well, Jovran... I mean Harelo, slipped you the regenerator in the Great Hall to fix your side," Dav began.

So that's why Artus was doing better! It also explained what he'd slipped to Dav a few minutes ago.

"Because of him, we're both ready and able to fight if we have the chance. Then he gave Allie a gun."

"You saw that?" Allie asked, surprised.

"You bet." Dav chuckled. "He's smooth, but I was already watching for it," Dav added, a bit of pride showing in his voice. "He slipped Allie something else, too."

"No, just the gun," Allie said, feeling it through her jacket pocket.

"Check a little deeper," Dav told her.

She did, her hand going to the bottom of the pocket. Sure enough, her fingers felt a smooth, hard object. Her heart leapt as she recognized the shape.

"That's impossible!" she exclaimed. "We saw Tyren destroy it!"

"I saw Harelo palm the crystal when he searched Raith," Dav said. "The one he slipped back was from his other hand. Tyren destroyed a fake."

Allie was stunned, but she felt the proof of Dav's words with her own fingers. The unusual cut of the crystal was unmistakable.

"We're still locked in here," Artus pointed out.

"You three are," Dav corrected. "Harelo left my pocketknife in my pocket when he frisked us back in the Great Hall. I used the blade to block the latch when he closed it."

"Dav, I know I've said this before, but I just have to say it again. You're a genius," Allie said.

Dav laughed.

"Thank you, thank you," he said.

Allie could almost picture him bowing dramatically.

"Now, when we're all ready, I'll get to the control panel on the other side, open your doors, and we can tear through those over-sized gorillas on the other side of the door there. With Allie's gun, and the three of us providing the muscle, eight shouldn't be…"

"Two of you," Raith interrupted softly.

"What?" Dav asked, momentarily confused.

"I'm under orders," Raith replied. "I can't escape or try to help you. I'm just glad that Tyren didn't order me to stop you if you tried. He's pretty smart, but he has a hard time focusing sometimes. I've never figured out why, but it's almost like he has to fight to keep his thoughts ordered."

"We can't go without you, Raith!" Allie exclaimed.

"Yes, we can," Artus argued. "He's still bound by orders, and even if we took him with us, one order from any of the Coalition, and he'd turn on us. We can't trust him, and he can't escape anyway. I'm ready when you are, Dav."

Allie opened her mouth to protest, but Raith beat her to it.

"He's right. The best way I can help you now is to let you go without me. You have to, Allie. You're carrying the only crystal key left in the galaxy, and only you can use it."

"I hate to admit it, but he's right," Dav agreed. "We have to get out of here. We're the only ones that can stop Tyren."

Allie was torn, wanting to help Raith, but knowing the others were right. Raith couldn't escape and couldn't really be trusted even if he could break out with them. One order and he'd have no choice but to do what he was told.

"I'm sorry, Raith," she said, feeling a lump building in her throat.

"Don't worry about it, Allie. I'm a machine, remember? The recycling process is pretty quick, and it won't hurt me. I was supposed to have powered down years ago, anyway. I've had a seriously good run for a Theta."

"It's still not fair," she said softly.

"Not many things are," Raith replied. "Get out of here, Allie."

After a long moment to compose herself, she nodded, though none of them could see her. Allie took several deep breaths, then put her hand around the grip of the gun.

She had no idea if she could hit the broad side of a barn with this weapon, but those maruck seemed very nearly the size of a barn to her, so it's not like her aim would have to be amazing. She didn't know if Dav and Artus could take eight by themselves, so she intended to help as much as she could.

"Goodbye, Raith," she said softly, "and thank you. You're a good friend. Okay, Dav, I'm ready."

She forced the knot in her stomach out of her mind, forced Raith out of her thoughts, and then focused on the maruck outside the door.

One of them was looking directly at them. He might be suspicious, but with those ugly faces, Allie wasn't sure she could tell the difference, so something as subtle as suspicion was completely beyond her ability to read on the brutes.

"Go!" Dav shouted as he burst from his cell. He crossed the room in less than a heartbeat and hit buttons rapidly on the control pad.

The maruck watching them cried a warning and charged the door. It opened the same time the other cell doors popped open.

Allie didn't bother charging out, she just raised her gun and pulled the trigger. A pulse of neon green light flashed out of the little weapon with a sizzling sound, striking the maruck in the shoulder. The impact was tremendous, spinning the massive maruck backward and into the beast behind him. She couldn't help but stare at the little gun in awe. There hadn't even been a kickback. A grin came unbidden to her lips, and she aimed again.

Artus was there already, though, so she had to hold her shot. He went through the doorway like a bullet, moving hard, straight, and with astonishing speed. He leapt the falling maruck Allie had shot with ease before it even hit the floor, slamming a foot into the jaw of the one behind, sending him sprawling, as well. Dav dove through right after, rolling to one side to get out of Allie and Artus's way.

She moved toward the doorway, accompanied by the sounds of roars, snarls, and that peculiar, fierce, terrifying growl that Dav had given what felt like forever ago when he stood against the maruck back on Earth. Artus made a similar sound as he fought, though deeper than his little brother's, something between the snarl of a wolf and the growl of a panther.

The two moved outward, each trying to hold back three of the maruck still standing. Allie took aim at one of them to Dav's side and squeezed the trigger. Another angry green bolt hissed out, hitting the creature on one hip. It knocked the beast sideways and down to one knee.

Dav didn't miss the opportunity and slammed a fist into its head. No blue sparks, his strike rings had been taken from him back on the planet, but the impact was still enough to slam the beast to the ground, unmoving.

Allie turned toward Artus, but he was moving so fast that she didn't have a clear shot. Another glance at Dav, and she realized she had the same problem on that side now. The maruck roared as they swung their huge, club-like fists at the smaller men, but could never quite catch them. The maruck were faster than they looked, but they were no match for the two Sy'hli.

A shot opened up on Artus's side, and she took it. The beast moved just in time, the green bolt hissing down the hallway. It struck the wall beside the entry to the passageway, just as another figure rounded the corner.

Tyren!

"He's coming!" she managed to shout.

Dav spared a quick glance, but Artus had already seen him.

"Dav's side!" Artus yelled, kicking one maruck in the chest hard enough to send its massive body sprawling. Allie moved toward Dav, who dropped the last of his opponents with a swift uppercut that snapped the tusked jaw upward with a resounding crack.

Allie ran past him, but he caught up and quickly moved a few paces ahead of her. She cast a glance over her shoulder, and saw Artus right behind her, his own felled maruck creating a bit of an obstacle for the guard squadron coming fast. Tyren was right behind, but he stopped at the cell door. She looked forward again, unable to watch behind herself and keep her balance at the same time. That didn't stop her from hearing Tyren's shouted order.

"Theta! Get to the recycling chamber immediately! Enter the chamber and wait there until Preston activates it! Preston! Get rid of that blasted android!" came the angry shout behind her. "Harelo! Get every soldier on the station to close off this quarter! Weapons hot, and fire to kill!"

Allie wondered how long it would take for them to be completely hemmed in and back in Tyren's hands. She was sure he was running after them, and just as certain that she couldn't outrun him. Arcs of energy flashed past them as the Coalition Guard opened fire.

Dav moved fast, but she knew he was holding back to protect her. Artus also didn't pass her up, which told her he was trying to protect her, as well. A blast hit Artus in the shoulder. He stumbled but didn't fall. These Sy'hli were something else, she thought to herself in awe.

They approached the end of the hallway and the door on the far side. It was already open, but Dav moved immediately to the control panel on the far side as he went through. Allie went through, too, almost stumbling through the doorway.

She looked at Artus. A long section of his upper arm was scorched and emitting trailing wisps of smoke, though it looked like the strange body armor he wore absorbed most of the damage. By the look on his face, it sure hadn't made it hurt less, though.

The door slid shut behind them, and Dav slammed a fist into the control panel. It shattered inward in a shower of sparks and debris.

Dav gave Artus's arm a quick look, but Artus shook his head, indicating now wasn't the time for it. Dav nodded, and they turned to run down the hallway at a right angle to the passage they'd just left. They hadn't made it more than two dozen steps before the door behind them opened.

"What?" Dav cried in exasperation. "That always works in the movies!"

"Hate to tell you this little brother, but this isn't a movie," Artus pointed out between breaths as they raced down the hallway.

Allie couldn't spare the breath to comment as she

put everything she had into her speed. The hallway was long and straight, which wasn't good for any of them, as it gave a clear line of sight to the guards behind them.

Huge windows lined the right side of the wall. We are at the outer edge of the station, she realized. She glanced out the windows as they passed and almost stopped in awe.

The view outside was breathtaking. A clear view of a starlit expanse framed a massive, green planet. The planet almost seemed to glow in the reflection of the light from its sun.

Wispy traces of clouds hung, seemingly suspended, in the atmosphere of the strange world. She couldn't see any oceans, or color of any kind other than that luminescent green, accented by the drifting white wisps.

Allie would have given almost anything for a few peaceful minutes just to stare. She couldn't afford it, though, and she knew it. They passed an enormous set of doors, and Artus glanced in as they ran past.

"Wait!" he called. "In here!"

Dav and Allie backtracked, Dav ducking low when another barrage of arc blasts tore past them as the guards drew nearer.

The room was obviously a storage area. Massive shelves lined the walls, and several large racks stood in the middle of the room, as well.

Artus grabbed a large, metal pole with a curved end. It was nearly as tall as he was. Allie couldn't even begin to guess what the tool was meant for, but she was pretty sure Artus didn't intend to use it properly.

As it turned out, she was right.

"Grab onto something!" Artus yelled.

Just as Allie and Dav wrapped their arms around the

support bars of the nearest massive rack, Artus threw the pole end over end, straight at the doorway.

The first two guards who made it to the door barely managed to leap out of the way as the pole whistled by them. They turned back to Artus, looking smug.

An instant later, the pole hit the window behind them.

CHAPTER TWENTY-ONE

ALL IN THE PHRASING

The pole slammed end-first into the window, Artus's powerful throw sending it through even the strong, reinforced material that it was composed of. The pole speared the pane, lodging itself halfway down its length. For one terrifying second, all was again still.

The guards stared at the window in horror as the slow, crackling sound of the window losing its integrity became the only sound any of them could hear. In a frightening absence of more sound, the window exploded outward.

Allie was immediately hit with a tremendous force as all the air in the room behind her violently blasted forward in a desperate surge to get into the lower-pressure space beyond.

She clung in a panic to the rack, her heart pounding and a scream tearing free as she felt it slide a few inches. Dav planted his feet firmly, one arm around the frame, leaning all his weight and leg strength into holding the shelving where it was.

The two visible guards were the first out, flying into the emptiness of space. Allie couldn't hear their screams over the sound of the rushing air. She couldn't even hear her own panicked cries, for that matter.

Several more guards followed, having nothing to grip in the smooth, unadorned hallway, joining their comrades in the darkness beyond. Crates and boxes began flying off the shelves past her, racing in a mad bid to see which of them would escape the station first.

It was almost ten full seconds before a massive metal panel slid down over the opening, an emergency seal in case something broke a window, she assumed. The force shoving her toward the breach didn't stop until the metal plate clamped down, a hiss indicating it was sealing itself. In the sudden stillness, she realized an alarm had been sounding for some time.

Allie inhaled sharply, but there wasn't enough air left in the room. She gasped, desperately trying to fill her lungs. With a loud hiss, the vent in the room began pumping more air into the storage room to replace what had been blown out. Slowly, too slowly, she felt, the air returned.

She fell immediately to the floor, taking in loud, deep breaths. She could hear Dav and Artus gasping, as well, and a quick look their way showed her that they were all right. She glared at Artus.

"Don't ever..." she paused for another gasp of air, "do that..." another gasping pause, "again!" she scolded.

Artus laughed, an odd sound, considering his gasping breaths inward every few seconds.

Dav grinned.

"It worked... didn't it?" Dav said between breaths.

She couldn't really argue with that, so she simply settled for sending a glare his way.

"Come on," Artus said. "We won't have long before another squad comes."

The three stood and moved back out into the corridor. The hallway was empty, with no sign of any remaining guards. The entire group had been blown out the window.

Artus breathed an audible sigh of relief, then turned to continue the way they had been going at a steady, but manageable, run. Allie followed, Dav taking up the rear this time. She winced at the sight of the black scorch mark along Artus's arm, but he didn't seem too troubled by it, so she didn't say anything. She was still a bit out of breath anyway and probably couldn't have talked while they ran even if she'd wanted to.

"What's the plan?" Dav asked as they took a series of turns.

Allie was completely lost, but Artus seemed to know where he was heading. Her thoughts kept drifting to Raith. The poor boy… android, she corrected herself.

Raith was probably climbing into the recycling chamber at that moment. The power seemed to have stabilized, too. Tic was no longer wreaking havoc in the environmental controls. Tyren had probably caught her little friend.

"Escape pods," Artus replied simply.

Allie was only half paying attention. It was ridiculous to build a machine as complex and incredibly human as Raith was, and then make him unable to defend himself even against a suicide order.

Allie couldn't help but think of the spiteful and mocking comment Highlord Tyren had thrown Raith's way; he'd never have to obey another order he didn't like once he'd climbed into the recycling chamber and it had been activated. The cruelty of a comment like that was almost more than Allie could understand. Of course, he wouldn't have to obey any more orders, he'd be dead.

"What?" Dav asked incredulously. "That's a stupid move! Their systems will pick up the launch sequence before we even launch! Once out there, we can't move fast, have no weapons, and the only place to go in the thing is Pahrvic, where the guard has dozens of ships and hundreds of men stationed."

If only Raith didn't have to obey orders, Allie thought again. Then he'd be running along with them, helping them escape.

"All true," Artus said. "But we won't be on the escape pods when they launch."

"They?" Dav repeated, his tone betraying his sudden curiosity.

"We'll launch a whole string of them, then steal a guard cruiser," Artus clarified. "Nobody will think twice about a guard cruiser leaving the same time several others are heading out to chase the escape pods." Dav was quiet for a long moment.

Allie didn't know how the recycling chambers worked, but she hoped they were fast so Raith wouldn't feel anything. Probably not faster than Raith could process, she thought wryly.

"That's… actually a really good plan," Dav responded finally.

Allie heard Artus snort.

"Don't sound so surprised. You're not the only genius in the family, little brother."

"I didn't mean it like that," Dav began, but was

interrupted as Allie screeched to a halt. "Hey!" he shouted in surprise, almost stumbling into her.

He stepped around her and caught the look on her face. So did Artus as he turned around. The tall man frowned as he regarded her.

"What is it?" Artus asked.

"We have to go back," Allie said softly.

"No thanks, I'd rather not get fried in a recycling chamber," Dav retorted, clearly unhappy with their delay.

"I have to go back," Allie clarified, looking at the two brothers.

"Why?" Artus asked, completely baffled.

"I have to save Raith," she told him.

"You can't save Raith, we went over this," Dav said, sounding exasperated.

"Yes, I can," Allie replied, her tone becoming frantic. "Trust me. We may not have any more time. Please, Artus, do you know where the recycling chamber is?"

Artus's frown deepened, but he considered only a moment before answering.

"I do," he said. "That way." Artus pointed at a side passage branching off their corridor about twenty feet behind them.

Allie didn't hesitate an instant; she simply started running. Her two companions had no choice but to follow. Artus quickly overtook her, then moved ahead of her, leading the way.

"Are you going to explain?" Dav asked.

"Can't," Allie panted. "Have to… run."

She was infinitely grateful that they had both trusted her so quickly, willing to risk themselves on her word alone that her plan was a good one. She couldn't have done anything without their help.

Allie most sincerely wished she could run like they did and not get tired. Neither of them even seemed winded. She'd have to settle for what she could do, though, and not waste time wishing she could do more.

Artus led them through a series of corridors and doorways, having to make a couple of sharp and unexpected detours to avoid patrols that he seemed to be able to hear coming far sooner than she could. A short time later, they arrived at a massive, metal door. Artus stopped and gestured to it.

"There you go," he said. "Now what?"

"Now, we surrender," she said simply, then turned away from their dumbfounded expressions and headed for the door.

Dav grabbed her arm.

"We what?!" he almost shouted at her.

"Please, Dav, we don't have time. Trust me?" she begged.

His eyes seemed to bore into hers, digging for something deep within her. He must have found whatever it was he was looking for, because he nodded.

Artus gritted his teeth loudly.

"This is not wise," he told them.

Allie grinned.

"It's also not wise to eat school lunch on mac and cheese day, but that's never stopped me," she retorted.

Dav laughed. Artus did not.

Allie turned and entered the room, the doors opening before her. The inside of the room was massive, lined with enormous racks filled with what looked like eight-foot cubes of crushed, melted, and compacted metals. The center of the room was open, and ten figures stood within it; six maruck, two Coalition Guards, Preston, and Highlord Tyren himself.

They were gathered around a large door on the far side of the room, looking through the small window in the front of it. The door was just sealing itself as Allie and the others entered. Preston stood at a control pad beside the door. All ten figures turned and looked their way.

Preston blinked in surprise, the two guards cursed, and Highlord Tyren simply stared, his expression radiating his absolute, unyielding confusion and shock. He opened and closed his mouth more than once, unable to find words.

The effect would have been comical if it weren't for the six maruck charging toward the group, looking for all the world like a herd of angry, tusked, stampeding buffalo. Allie threw her hands high above her head and shouted.

"No, wait! We surrender!"

The maruck didn't even slow.

"Stop!" a voice from behind the charging beasts called.

The enormous creatures slowed and stopped, uncomfortably close to the trio.

"Bring them here," Tyren continued in a smooth tone.

The maruck grabbed them all roughly and practically carried them forward.

Allie looked up at the hideous face of the brute holding her. It looked back down at her, black eyes glinting, a trickle of drool trailing from one of its awkwardly angled tusks.

She winced, and it grinned. Its breath washed over her like a tide of sewage. She didn't know for sure what these things ate, but from the stench coming off the beast's breath, it was probably rotted meat. It took all her willpower to suppress her gag reflex.

Tyren was smiling in an impossibly smug fashion, as though he were singlehandedly responsible for capturing the three fugitives.

As the maruck brought them closer, Allie breathed a sigh of relief. Inside the chamber beyond the door, Raith stood. He looked unharmed, though he was watching Allie with a mixture of horror and disbelief, one hand on the glass window, as though trying to reach through and make this not happen.

"Excellent," Tyren said, drawing Allie's attention. "You've just saved me the trouble of having to hunt you down myself, since my idiot guards can't seem to manage it."

He cast a dark look at the two guards, as though the other squads' failure to capture Allie was their own personal responsibility, and that punishment was inevitable.

The two men shrank back under the glare.

Tyren looked back at Allie.

"Besides, now you're here in time to say a final goodbye to your little mechanical pet in there. Don't worry about him, though; we're putting you three in next." Tyren smiled. It was not a happy expression.

He gestured to Preston, who again turned to the console.

Allie locked gazes with Raith. He was looking at her, and only at her. She had only one hope at this point. Her saving Raith was the key to saving all of them now.

"Remember," she silently mouthed, glancing pointedly at Tyren. Raith frowned, obviously confused.

The maruck holding her looked down at her suspiciously. She glared back at it, and it turned its black eyes back to Raith. Allie looked back at Raith and tried again.

"Your… last… order…" she tried again, "remember!"

Raith glanced at Tyren, then back to her, still frowning. Then, she saw the realization hit him. His eyes went wide with shock as the implication of her words struck him.

Allie was so relieved that he'd understood that she would have collapsed right then and there, allowing her racing, panicking heart to simply overwhelm her, if it weren't for the hand of the maruck completely enveloping her arm and holding her up.

Raith shifted position slightly, one leg moving back a bit as his body turned. Allie glanced at Dav as a soft glow began to build in the chamber around Raith.

Dav was frowning at her, not having caught her words, or understanding the profound impact they were about to have on their immediate future. He had clearly noticed the change in Raith and where the android's gaze had been, however.

Allie grinned at him and mouthed, "Wait for it." She was incredibly glad that they were standing to the side of the door, not directly in front of it; she had seen Raith's body shift and had a pretty good idea what was about to happen.

As carefully as she could, she pulled the little gun out of her pocket, easing it over to point across the front of her belly at the side of the monster holding her captive. In their excitement at capturing the prisoners, nobody had bothered to search them again.

Arcs of white light began dancing from ceiling to floor inside the chamber. One of the bolts of light cut across the left side of Raith's face. He didn't flinch, but when the light vanished, a narrow streak from above his left brow down to just below his cheekbone glowed brightly. The pulse of energy had burned away the skin and melted the metallic plating beneath it into a solid, white-hot band of super-heated metal. His eye was glowing as well, clearly heated almost to its own melting point.

Allie cried out, suddenly a lot less sure of her plan's success. Tyren laughed. Raith stood as still as a statue. A high-pitched beep came from the panel Preston was working on, indicating full activation of the machine and the beginning of the recycling process.

And then, Raith moved.

CHAPTER TWENTY-TWO

UNLEASHED

The word "moved" wasn't nearly strong enough, Allie thought. Raith *exploded* into action. That would be more accurate. One instant, he was as still as a statue, expression serious and focused; the next, he shot forward like a bullet.

His android foot struck the door, and it burst outward with a violent screech of metal as the hinges tore like paper. The mangled panel of metal flung forward, striking one of the maruck standing in front of it and knocking it back several feet to the floor.

Raith came out of the chamber in a blur. She'd never seen anyone, not even Dav or Artus, move that fast. She could barely follow his movements at all. Beside her, Dav and Artus, despite their surprise, made their own efforts toward freedom.

Dav grabbed the hand of the maruck holding him on one arm, and with a double-handed twist, broke the grip with a snarl.

Artus simply threw a punch into the side of the brute holding him, bringing from the massive creature a squealing gasp that sounded surprisingly like a pig's. It dropped Artus's arm, and Artus turned a different direction, throwing himself at the maruck holding Allie.

He was too slow. Allie had already pulled the trigger on her gun. The angry hissing sound announced the blast a fraction of a second before the bright green bolt struck the creature squarely in the side.

It folded over the impact, falling to its side away from her, massive hand almost pulling her down with it, despite its grip relaxing. She scrambled back, trying to keep the gun up, and looking for a target.

A hand shot around from behind her in a snakelike strike, grabbing the wrist of the hand holding the gun. The grip felt something like getting your hand slammed in a car door, she thought.

She cried out in pain as the gun fell from her loose fingers. The hand gripping her spun her around and hauled her right off the floor. She found herself staring into the cold, blue eyes of Highlord Tyren himself. His expression was one of cold satisfaction. She screamed as he growled at her.

Any second, he would reach out with his other hand and break her neck, or something even more horrible, she knew. Her free hand frantically sought a weapon, though none was in reach.

As Tyren's other hand came out toward her neck, her hand found the crystal in her pocket. It wasn't a weapon, but she held onto it like her only lifeline as her hand came out of her pocket anyway. She threw a punch at the man's head. He didn't even try to dodge it, knowing her pathetic blow couldn't possibly hurt him.

The instant before her fist struck him, the crystal, clutched tightly in her hand, flared to life, brilliant white light shimmering around her hand.

As her fist connected with his face, something odd happened; Tyren screamed. It was not the scream of a man. It was as if a thousand voices from far away were screaming in unison, resonating off one another. It was an eerie, echoing, haunting sound.

A faint haze of red mist sprung into being around him, seeming to pour from his very skin, writhing in tendrils like a nest of snakes.

Tyren dropped her, and she fell to the ground, scrambling backward on her hands, wanting to get away from him even more than she wanted to regain her footing. The crystal slipped from her grip as she backed away from Tyren, making a faint bell-like sound as it skipped across the metallic floor.

Tyren thrashed for a moment, fingers clawing at the spot where she'd touched his cheek. He staggered backward, gasping. The red haze seemed to absorb back into him, and he turned his gaze back to her. This was no longer the stare of a hungry snake at a defenseless mouse. This was the white-hot, furious glare of an angry demon.

Allie had to get the crystal back. For some reason, it had hurt him. She didn't know how or why; she just knew it was her only defense. She turned and reached for it, just beyond easy reach, but Tyren's foot whipped out, catching her hand.

If she'd thought his grip before had hurt, this made that feel like a minor inconvenience. She screamed out in pain, certain he'd shattered her hand. He moved between her and the crystal. A quick look around showed her Raith was single-handedly dealing with three maruck, and Dav and Artus were fending off an entire squadron of guards who had come in while she was distracted. There would be no help.

"I don't know where you got that wretched stone, but I'm going to tear all of your limbs off before I kill you," he told her in a snarl. He reached down for her, and she knew she was finished.

Allie was closing her eyes to brace for the pain when she caught movement. Something rapidly flew in from the side straight at Tyren's head.

It was small, it was fluffy, and it was angry!

Allie felt a profound surge of relief, not only at her unexpected rescue but at the realization that her little friend was okay.

The little purple jicund was clawing, screeching, and biting at Tyren's head in a rage-filled fury that could only be described as psychotic. Tyren desperately tried to get a grip on the creature but couldn't seem to catch hold as Tic scrambled around the Highlord's thrashing head. A vicious snarl came from the chaos, but Allie wasn't sure if it came from Tic or the Highlord.

Allie didn't know what had happened when Tyren had tried to catch her little friend in the environmental systems, but whatever it had been, Tic clearly wanted the Highlord in as many pieces as possible, and she wanted it right now!

Allie reached quickly around Tyren's leg, grabbing the crystal. Just as Tyren finally got his hands around Tic, she hit him again, crystal held tightly in her fist. She hadn't had time to stand up, so she struck him in the upper thigh. The crystal flared with power once more, and the Highlord's leg buckled.

Tyren flung Tic aside as he screamed that inhuman,

evil sound once more. The red mist burst from his skin again, as though torn from his body by the crystal's light. He staggered backward, trying to keep his footing. The expression on his badly torn face as he looked at her was still filled with that terrible rage, but there was something else in it now; fear.

As the red haze absorbed into his body again, he turned and ran with inhuman speed, straight toward Artus's back. Allie shouted a warning, but Artus didn't seem to hear. Three steps from Artus, Tyren suddenly folded over, falling to his knees as if struck, hands clutching at his head.

"No!" Tyren screamed. "It's mine!"

He clenched his head as though trying to hold something inside. He shook his head violently, almost falling over completely as the red mist writhed again.

Allie hurried to her feet and began to run toward him.

Tyren recovered first, climbing to his feet and charging Artus again.

He staggered once more only a step from reaching his chosen prey, gripping his head in both hands, and then turned toward the door, moving straight for the exit.

Allie started after him but realized she'd never be able to catch him. Instead, she headed for the gun.

Tic ran along beside her, apparently not injured by being tossed across the room. She looked down at her little friend as she ran.

"Tic!" she called. Those big blue eyes looked up at her questioningly. She hoped Tic understood her. "Go help the boys!" Tic immediately turned and raced toward Artus, Dav, and Raith. Just how smart was this little creature, she wondered?

She grabbed the gun and spun back toward the fighting. Raith had taken care of all three maruck and had turned to help Artus and Dav when a massive maruck, big enough to be easily a full head taller than any of the other monstrous brutes, loped through the doorway carrying a spiked, ridged club that was significantly longer than Allie was tall.

Raith saw it, too, and moved for the beast before it could broadside Dav and Artus, who were distracted by the fight with the last of the Coalition Guards.

The beast saw Raith charging and roared with excitement. The massive club came up, and with terrifying force, came rushing downward so quickly that Allie could hear the air tearing past it even as far back as she was.

Raith slid to a stop in front of the behemoth, reached up, and caught the massive weapon with both hands, stopping it cold. The monster stared at Raith in complete astonishment for a long moment.

Then, it adjusted its grip, and leaned in, putting all its force behind the effort to crush the little android. Raith's knees bent slowly, even his strength not quite enough to fully suppress the magnitude of the gigantic, tusked alien.

Allie, feeling close enough for a clear shot, stopped where she was, gripped the gun with her good hand, aimed, and squeezed the trigger. The rolling green bolt flashed out and struck the towering brute squarely in the face. It fell backward, stumbling several steps before dropping to the ground, thrashing as it roared in pain.

Raith, still gripping the club that the brute had dropped when she hit him, flipped the enormous weapon like it weighed nothing, caught it by the handle, and slammed it downward in a double-handed grip onto the fallen maruck. Its movement stopped instantly. Raith dropped the club, turned to meet Allie's gaze, and smiled slowly.

The smile wasn't just a show of thanks, though gratitude was in it. In his eyes, she could see a surge of his gratitude and relief for everything she had done, from forgiving his betrayal to risking herself to save his life.

Allie smiled back at him, nodding once to show him that she understood, then hesitated as she saw the extent of the damage to his face. A line of metal now showed through where the recycler had burned through his skin and fused the metallic surface underneath. It spanned several inches from above his eye to below his cheekbone.

To her relief, his eye didn't seem to have melted with his skin. The arc must have just missed the front of the eye itself. It didn't look quite right, though. The color was a lot lighter than the other one, and the iris looked smoky. He moved toward her.

"Oh, Raith," she started, reaching one hand instinctively up toward the shining line of silvery metal that marred the once-perfect contours of his face. She stopped before touching it though, suddenly uncertain.

His smile didn't falter.

"Don't worry about it," he told her. "Androids don't feel pain. It doesn't hurt. Didn't hurt when it happened, either. It is a bit of a shame, though. I used to be so pretty…" He looked playfully mournful as he touched the streak of metal.

Allie laughed, relieved that it didn't cause him any pain, though secretly, she agreed. He had been very good looking. Oddly, the silvery scar changed his looks a great deal, although not negatively. He was still very good looking, he just looked… tougher. Maybe that's why boys like scars so much, she thought to herself.

"You're just going to have to find some other way to impress all the android girls," Allie teased.

For some reason, his smile slipped a little at that, but it reappeared so fast that she wasn't sure that she'd seen it at all.

"I guess so. Good thing I'm impressive in all sorts of ways," he retorted, winking his good eye.

Both of them turned sharply at the sound of another vicious snarl from one of the brothers, Allie couldn't tell which.

Raith's smile turned into an enthusiastic grin as he broke into a run, heading for Artus, Dav, and Tic. In an impressive show of acrobatics, he leapt into a spinning kick and brought down the last of the men that Artus and Dav had just turned to face in a joined assault.

Allie saw Tic jumping up from another man that the little jicund had most likely just taken down by herself. Tic scampered over to Allie, and with an easy leap, perched upon her shoulder. She reached up to pet the animal with a smile. Tic leaned into the touch and trilled happily.

"Oh, sure," Dav said to Raith with a bitter tone, drawing Allie's gaze, though his expression was one of amusement, not anger. "Steal the last one for yourself."

Raith laughed.

"Sorry. You guys were just doing so well, I thought you wouldn't save me any," Raith said.

"We wouldn't have," Dav admitted with a smile.

Artus looked to Allie, noticing the way she held her hand. He winced.

"You okay?" he asked her.

Dav and Raith turned toward her, both looking confused. Raith apparently hadn't noticed when they'd spoken earlier. Dav ran a hand through his hair as he approached, clearing the sweat from his brow.

Allie looked down at her hand. It was a mass of angry red, several fingers swollen and awkward. She gasped, feeling the pain surge as the adrenaline of the fight faded and awareness of the injury sank in.

Dav ran forward, sliding something from his pocket. He reached her before the other two did. Raith gave Dav a look she couldn't interpret, then moved toward the door. She looked back to Dav. He was holding the same little object Harelo had given him in the cell.

Dav pressed it against her hand, pressing the small button on the side. She winced at the contact, but as soon as he pressed the button, the pain lessened. It still hurt, but it was manageable. He met her gaze, looking apologetic.

Artus moved to the doorway and stood by Raith, on guard for another squad of guards or maruck. Or the return of Tyren. Artus had picked up an arc rifle at some point in the fight and held it like he knew how to use it.

Allie couldn't imagine what Tyren was up to at this point. No doubt figuring out how to kill them without getting close to her, she thought with a slightly smug smile to herself.

"This is going to hurt, but I have to do it, or they won't set right," Dav told her.

She nodded as her attention turned back to him. He yanked on one of her fingers. It felt like he'd torn it off, and she cried out in the sudden explosion of agony that tore through her hand.

He winced, looking pained himself. She gritted her teeth, determined not to scream again as he moved to the next finger. She couldn't suppress the whimper as he straightened the next one, but she was proud of herself that she didn't cry out.

Dav looked closely at her, but she nodded for him to continue to the last one. Another whimper, but no cry, to her great satisfaction. Her eyes were filling with tears, though. She'd never felt anything so terrible in her entire life. Dav reached over and adjusted a small dial on one side of the device on the back of her hand. He held it tightly, and the pain eased again.

"Here, use your other hand to hold this in place. I'll take the gun," he said.

Allie handed the gun to him with a nod, placing her other hand across the device to hold it securely against her skin.

"We need to go," he told her.

She nodded again and moved to the door.

"My plan is still good," Artus said as he saw them approach.

Raith looked at him with a raised brow in question, but Dav nodded.

"Right," Dav said. "Trigger as many escape pods as possible, steal a guard cruiser."

Raith nodded at the quick breakdown of the plan.

"That is a good plan. This way, then," Raith said, leading the way.

Allie could hear shouts the other way down the hall and knew another squad of guards was coming in fast. She hurried after the others. The pain was even less in her hand now. Whatever this device was, she decided then and there that it was pure magic and vowed she'd never be without one.

They ran down the hallway, Raith in the lead, Artus running beside Allie, and Dav taking up the rear. Tic held comfortably onto Allie's shoulder, still happily trilling, almost like a purr, now that she was back with her friend. The sound was incredibly comforting.

Raith led them through the halls easily, clearly having learned the layout of this place at some point. The guards sounded closer behind them, and Allie knew they were outrunning her. Her three friends were staying slow enough for her to keep up, but it was going to cost them all if they didn't reach their destination in time.

A long minute later, Raith led them into a hallway lined on only one side with narrow doors. Artus moved forward and immediately touched the control pad beside the first door.

It slid open, and Allie glanced inside. It was a small chamber, with what looked like eight seats tightly packed together. Several small control panels were visible, but that was basically it. Definitely not a luxury vehicle, she thought.

Artus pressed buttons on the touchscreen console quickly, then reached inside and hit another button before backing out of the doorway. The door closed, and Allie heard a sharp hiss, like a sudden rush of air, and the hum of an engine. He moved to the next console and began pressing buttons again.

"This is taking too long," Raith said, moving in front of Artus to the second console.

He placed his palm flat against the touchscreen. Dav and Artus watched curiously.

The image on the touchscreen began to flicker, rolling through command menus so fast that the little screen looked like a strobe light. Allie looked down the hall and saw that every one of the two dozen consoles in this hallway was doing the same thing.

Less than five seconds later, every door in the hallway opened, closed, then emitted the same hissing, humming noise. She assumed that meant all the pods on the other side of the doors were launched.

"Wow," Dav said simply. "That's cool."

"Being robo-boy has its advantages," Raith replied with a grin.

The others laughed as they began running down the hallway again.

The guards sounded quite a bit closer now. If they ended up in a long enough hallway, she was sure that they would end up in line of sight and get shot in the back. Dav would, she realized in horror. He was taking up the rear. Allie leaned forward and ran harder.

A few short turns later, and they went through a large door into a huge bay. A line of ships she recognized as the guard cruisers sat parked, facing what looked like a vast doorway in the far wall into empty space. If it weren't for the slightly bluish glow over the opening, she'd think they were all about to be blown out into the emptiness beyond.

Allie followed the others up the ramp and into a guard cruiser. She moved with them up to the cockpit. Dav took the pilot's seat, of course, Artus sliding into the navigator position. Raith moved to the side, where the gunner's post was on the last ship she'd been in. She moved to the last seat, not even sure what the person who sat here was supposed to do.

She wondered idly if all ships had a standard cockpit layout like this. This one was surprisingly similar to the one she'd been in before, at least on the inside.

They'd passed a few small doors in the narrow hallway from the ramp leading in, though they'd been closed, and she hadn't been able to glance inside. They were probably rooms with bunks like the last ship had.

The engine began to hum to life as Dav activated the controls. Holographic displays popped up in front of each of the four stations. She looked at hers and could see a virtual image of the launch bay around them.

Allie put her hand on the control bar and mentally thought about her view moving around in other directions. Sure enough, the display shifted with her thoughts, showing her a large number of Coalition Guards pouring into the room, and into the other ships. Other ships began to lift off, moving straight forward. A glance at the front window and she realized they were moving, too. She hadn't even felt the ship lift off.

"Okay, folks, now all we have to do is blend in for a bit," Artus said.

Allie was excited to realize that, so far, the escape plan was working perfectly. On her display, Tyren entered the bay. He was accompanied by almost twenty maruck. How many of those thugs did he have on this station, she wondered, slightly annoyed. They didn't even appear to have made a dent in his forces.

Tyren was shouting something, but she couldn't hear anything through the display. Tyren pointed at their craft, shouting something to the guards running around the room. Several turned and leveled their arc rifles at Allie's ship.

"Too late," Allie said in frustration. "Tyren's spotted us." Just then, the first of the arc blasts hit the ship. She may not have felt the liftoff, but she felt this. The ship shuddered with each impact.

A small readout appeared on her display. It wasn't in English, but she found that it made sense to her, almost like she knew most of the words, and the rest just sort of fell into place.

The readout was a simple, but clearly important, measurement of the integrity of the hull as it took the blasts. In short, it told her how many more shots they could take in any given section before the hull ruptured.

"Can we go faster?" she urged.

Dav chuckled.

"Oh yeah," he said, and she felt a faint pull as the ship darted forward.

They passed through the blue energy field and into open space in a fraction of a second. Dav dodged around several guard cruisers before they could get out of the way, and Raith activated the weapons interface.

Her display shifted at her thought to a more overhead, two-dimensional perspective of their immediate area. This interface was seriously awesome. She could see where all the other ships were around them, and she could see the plasma bursts as they came both from and toward their craft.

Dav's flying skills showed plainly from the instant he kicked the ship into high gear. He rolled, banked, and maneuvered with phenomenal ability around the plasma bursts and the guard ships.

Raith showed similar expertise as his rapid, terrifyingly accurate shots hit ship after ship.

"Raith!" Artus called over his shoulder. "Aim here!"

She looked back at Raith. He must have gotten coordinates from Artus, because he fired a shot back at the station, directly through the launch bay entryway.

A massive explosion followed, and Allie wasn't sure if he'd blown up a ship inside, or if something equally destructive had been ignited, but the explosion was enormous. Not only did fire burst from the opening in huge, rolling waves, but the wall all around the bay entryway fractured, flames licking through small cracks, and a few larger holes. She couldn't even imagine what kind of damage had been done inside the station.

"Thanks!" Raith called, a smile in his voice.

Artus chuckled.

"Man, I hope Tyren was still in there," Dav said softly to himself.

"We're probably not that lucky, little brother," Artus replied.

Allie, watching her display of the station, noticed it first. A colossal weapon, looking like a flattened cannon mounted atop the station, was slowly turning their way, and was nearly pointed right at them.

"Dav!" she called, mentally sending the image to his display.

"Oh, great," Dav said bitterly. "Every time we start to get ahead…"

The cannon fired. The blast coming from the weapon looked more like a wave than a bolt, shimmering energy rolling forward in a swath toward them.

Other guard ships behind them were flung about like toys as the wave hit them, some were even caught up in the rolling motion and dragged along, being torn into smaller and smaller pieces with each roll.

Dav tried to dodge, but the wave was enormous, and they were caught on the edge of the rippling energy surge. It hit them with enough force to knock Allie completely out of her seat, sending her crashing into the wall of the cockpit.

I should have buckled up, a stray thought chided her. Always buckle up.

Dav was buckled in, as were the other two, and seemed fine. Tic's reaction time was good, and she'd managed to dig claws into the seat back and hold on.

"Status!" Artus called.

"Not good," Dav replied as the shaking of the ship stopped. "Thrusters are trashed. Exterior plating is seriously damaged. We're leaking air." He turned and looked at Allie, concern on his face as she got back into the chair.

"How long do we have?" Raith asked.

Dav checked his display.

"Maybe three minutes of air left, assuming we survive the guard that long," he said softly.

"No!" Allie yelled angrily. "He can't win like this! Not after everything we've done to get away!"

The other three turned to look at her, expressions filled with sorrow, regret, and resignation. The resignation in their eyes angered her even more than the thought that Tyren might win after all.

"We don't have any options, Allie," Dav said gently.

She thought frantically but couldn't come up with anything for a long moment. Then it hit her.

"Dav?" she asked. "Can I bring other people along when I Jump?"

Dav stared at her, a smile slowly forming on his face.

"If they're in direct contact with you, and you mentally will them to come with you," Dav replied.

The three hurriedly unbuckled and approached.

"This is too dangerous," Artus told them. "She doesn't know anywhere well enough to Jump to, and she isn't experienced enough to bring people along. She might not even manage to Jump successfully in the first place."

"Sure, I do," Allie retorted. "Home. And do you have a better idea?"

"We'd be stuck there, and Tyren would know to look for us there," Artus argued.

"Not necessarily," Dav interjected. "Tyren will probably think we're dead. And we could talk to the uhran colony in the Mariana Trench. I'll bet they'd sell us a ship."

"Yeah, for your first-born child," Raith laughed.

"If we're not out of here before the hull ruptures completely, I'll never have a first-born child anyway," Dav replied with a grin. He looked back at Allie. "Do it."

Dav put his hand on her arm. Tic, already back on her shoulder, watched curiously. Artus hesitated a second, then nodded and put his hand on her other arm. Raith put a hand on her shoulder opposite Tic and nodded once to her.

Allie took a deep breath and looked out the front window at the vast expanse of stars. Another blast rocked the ship.

She could do this. She had to, for all of them.

Allie did her best to clear her mind and focus on what she had to do.

Raising her hand, she spun the crystal.

NIGHT VISITORS

Allie held the small, wooden box almost reverently. Her fingers traced the elegant writing around the outer edge.

It made perfect sense to her now. She didn't have to concentrate on it at all. "Breath of the Bearer", she read. She didn't know why she could read the words now, but they were as clear as English to her.

Looking at the spiral pattern in the center of the lid, she recognized it now for what it symbolized. It was the Milky Way, though highly stylized. She thought she understood the symbolism too, the design showing the entire galaxy, telling her that it was all open to a crystal bearer. Simple and elegant.

"You know," she told Dav softly, turning to where he stood lookout at the window, "I don't really like the term 'crystal bearer'. It's sort of… dull."

Dav grinned at her as he looked her way, eyes sparkling in the moonlight filtering in from the window overlooking Allie's backyard.

"Oh, and I suppose you have a better idea?" he asked with a smirk.

"As a matter of fact, I do," she said, tucking the box into her backpack, along with several changes of clothes and a few other necessities.

Dav insisted they would be fine and that she didn't need much, but she preferred to be prepared.

Her backpack was filled almost to capacity. It would be a trick to zip it, she knew. She thought about leaving home again, after the hour walk back here from where she'd managed to Jump them all. Not exactly where she'd been aiming, but close enough.

They'd only been in the house for a few minutes.

The thought made her feel like a huge weight had settled in her stomach. She knew it had to be this way, though. Katherine wouldn't understand, she'd try to stop Allie from leaving, and it would take far too long to explain what was going on, and even longer to get her to believe it. Every minute they stayed here was more risk to Katherine, and Allie wouldn't tolerate that.

It was nearing three in the morning here on Earth, and Katherine, always a heavy sleeper, was sleeping soundly in her room down the hall. After a moment's struggle with the zipper on her backpack, Allie moved to her desk and withdrew a small pad of pink stationery from a drawer, along with her favorite pen.

"Well?" Dav asked, interrupting her train of thought. "What is it?"

It took her a moment to remember that she'd been talking about the crystal bearer description and had left him hanging on the answer. She grinned over at him.

"Starjumper," she said with a grin. "Much cooler, if

I do say so myself. Allie Bennett: Galactic Starjumper. Yeah, I like that. I should have business cards made."

Dav rolled his eyes, but he couldn't hide the chuckle he let slip.

"Okay, Miss Starjumper. Hurry it up; we have to get going," he said. "Artus and Raith are waiting outside."

Allie nodded and turned to the notepad as she sat at the desk.

She couldn't just ditch Katherine. It killed her to know she wouldn't get to see her adoptive mother before leaving again, but even staying this long was unsafe. Who knew how many ships Tyren had initially sent to get her from this place, and they knew where she lived.

The longer they stayed in familiar territory, the more likely they were to be caught. They didn't have many weapons to defend themselves. The little silver gun Allie had kept and the arc rifle Artus had grabbed were all they had.

Dav kept complaining that they didn't have his crafter. She didn't know what that was, but she knew she really didn't want to fight a squad of maruck with one little pistol and a single rifle. Both of them were fairly effective, but still, a risky game, depending on how many of the beasts were sent.

A letter was the best she could do for Katherine. At least enough to let her know that she was okay and that Allie's mom, Katherine's closest friend, was alive. It was the least she could do. Her attention turned to what to write. She struggled with the beginning, but finally worked out what she wanted to say.

Mom,
I'm so sorry for leaving you the way that I did. I had no

choice. Staying here put you in danger, and I couldn't stand that. I wish I had the time to explain everything to you, but I don't. I'll do the best I can with the time I have left.

First, there are some very bad people after me. Dav and Artus saved my life. They're with me, and they're keeping me safe. It has to do with my birth mother. She's alive, Mom, and my friend, Raith, knows where she is. We have to help her.

Once she's with us, she can help us with the people that are after us. Maybe she knows where my father is, too. There's so much I want to tell you, but you wouldn't believe it unless you saw it. We're going to the Mariana Trench. I'm pretty sure that's in the ocean, but you know geography isn't my best subject. I don't know how we'll manage it, but Dav says he has it all worked out. As always, right?

Please, don't worry about me. Artus, Dav, and my new friends, Tic and Raith, are taking great care of me. I'll send messages as often as I can to let you know how things are going, and I promise I'll come back as soon as this mess is all taken care of.

I took some of my clothes and things, and I borrowed that picture of the two of us from the mantelpiece, so I can keep you close. We also raided the fridge. Sorry about that, but we needed supplies. It's a long drive to the coast.

You've been the best mother anyone could ever ask for, and even after we rescue my birth mother, you'll always be my Mom. I'll tell her you said hi. We'll be back as soon as we can.

Love,
Allie

Allie sighed and stood, folding the letter up and writing Katherine's name across the front of the paper. She moved to the doorway, glancing back at her bed.

"Come on, Tic," she said.

Tic looked up from where she'd been curled up on Allie's pillow, trilled softly, stretched, and then bounded over and up onto Allie's shoulder. Allie reached up and stroked her hand along the remarkably soft little creature's strange fur as she moved into the hallway.

There was a small, decorative table at the end of the hallway, right by Katherine's room. She set the letter neatly on top of the table, knowing Katherine would spot it as soon as she came out of her room in the morning.

Allie looked at the door, aching to open it, race in, and embrace her mom. She knew she couldn't, though. She looked at Dav, who nodded, reaching out to touch her arm comfortingly. He understood, she knew.

They moved down the hall, down the stairs, and outside to where Artus sat behind the wheel of an idling old car, the one Artus had been driving around in for years. Raith stood by the back door, scanning the area with watchful eyes and sensors.

She climbed into the back seat as Raith held the door for her, Dav climbing in beside her. Raith moved into the passenger seat.

As Artus pulled away, Allie felt her gaze drawn to the house. Her home, her whole world; or at least, it used to be. Her world felt so much smaller now, just a tiny speck in a massive galaxy, and while she still felt drawn to the house she knew of as home, she also knew that she didn't really belong here anymore.

There was so much more, and she was involved in all of it. Allie felt important, really important, for the first time in her life. She could help people, make a difference. Her actions could save countless lives.

A lot of responsibility, she knew, but if she didn't do

everything she could to help them, she would be as guilty as those who threatened them. Tyren had to be stopped, for the sake of so many people; human, Sy'hli, and all the others. So many others, she thought.

Too soon, the house was out of sight. She closed her eyes, resting her head back against the headrest. She was so tired. She could sleep all she wanted on the drive, Dav had promised her. She intended to take him up on that. Dav reached over and took her hand.

Allie smiled and squeezed it, opening her eyes enough to smile at him. She caught Raith's expression as he looked back over his shoulder at the two of them, but it disappeared faster than she could identify it as he turned forward again. Allie was too tired to think about it. She closed her eyes again and fell asleep as Tic curled up in her lap.

From an upstairs window in the house they had just left behind, a figure moved in the shadows of the bedroom, watching the car pull away. It moved silently and gracefully through the darkness with the confidence of a predatory cat.

The form moved into the hallway and to the small table at the end of the hall. A hand reached out and opened the letter. Instantly, the information within was scanned, processed, and stored. The tall, dark figure moved again, down the stairs and out the door, closing it quietly behind itself. The figure looked up and activated its transmitter.

"C.A.D.E.-16 reporting, private communication directly to Highlord Tyren," he transmitted. A moment later, the response came.

"This is Highlord Tyren. Report, Epsilon."

Voice pattern was confirmed, C.A.D.E.-16

registered. Authorized to proceed.

"Fugitives identified, destination marked. Data incoming. Prepare to receive," C.A.D.E.-16 transmitted.

"Transmit," the Highlord commanded. The data flowed through a place between space, far faster than light ever could, all necessary information sent halfway across the galaxy in the span of a heartbeat.

"Requesting instructions," C.A.D.E.-16 said. There was a long pause as the Highlord reviewed the data.

"Pursue, remain unobserved. Maintain contact and continue to inform me directly as new information develops. Do not contact the fugitives or allow yourself to be discovered. Out," the Highlord instructed.

C.A.D.E.-16 frowned. No contact? He could easily destroy the fugitives. He was designed for it. Personally, he'd have preferred to have been ordered to eliminate them with extreme force.

Ah well, he thought. He followed orders, and his orders were to avoid detection. That's what the reconnaissance series androids were for, not the combat series androids, but apparently, Highlord Tyren had lost his only remaining recon unit. A Theta, no less. Valuable bit of property, those were. They were inferior to the combat Epsilons, of course, but still a decent piece of machinery. And this particular Theta was unique in several ways, C.A.D.E-16 knew.

They were… acquainted.

C.A.D.E.-16 began to run, moving through the night silently and just as fast as the old car the fugitives were driving. Perhaps eventually, the Highlord would authorize him to destroy them all.

That thought brought a cold smile to his face. He hoped he would be permitted the opportunity to kill them sooner or later. Nothing else in his existence gave him the same pleasure. It wouldn't be long, he knew.

Soon, the girl would meet Death.

COMING SOON

STARJUMPER LEGACY

BOOK TWO

THE VANISHING SUN

CHRISTOPHER BAILEY

NOVEMBER 2014

ABOUT THE AUTHOR

Christopher Bailey lives in Washington state with his amazing wife, happily expecting their first child. Working professionally with children for more than twelve years has helped him develop a fondness for children's literature, and a frustration for the lack of good stories for older children that are family friendly.

Inspired by an argument between two children in the school where he worked, he decided to write his first novel, "Starjumper Legacy: The Crystal Key". In answer to that argument, magic and science are one and the same, only divided by level of understanding. The real truth is that both exist in our world today, if you only take the time to look closely enough.

With half a dozen more novels already in the works including the exciting sequel to "The Crystal Key", he looks forward to the chance to publish many more stories yet to come and hopes his readers enjoy reading his stories as much as he enjoyed writing them. The adventure continues…